ISBN: 1502570521
ISBN 13: **9781502570529**

-PROLOGUE-

I didn't know if I was in a war or if Psychodrome was playing mind games. It works both ways. You play Psychodrome and Psychodrome plays you. If this was a hallucinact, the only way to tell would be when it was over. Assuming I survived. A hallucinact is not supposed to kill you, but if your mind believes your death is real, it might persuade your body. And my body was getting some heavy doses of reality.

The combat armor I was wearing was supposed to be state-of-the-art equipment, but it was state-of-the-art equipment that had been contracted out to the lowest bidder, something you don't really want to think about while under heavy fire. I couldn't help thinking about it because the recirculating and cooling system in my suit wasn't working properly. I was sweating like a pig and having trouble breathing. It felt like being locked in an ambulatory sauna bath. The home audience was getting a graphic taste of what it felt like to be a human tank, advancing through a bug-infested jungle that was bursting into flame. Of course, if this particular tank took a direct

1

hit from a plasma rocket, the "death" of the home audience would only be a vicarious experience—appropriately edited— and they could then switch channels and tune into another fantasy. I, on the other hand, would either wake up screaming or experience an incredibly brief instant of unutterable agony before I turned into a smoking, gelatinous puddle on the jungle floor. That's entertainment.

A war always got good ratings. There was a time when I didn't understand that. As a child, I played with toys of violence and rained death upon my playmates, who usually stubbornly refused to die, insisting that I'd missed them. There would then ensue heated arguments concerning their mortality. Sometimes the consensus of opinion would declare a prepubescent little soldier KIA, but it didn't really matter except as a momentary blow to pride. We all lived to die another day. I didn't understand it—then.

The ugly truth is that violence is life affirming. If it's a fantasy, it gives you the illusion, the vicarious experience, of confronting the reality of your own ephemeral existence. If what you're witnessing is real, it especially compels your fascination. It may frighten you, outrage you, shock you, or depress you, but in some deeply buried aspect of your psyche, there is a frightened little guilt-racked thing that huddles like a Judas, making you feel good because it isn't happening to *you*. No matter how real the illusion or how graphic the reality, you will survive to die another day. Escapist entertainment. With the accent on escape. They say it's cathartic, but if it really is a cleansing, purifying thing, we seem to need repeated doses of it. And Psychodrome supplies them in abundance.

I glanced over to the right and saw Breck advancing on my flank, looking like some giant, ugly robot painted O.D. green. Winters was about a dozen yards or so ahead of us, taking the point. Behind us were about thirty other grunts, mercenaries all, encased in combat armor and moving ponderously through the jungle with a whine of servo-motors while the enemy laid down a barrage of plasma rockets all around. They couldn't see us yet, but they had a fairly good idea where we were and their idea was getting better all the time.

There was a major difference between the other mercenaries and Breck, Winters, and myself. The others were getting paid extremely well to risk their lives for Consolidated Developers, Inc., while the three of us were being provided free of charge in exchange for exclusive broadcast rights. Oh, and there was one other difference, too. All they had to do was stay alive and defeat the opposition, the forces of a rival multinational disputing CDI's claim to this insect-ridden hothouse of a planet. The three of us had a somewhat loftier objective. Together or independently, we were supposed to win a combat decoration. And, with any luck, we'd win ours before players on competing teams won theirs, which would enable us to advance to the next stage of the gaming round.

There was no safe way to make an overflight of the objective and drop down on the enemy, because a high-altitude drop meant plenty of time for them to pick us off and a low-altitude drop meant making easy targets of the personnel carriers. Bombing was out of the question, as was the use of orbital particle beam weaponry, not only because it would destroy the equipment and facilities we were hoping to capture intact, but because it was against the rules.

It was all right for corporations to have private armies pounding each other into jelly on some undeveloped piece of rock, but it had to be done in a way that didn't violate any international weapons treaties. No government wanted to get involved officially, not only for political reasons, but for economic ones, as well. No one wanted to back what could wind up being the losing side. It was easier to sit back and let the corporations fight a limited war that jeopardized no one except the mercenaries fighting it. The executives battled in their boardrooms while the soldiers fought on the disputed territory and, one way or another, the claim was eventually settled. Then the winner came in, developed the real estate, and once a colony was formally established, the politicians recognized it and took advantage of a *fait accompli* with no territorial disputes and no investment outlay.

The political ramifications of this conflict did not concern me any more than did the outcome. I couldn't care less who won, so long as one of the three of us managed to win a combat decoration. The sooner that happened, the sooner we'd be out of the jungle and on our way to the next scenario of the gaming round. Some game! You could get killed playing this game. And to think the only reason I got into it was because I wanted to survive.

A plasma rocket hit so close that I was caught in the blast and almost knocked over, no mean feat considering the suits weigh several tons. A huge sheet of flame washed over me as I continued to advance through the roiling black and orange cloud and I felt the temperature inside the suit rise appreciably.

Breck's laconic chuckle came over my helmet speaker. "Getting a bit warm for you, O'Toole?"

"Cut the chatter!" the group commander broke in.

"With all due respect, Major," I heard Breck say, his smooth Teutonic voice as dry as sherry, "the enemy now has a fix on our position. I would advise a change of strategy before several well-placed rockets take out the entire unit."

The major hesitated. When a man like Rudiger Breck spoke, even a veteran mercenary group commander listened. Before Breck lost his arm, he was an officer in the SS. The commandos of the Special Service are a very strange, rare breed. They're bio-engineered and trained for service from the crèche. Their motto is "Born to Raise Hell" and they are utterly capable of it.

"What would you advise, Breck?"

"Open skirmish formation. And I would send out several flankers to deploy jet paks and lay down covering fire. We cannot effectively return fire until we break free of the brush. Without covering fire, we may never have that opportunity."

"Anybody who takes to the air is going to be a target," said the major. "And if the insects foul the jet paks—"

"A jump is necessary for the flankers to get into position," said Breck. "As for their being targets, it will help the unit if they draw enemy fire. At the moment, all of us are targets, are we not?"

"That's asking several men to commit suicide just so the rest of us can get into position," said the major.

I could almost hear Breck shrug. "A calculated risk," he said. "One I am well prepared to take. O'Toole will join me, won't you, O'Toole?"

"Thanks, Rudy. Thanks loads."

"There, you see? You have two volunteers already. Stone, what do you say, shall we make it a party?"

I couldn't see Stone Winters anymore, she was too far ahead, but her voice came back strong and steady. "I'm game."

"You realize they can probably hear every word you're saying, don't you?" said the major.

"And what difference does it make?" said Breck. "It's getting a bit warm down here and I could use a little air."

"Okay, Breck, go ahead," the major said. "It's your ass. Form open skirmish line!"

"Stone, you jump flank right, I'll take the left," said Breck. "O'Toole, you take left flank with me."

"I got it."

"Breck," I said, "I sure hope you know what you're doing."

"You can't win the game by playing safe, O'Toole. We jump on three. Do try not to get shot down immediately. Stand by . . . One! Two! *Three!*"

I damned Breck to hell and hit the thrusters on my jet pak. The audience at home was going to get a first-class show. I could imagine some fat slob sitting in his living room, plugged into his psych-fidelity set and sharing my experience. He was about to lift off with me into a blaze of glory, flying high above the jungle in his combat armor with his trusty auto-pulser spitting death down at the enemy while the air around him was full of bugs and plasma rockets and autopulser fire and more bugs and I hoped he had a heart condition so the blind panic I was feeling would rupture his aorta. No such luck, though. Psy-fi sets had bio-feedback sensors that would shut down the system if the armchair gloryhound got too excited. Unfortunately, I had no such safeguards.

I felt the press of G-forces as the suit jets fired and hurled me above the treetops as if the armor didn't weigh a thing. Several thoughts flew through my mind at once. I thought about what would happen if the jets got fouled or if the retros wouldn't fire: I'd make a large hole when I landed. I thought about what would happen if I flew right into a plasma rocket or autopulser ground fire. I could take some autopulser fire and still retain my suit integrity, but a plasma rocket would incinerate me in an instant. And I thought about what I would do to Breck when I realized that only Stone and I had made the jump. The son of a bitch had suckered us and now we were committed.

I saw the giant dome of our objective below and directly ahead of us and then I had no more time for thinking as the air around me filled with enemy fire. Stone had angled off away from me, to the right of where our unit was positioned, and I angled to the left, then started my descent. I spotted the enemy batteries in their small emplacement domes and opened up on them from the air. Amazingly, I hit one and was gratified by the sight of a lovely fireball where a rocket launcher had been a moment earlier, making things highly unpleasant for me. And then I realized I had made a very bad mistake. I was coming in too close. It was all happening too fast for a combat rookie like myself and I was not only going to land too close, I was going to land right on *top* of them.

I felt autopulser blasts slamming into my suit as I hit my retros and burned several enemy soldiers who weren't quick enough to dive out of the way. I crashed through the hole my retros had burned in the emplacement dome and felt the shock through my spine as I landed, a shock that would have driven my legs clear up into my shoulders if the suit had not absorbed most of it. I started firing blindly in every direction. I was so scared that it wasn't until almost half an hour later that I noticed the smell inside my suit.

I was still firing when I suddenly realized there was no one left to shoot at. I stepped over several bodies and took control of the rocket launcher. All I could think about was taking out the other gun emplacements before they decided to drop a rocket on me. I didn't really know how to handle the controls, but the knowledge must have been programmed into me during game orientation, because I was functioning on automatic pilot. I felt the entire emplacement swivel on its pad and the launcher lowered its elevation, angling down toward the other gun emplacements. They had to see what I was up to and I was praying that I could do it to them before they did it to me. I saw one of the other batteries start to swivel towards me and I opened fire. I scored a direct hit and an orange and black cloud shaped like a giant ball flowered and rose into the sky.

I immediately tracked onto another target and opened fire again and saw a wonderful repeat performance, then the unit was breaking cover and moving out into the open in a spread-out skirmish line, firing at will.

Then there was a flash of fire and I don't remember what happened after that. I woke up flat on my back a considerable distance from the emplacement dome. My suit integrity was intact, which was astonishing when I saw how battered and blackened it was on the outside. There was an incessant ringing in my ears and blood was running from my nose and mouth. Breck's handsome, hard-featured face was staring down at me from behind the faceplate of his helmet. His glittering, ice-blue eyes were gazing at me mockingly and I heard his chuckle over the ringing in my ears.

"Well done, O'Toole. Congratulations. You're a hero."

"Where the hell were you?"

"Jets malfunctioned. Damnedest thing—they seem to be working perfectly now." He grinned. "I just heard from Mondago. You were a major hit. The ratings were spectacular. They had to edit out certain involuntary reactions, so you came out looking like a one-man war machine. The major's putting you in for a commendation. We can leave soon as you've changed your shorts."

The last thing I heard before I passed out again was that goddamned chuckle. I was growing to hate that chuckle almost as much as I was growing to hate Breck. Some teammate. Some game.

-ONE-

"Honor is a word for virgins and tombstones, O'Toole."

Hakim Saqqara was smiling when he said that, but somehow I did not find that very reassuring. He was tall and slim, elegant and darkly handsome, soft-spoken, charming, and utterly deadly, with about as much regard for human life as his pharaonic ancestors.

My own ancestry is Irish and Russian, which means I believe in luck, but don't really expect to get it. The Irish part of me was counting on all the magical companions of my race to pull me through while my Russian half was trying to plunge me into black despair, fully expecting a cruel and vengeful God to punish me. My life was a constant battle between my Irish and Russian aspects. My leprechauns were what got me into this mess in the first place and now there was a chorus of Russian archbishops singing in stentorian baritone at the back of my mind, sounding an ancient Orthodox funeral dirge.

"Honor means a little more to me than that, Hakim," I said, summoning up my most sincere voice. There's nothing

like fear to bring out sincerity and even as an image on a screen, Hakim Saqqara scared me. "You know my word's always been good."

"True," Saqqara said, "but think how it would affect my other business interests if I were to let you off. I'd be more or less expected to offer the same leniency to others. You see my problem, don't you?"

He sounded so regretful that I almost felt sorry for him. I wished there was some way I could be more helpful and give him a reason not to have me killed.

"Look, Hakim, let's stop being so formal and polite and get down to the bottom line here. The bottom line is that I owe you a rather large sum of money and I haven't *got* a rather large sum of money at the moment. Now I wouldn't be much good to you lying at the bottom of Tokyo Bay, except as an object lesson to your other so-called 'business interests,' but alive and kicking, I'm at least a piece of functional meat you can still get some use out of. Does it make sense to ignore my potential value? Would that really be good business?"

Saqqara stopped smiling. Now I knew I was in trouble. The Russian chorus in my brain began to bellow in full voice. The leprechauns started to scream Gaelic obscenities at them and my head began to hurt. Saqqara's voice cut through the mist of pain and panic like a katana.

"You are an imprudent man, O'Toole," he said, steepling his fingers and gazing at me over them. "You are like a little dog that barks at a hound four times its size. You do not give enough thought to the consequences of your actions. I might have chosen to regard you as nothing more than an annoyance, but even the largest dog cannot ignore a puppy once it stops barking and decides to bite. You have figuratively fastened your tiny teeth upon my ankle and you have left me no choice but to shake you off . . . decisively."

I swallowed hard and cleared my throat. "What do you mean by . . . decisively?"

He spoke very softly. "There are people within my organization who specialize in making difficult decisions."

My mouth was very dry. "That's one of the reasons why I called you. I was hoping there was some way we could avoid your having to . . . make a difficult decision. I seem to be doing pretty well in the game so far—"

He smiled. "Yes, I know. I have been following your exploits. Quite amusing, really, knowing you as I do."

"Well, what I was getting at . . . that is, if my team wins, I stand to make a fair amount of money. I was thinking—"

"That you could buy me off?" Saqqara said. He shook his head sadly. "I'm afraid not, O'Toole. It's more than the money. You've caused me to lose face. If it was just the money, perhaps we could arrive at some sort of rapprochement, but you've made it a matter of personal pride. I wish you the best of luck in your new career, I really do. Actually, it isn't all that new, is it? You're still a gambler, only the stakes are higher. Care to make a little side bet?" He smiled. "I'll wager that my, uh, 'decision makers' dispose of your assets before the game does. What do you say? Even money?"

I sighed. "No bet. Good-bye, Hakim."

"Nice knowing you, O'Toole."

The screen went blank. So much for any chance of quitting the game and going back to Tokyo. I'd been hoping there was some way Saqqara and I could cut a deal, but my call to him had settled the matter once and for all. I had to give him credit for being straight with me, at least. But on the other hand, I knew him well enough to understand his motives. He could have lied to me and tricked me into going back to Tokyo, thereby drastically reducing my life expectancy, but that would have been too easy. He knew me well enough to understand exactly how I felt about playing Psychodrome. I'm basically a coward and Psychodrome can be a terrifying game. However, his "decision makers," as he euphemistically referred to them, were still more terrifying.

They were properly called ninjas, a term stemming from the word *ninjitsu,* which means "the silent way." Originally a secret guild of assassins dating back to the days of the samurai, they were trained almost from birth to kill quickly, silently, and efficiently. They were so good at it, they were believed to be supernatural. Supposedly, the guild had disappeared when Japan became westernized, but the Yakuza revived them, adding a new wrinkle with bio-engineering. The modern ninjas were supposed to be quite capable of giving Special Service commandos a real run for their money. That ancient, quasi-mystical, octopoid entity known as the Yakuza has controlled organized crime in Japan for generations and they had come a long, long way since their sword-wielding beginnings. I didn't know who the shoguns of the Yakuza were now and I didn't want to know. I only knew one of their minor factotums and Saqqara was frightening enough.

It amused him to be able to plug into the net and experience me sweating out the game scenarios of Psychodrome, knowing that when his assassins finally caught up to me, my termination would become a mass media event he would be able to experience vicariously. It was an elegant way of saving face and Hakim preferred to do things elegantly. Just staying out of Tokyo would not guarantee my survival.

I remembered what it felt like seeing Tokyo for the first time, looking up at its purple sky with the massive spires of the city towering above me and skycabs threading their way between the spanways. It was September of 2425. I was twenty-six years old, fresh out of the service, without a job, but I had enough money in my pockets to last me for about a month—or about two days if I decided to enjoy myself. I was only passing through. Five years later, I was still there, because like a fool I had decided to enjoy myself.

The first thing I had done was get drunk. I'm not sure what the second thing was. Sometime during that night, I had picked up a tattoo of a dragon—never mind where—and a girl named Miko. I woke up in a tiny cubicle on ground level in a section of the city known as Junktown. There was about enough room in that little prefabricated cell for two people to turn around in if they knew each other really well; there were five people living there. I woke up to the sight of Mama-san, Papa-san, and two prepubescent daughters-san sitting cross-legged around the bedpad, grinning down at me and nodding. Miko was lying next to me, as naked as I was, and the reason they all seemed so pleased about it was that at some point she had become Mrs. Arkady O'Toole, which meant she was my responsibility and there would be more room in the apartment. My Irish half was still hung over from the nuptuals and my Russian half was contemplating suicide.

I felt I was too young to settle down. I had no idea of Miko's age. She didn't look a day over sixteen. I never did find out exactly how old she was. I don't think she knew herself. She and her family were nonregistered, along with everybody else in that slummy neighborhood, and at the time, she spoke almost no English. She couldn't even pronounce my name. She called me "Akadee" and when she tried to say my last name, it came out "Otto."

From a strictly legal standpoint, there was no way to make the marriage stick. As nonregs, they had no civil rights of any sort. You can't take legal action against someone if, legally, you don't exist. But I didn't know that at the time. They had scraped together what little money they had and hired a priest or monk of some sort to officiate and make it legal, at least in the spiritual sense. The signature on the scroll they showed me was little more than a drunken scrawl, but it was recognizably mine. The marriage was real in the eyes of their ancestors and I had enough trouble with mine without taking on a bunch of Japanese.

Under the circumstances, I could have done a whole lot worse than Miko. She had long, jet black hair which she wore in a thick braid down the side of her chest and the biggest, loveliest almond-shaped eyes I had ever seen. Her figure was slim and coltish, she had long and shapely legs and a face so innocently pretty it was impossible to believe there could be any guile behind it. How a place like Junktown could produce a flower of such fragile beauty was beyond me, but Junktown produces them by the thousands every year and, if they're lucky, they manage to find their way out into the upper levels of the city.

To give you a rough idea what it's like down there, a career as a prostitute on the Ginza Strip is considered a step up for a pretty young girl from Junktown. Parents often go out of their way to cultivate good contacts with the sleazy Ginza pimps who scout the territory every now and then, in the hope that a pretty daughter will be able to buy passage for the family to a somewhat more survivable environment. A hard life brings hard priorities. Miko's parents were ecstatic. She had actually found a husband.

I was in a considerable state of alarm. Not only was I married, but I had suddenly inherited five dependents and I had no place to live and hardly any money left. There was no one on Earth to whom I could turn for help. The only family I had left was my dad back in Bradbury, on Mars, and if he knew of my predicament, he would've laughed himself silly. Sean O'Toole was not the kind of father a son could ask for help. I knew just what he'd have said, after he had finished laughing. "Fucked up again, huh? Well, I'm sure you'll figure something out. Be sure and send me holos of the kids."

Spending the rest of my life in a Junktown closet wasn't my idea of domestic bliss, so I assigned my hangover to my Russian ancestors and sat back to see if the leprechauns could come up with anything. Luck, for a change, was with me. That is, if you can call what happened in the long run luck.

The Lord giveth with one hand and smiteth with the other and my leprechauns figured that since I had already been duly smitten, I was in line for some of the good old giveth. So I did what any self-respecting Irishman would do when he was truly up against it. I had a couple of drinks and went looking for a game of poker.

Now when you've set your mind to lay the cards down and take a risk, there's no point in being small-time about it. I learned at least that much from the old man. I wasn't going to find a game in Junktown, so I headed uptown, straight up to level three and the Ginza Strip, the only other place I'd seen so far in Tokyo. It was where I had met Miko, I suppose, though I had no recollection of the meeting.

The Ginza Strip is a small city unto itself. It's like a giant arcade. I've come to know it very well since then, but that day was only the beginning of my education. I heard about the Ginza of Tokyo from other guys in the service and I'd always wanted to see it for myself. I never thought I'd wind up living there.

The first thing that hits you on the Ginza are the lights. Red lights, green lights, blue lights, purple lights—every color of the rainbow flashes from a thousand different signs advertising everything from gambling saloons and tattoo parlors to drug emporiums and whorehouses. The second thing that hits you on the Ginza Strip, unless you're either quick or lucky, is usually a scooter.

According to some arcane and ancient custom, the moment a socially awkward Japanese boy reaches the earliest stages of approaching manhood, complete with undirected sexual stirrings and homicidal impulses, he's issued a set of lycras and a scooter. These bushido bandit gangs in their skintight lycras, studded boots and gloves, and crested full-face helmets slalom through the traffic on garishly painted skimmer sleds covered with aerodynamic plastic bodyword at speeds you'd have to see to believe. They make amazing turns with thrusters on full power, hanging off the sides of their "scooters," and they ride in packs. Quite frequently, they hit things. People, cabs, each other, the sides of buildings . . . The results are nearly always fatal.

The Tokyo police don't really interfere because the bandits hopelessly outnumber them and if the bandits crash and burn, it's worth the price of the occasional window or civilian. The Tokyo police don't concern themselves too much with what happens on the lower levels of the city anyway and they know better than to venture down below the third level. There are no crime statistics among the nonregs. How can there be crime among people who don't exist?

The third thing that hits you on the Ginza Strip is usually either a hooker, a mugger, a pickpocket, or a shill for one of the gaming houses. I had already seen the lights and had somehow avoided being jellied by a bushido bandit. I preferred not to think too much about the circumstances under which I had met Miko. I was still in uniform and that meant I was a prize mark, so what hit me was a shill.

My Russian archbishops were entirely too hung over to exercise their usual cautionary influence, so my leprechauns were free to go berserk. I had a run of luck the like of which I hadn't seen before or since. Old Sean would have been proud of me. I also had a little bit of help in the form of a token I had obtained from an old friend in the service. I had told him that the first thing I was going to do upon my discharge was visit Earth and hit the Ginza, so he had slipped me a set of SS insignia. The insignia consists of two collar pins with the stylized scarlet double lightning bolts and a silver breastpin of the double helix strand of DNA, meant to be worn above the rows of campaign ribbons and decorations.

The people on the Ginza know about SS commandos, even though they've rarely seen them. The Commandos consider the Ginza a bit too tame for their sort of R & R. Still, the few times soldiers of the Special Service had done some unwinding on the Ginza, they left a lasting impression. The greatest risk I faced wearing the insignia was running into someone who was born to wear it, but it was a negligible risk considering the margin of safety it gave me.

There are straight games on the Ginza and there are crooked ones and it takes either professional instincts or Irish ancestry to tell the difference. The odds are with the house in either case, but the crooked ones generally sucker in the mark by letting him win a few times before dropping the hammer. The trick is in anticipating when they're going to turn on you and my leprechauns, bless their larcenous little hearts, didn't let me down. Somehow, I sensed the burn each time and got out before the house nailed me. Ordinarily, things can get a little tense when you do that, with people prevailing on you not to leave, but even on the Ginza they thought twice about getting on the wrong side of someone wearing SS insignia. All it took was a long silence and a serious look to convince them they could make it up with the next sucker. That was fortunate, because I can *look* real serious if I want to, but I generally *act* real foolish.

I eventually wound up in a very intense game. Indeed. It was the game I had started out to find, though I never dreamed I'd end up with such a group of heavyweights. It was in the plushest nightclub on the Ginza, a place where if you walk in and you look like you don't belong, they carry you out in pieces. A place called the Pyramid Club. A place owned by a sophisticated, charming, snakelike Egyptian gentleman named Hakim Saqqara.

The flash of satori came to me when I drew to an inside straight and made it. I suddenly realized there was no way I could lose. I'd been having an unbelievable run of luck up to the time I got there, but when I sat down to that table with those very refined and very serious-looking gentlemen, I started feeling very apprehensive. I was way out of my league. The room was elegant and understated, with plush gray carpeting and antique furnishings. The refreshments they consumed so casually were eagerly sought after by gourmets and oenophiles and they were served silently by women guaranteed to break your concentration—only no one's concentration wavered except mine. And when I saw the size of that pot, I realized that unless I was fantastically lucky, I could survive for one or two hands at the most, despite all my previous winnings, and then I'd be right back where I started.

I had bluffed my way in by pretending to be something that I wasn't and by pretending also that I was a lot more flush than I really was. I couldn't exactly clear my throat, mutter polite excuses, claim an old war wound had suddenly flared up, and leave. They wouldn't have taken that very well at all. There was absolutely no way out. And then I drew to that inside straight.

I don't know how I knew, but I *knew*. And I knew it so damn for certain that they knew it too and one by one, they folded. All it would have taken was one bluff, one balls down "I'll see you and I'll raise you" and I would've been dead meat, but it didn't happen. The pot was mine and I was God. I rained the plagues of Job upon them for the next three hours, and then a little switch tripped inside my brain and I knew my lucky streak had ended. I managed to lose gracefully and conservatively for the next few hands, just long enough to make it look good, then I got my sweet alabaster ass the hell out of there and Irina O'Toole's dark-haired, blue-eyed baby boy had come a cropper.

I secured lodgings for myself and my bride on level fifteen and obtained a new home and registrations for her family. In the process, I discovered my marriage wasn't legal and was advised that I could either make it legal or ignore it. Officially, it had never happened. Well, I had been drunk and I hadn't known it wasn't legal, but I had slurred my troth or whatever and I was prepared to stand by it. Drunk or sober, a man's word is a man's word. However, Miko didn't really want to hold me to it.

Between her broken English and the help of an interpreter, she made me understand that my windfall had resulted in a situation for herself and for her family that was more than anything she could have hoped for. She said I was under no real obligation, but if I would consent to loaning her some money so she could get some schooling and find a job to help support her family, she would promise to repay it all eventually and let me go with the hope that we could still be friends.

I didn't believe the money would ever be repaid, but I didn't really care. I couldn't remember exactly how we came to the state of wedded bliss, but if she had taken advantage of my inebriated condition, who was I to blame her? A life in Junktown is a life of quiet desperation and desperate people are driven to do desperate things. I agreed to give her the money. We remained together for a while so we could help each other with our new beginnings, then after several months we went our separate ways, promising to keep in touch—though I doubted we would. I managed to convince a prestigious brokerage firm that I was just the lad to lend their establishment some panache, then I settled down in my new home with my renewed bachelor status and my brand-new bank account, prepared to embark upon a few profitable investments and a lovely, affluent life-style. And then Saqqara found me.

Luck can be a lot like magic. Sometimes it doesn't work for you, but when it does, it always exacts a price. But I was still naive then, a condition that wouldn't last much longer. I was naive enough to believe it was a simple case of serendipity. Saqqara was looking to make a few investments and "just happened" to contact my firm.

My pessimistic Russian ancestors must have been asleep. Russians grow torpid when they're being well fed. Saqqara played me like the pro he was. He remembered me and seemed surprised, but impressed at how I had parlayed my winnings. To show there were no hard feelings, he made friendly overtures. Invitations to dinner at his club and introductions to people a man in my position "could benefit from knowing" led to investment contacts and opportunities. I was suckered in because Saqqara was so smooth and charming and because he knew some very influential, very prominent people. And because it never occurred to me that very influential, very prominent people could have some very nasty skeletons in their closets—closets to which Saqqara had the key.

By the time my Russian ancestors finally woke up and started singing songs of doom, I was well and truly had. Businesses I had invested in on Saqqara's advice, both on my own behalf and that of many of my clients, turned out to be fronts for some highly illegal activities. That was when I learned Hakim Saqqara was a far more elegant poker player than I could have imagined.

He never forgave me for the drubbing I gave him. It offended his pride. He just couldn't bear to lose, especially to a small-time hustler like me. He was an Egyptian who had grown up in Japan and been initiated into the mysteries of the Yakuza, resulting in a Machiavellian creature of frightening complexity. For him, the game did not end at the table. He did not lose often, but if he lost heavily to some well-heeled business magnate with a weakness for the sort of entertainment his nightclub could provide, he made it up some other way, usually through exploitation of the contact. He could easily have had me rolled after I left the club and taken all my winnings, but that would have been too easy a revenge. He wanted to destroy me. He watched and waited and he must have smiled a lot when he saw how he could use me. He built my coffin, handed me the hammer, and I pounded in the nails.

The only solution was to buy my way out. And so I started buying. It was the beginning of the great big turnaround, a squeeze that lasted for four years. You might wonder what kind of man puts up with something like that for so long. The kind of man who's fond of living, that's what kind. Why didn't I cut and run? Because I had no idea of what I was letting myself in for. Because I had a comfortable, pleasant lifestyle to which I had rapidly grown accustomed; because I had a good job; because I had some profitable investments and because I thought I could somehow keep it all and wriggle off the hook. Instead, I gradually became more and more impaled until Saqqara owned me.

Bit by bit, I bought my way out of the pit my friend Hakim had dug for me, but to buy my way out of one thing that would incriminate me was to buy my way into something else that tied me more firmly to the Ginza Strip and to Saqqara. The scam was brilliant. I couldn't afford his upfront asking price, but he was more than willing to be flexible. All I had to do was sign something over to him "for security" and take over the "management" of his holdings on the Ginza. Little by little, the legal documents with my name naively on them that firmly established my credentials as a major shark and racketeer became exchanged for business interests on the Ginza that established me as something much closer to what I really was—a small-time operator and con artist who had lucked into some money. Saqqara pulled off a major coup of paper shuffling in which his interests on the Ginza became exchanged for mine, which he in turn managed with an acumen infinitely more acute. By the time it was all over, Saqqara was a well-respected business magnate who ran a seedy little empire on the Ginza traceable directly to yours truly, who took a minor cut for all his trouble. A cut the largest portion of which went right back into Saqqara's pocket.

Imagine the surprise of my respectable employers when they learned that one of their most successful account executives held a controlling interest in a chain of saloons, brothels, and gaming houses on the Strip. And imagine their chagrin and horror when they learned how I had implicated them, albeit unknowingly, in a number of business transactions which, if examined very closely, would bring their brokerage house tumbling down upon their heads. They wasted no time getting rid of me and scrambling to clean house, which meant dealing with Saqqara. I tried to warn them, but they weren't really listening as they kicked me out the door. Consequently, they were even more surprised a few months later when they discovered that Saqqara had moved in and taken over their establishment, lock, stock, and portfolios.

During all this time, I had been fighting desperately to find a way to get free of Saqqara and still manage to keep some of what I had, only there wasn't any way that I could find. Going to the authorities would have been suicide, partly because Saqqara had set things up so I would go down with him and partly because he had his fingers in that pie, as well. The minute I went to the police, he'd know and I'd never have survived to testify against him. In the end, I had sold everything I owned and was left without an income. No other brokerage house would touch me. The word was out that I was poison. I had no other skills and jobs were nonexistent. I was too old to reenlist and too broke to go anywhere else. I was already living on the Ginza, having been forced out of my fifteenth level conapt, and I had become a liability to Saqqara because I had nothing left to lose.

I knew him well enough by then to put myself into his shoes and decide what to do about me. I could, if I were him, use me as a flunky in fact instead of in name only to run my operations on the Ginza, but why bother? I had become a fabulously wealthy, well-respected businessman with friends and contacts in high places. People I ran into in my present life who knew about my past were people who had no business knowing unless they had a past as well and chances were I already had them well under my thumb. No one could connect me to the Ginza anymore. No one except O'Toole, who was uncomfortably well informed about me. And he had nothing left to lose . . .

I decided that if I were Saqqara, I would definitely have me killed. What a delightful, cheerful thought. There seemed to be only one thing left to do. Run. Jump into the ocean and swim to New Zealand. Get out of Tokyo, get out of Japan, get out of sight and stay there. I told myself to take what few lousy possessions I had left, everything except the clothes on my back, and sell them for whatever I could get—"Buy into a game and win your stake to a new life!" my leprechauns suggested, but I screamed at them to shut up—and then I got home to find a crowd of people waiting for me, shouting and jumping up and down. I had won the lottery. The leprechauns were giggling. I was going to be the next big star of Psychodrome.

It was a truly silly joke. Under other circumstances, I might have found it funny. Never, never, *never* antagonize the leprechauns. They'll get even in the most devastating way. My neighbors in the rats' nest where I lived had no idea I was the nominal owner of half the bloodsucking establishments on our little section of the Strip. They figured, and quite rightly so, that I was just a fellow down-and-outer and they were ecstatic. What happened to me had touched their lives. If it could happen to one of their own, that meant it might happen to them too and it gave them a little hope. Hope was a commodity in short supply on the lower levels of the city.

I never had much time for fantasy escapism. I had been too busy trying to escape from the reality of Hakim Saqqara, so "the ultimate experience" held little fascination for me. As far as I was concerned, the ultimate experience was death and I was anxious to avoid it for as long as possible.

During the time we were together, Miko had been a rabid devotee of Psychodrome, along with about three-quarters of the population, so I was familiar with the game. The word "game" was a bit of a misnomer for it. Psychodrome was played for real and the stakes were high. And, from a callous sort of viewpoint, it was the logical form of entertainment for the modern world.

I wasn't particularly fond of this modern world. I think I would have liked it much more in the past, say, in the twentieth century or maybe the nineteenth. Back then, there was lots of room for small-time hustlers. Mankind had not yet moved out into space, planets had not yet been terraformed, or colonies established or contacts made with other civilizations which, in several cases, turned out not to appreciate our saying hello at all. Geneticists were only beginning to play around with strange new life forms, little realizing what was behind the creaking door they were about to open. The human lifespan was much shorter—though not as short as mine now seemed to be—and robotics was a brand-new science I would have urged them to abandon. In those days, they were concerned that there were too many people and not enough jobs. If they only knew!

Still, in some ways, things had not changed all that much. Those who had nothing still vastly outnumbered those who had everything. There had been tremendous advances in technology, but not everyone could afford the benefits. Human nature hadn't really changed. We still had violence, we still had hunger, and we still had crime. Among those fortunate enough to have an abundance of leisure time, there was still a desire for more creative ways to fill it. Among the jaded few who had an abundance of everything, there was still a desire for the fresh thrill. Among the hard-working middle classes, there was still a desire for escapist entertainment and among the many who had little or nothing, there was still the dream, that vision of a golden opportunity that could lead to a better life. For all of them, Psychodrome offered a unique solution, a fantasy for every taste.

There were different levels to the game, some of which could provide sybaritic pleasures on a bacchanalian scale, while others provided adventure, challenge, and great risk. Players rich enough to afford the ruinous entry fees were free to choose their own scenarios from the adventures Psychodrome had to offer. The less fortunate could enter the lottery, with the grand prize being the chance to play, but these "winners" did not have the luxury allowed those who bought into the game. They didn't get to choose their game scenarios and they had no control over their experience. In that respect, there were two levels to Psychodrome; one in which the wealthy players got to use the game for interactive, exhibitionistic entertainment and one in which the game got to use the players. Those who fell into the latter category were generally diehard thrillseekers, gamblers, or desperate individuals. In other words, people very much like me. And there has never been a shortage of such people.

Players about to embark upon "the ultimate experience" were taken to the headquarters of Psychodrome International, the megacorporate entity that operates the game. There the prospective player was given a full medical and psychological examination and a definitive "player database" was assembled. The player was then taken into surgery, where a special biochip was implanted into the cerebral cortex.

About all I knew about this biochip was that it was semiorganic, incorporating hundreds of thousands of ultraminiaturized circuits and components. It gave the player the ability to interface directly with the Psychodrome computer banks, as well as with Psychodrome's "playermaster" satellite network. The player signed waivers assuming full responsibility and absolving the company of any legal culpability, then entered the final stages of "game initiation."

The game began when Psychodrome transported the player to a selected scenario where the player was supposed to interact with real people in real life situations in order to achieve certain game objectives. It was possible to win, of course, but still more possible to lose. And losing could mean death, which made for great entertainment. The game scenarios could be located anywhere on Earth or on another world or from a fantasy devised by Psychodrome. It could be real or it could be an illusory hallucinact. Only the playermaster knew.

As the player pursued the game objectives, the playermaster at Psychodrome International was capable of interfacing with that player to provide guidance or game clues, but never direct assistance. If a player got into a jam, it was up to the player to get out of it. And the fun part was that the playermaster satellite network enabled the tachyon transmission via biochip of the player's experiences in the game to Psychodrome, so they could broadcast those experiences on mass media psych-fidelity entertainment channels.

People using their psy-fi sets at home could follow the adventures of various players and experience the game with them by plugging into the net. Their psy-fi entertainment systems—which the company sold, of course—enabled them to achieve a sort of electronic sensory link with the players. Each player's experience was broadcast on a separate channel of the system. By switching channels, the home audience could switch players, vicariously "becoming" those players. Home viewers were also capable of some limited interaction with the players by voting on game options. The vote was electronically tallied and the results instantaneously transmitted to the players via tachyon beam. The players then had the option of following the "advice" of the home audience or not. However, since ratings were important, there was a certain amount of pressure on the players to act in a manner that would please the audience.

Realized game objectives resulted in fabulous prizes, as did accumulated "experience points." There was even a small group of Psychodrome professionals, people whose wealth and/or skill at the game allowed them to become full-time "psychos." These pros had the status of superstars among the psychodroid home audience. They were the modern gladiators, cult figures living a life of fantasy most people could only dream of (or experience vicariously).

Miko had been hooked on it, but I had never been a "psychodroid." I had plugged into the net with her a couple of times, at her insistence, and shared in "the ultimate experience," but, unlike most people, it left me with a feeling of distaste. It made me feel like a voyeur and I was left with the sensation of having raped somebody's mind. Which, in effect, was exactly what I had done, though the players were unaware of it on any but the intellectual level. The link was only one-way. I suppose it was the ultimate vicarious thrill in a sense, as if you were to rent someone else's body and consciousness in order to live out a fantasy. One of Miko's favorite psychos was a debauched socialite whose libidinous excesses she could share by plugging into one of the lust channels. To my way of thinking, that was exhibitionism on a truly gargantuan scale and it made me a little sick.

I guess I'm something of an anachronism. I was born too late and I'm too old-fashioned for my time. My ethics and morality aren't terribly flexible, though Saqqara did his best to bend them out of shape. I'm not a prude and I'm not the most sterling example of humanity, but I have no desire to become any more decadent than the good Lord already made me. He made me human and, being human, I'm . . . well, only human, but there is a limit. I've approached my limitations many times and looked out over the edge, but I've never had any great desire to jump. I'm just an average guy with a good line and an engaging smile, but I'm basically satisfied with who and what I am. Long ago, I decided that I didn't want a whole lot to do with The Man Upstairs, whether He's really there or not, so I simply told Him, "Look, You deal 'em and I'll play 'em and I'll try not to cry about it, however it comes out." And that's the way it's been. I've never wanted to be anybody else.

Sean O'Toole was a real hell-raiser and a bastard in his time and my mother, rest her gentle soul, was a patient and long-suffering woman who probably deserved a lot better than she got, but, unlikely a pair as they may have been, they stuck with each other most unfashionably and faced the world together back to back. I wasn't quite so lucky as old Sean had been, but I don't hedge my bets. If it's possible to be both a cynic and a romantic at the same time, then I guess I'm it. The only fantasy I have, really, is true love. But if there's one thing I've learned in all my peregrinations, it's that you don't find it by looking for it or by dreaming about it. You just take care of business and if it comes along and says hello, you don't weigh pros and cons. You just ante up and lay the cards down.

I was probably the last person in the world who wanted to play Psychodrome. And I had won the lottery. I hadn't even entered the damn thing. I had a vague memory of Miko telling me she had bought chances for each of us, but the odds against either of us winning were so astronomical that I'd promptly forgotten all about it. And I had won. The leprechauns were blowing raspberries and making rude gestures. The Russian archbishops solemnly intoned that no good would come of it, no good at all. If I could have sold my chance, I'd have done it then and there, but it was nontransferable. The computer had selected me and the only option I had was to refuse the prize. It was on all the news channels; my name was being announced over every psy-fi set as "the lucky winner" of the latest drawing and that meant Saqqara knew, as well.

I was suddenly famous. Saqqara would not want me to be famous. All I wanted was to run away and hide, go where nobody knew my name, and now *everybody* knew my name. I had to give Saqqara credit. He certainly did not waste any time. Even as my neighbors were congratulating me and slapping me on the back, I saw his "business associates" working their way through the crowd toward me. I offered up a silent prayer to the People of the Sidhe and made an O'Toole-sized hole in the crowd. I saw them pushing after me and treated several of my neighbors most discourteously by knocking them flat and running right over them.

I had no idea where I was going. I just ran as hard as I could down to the end of the street and turned a corner, screaming for help. There's one thing you can't find on the Ginza when you really need it and that's help, but my leprechauns must have been feeling guilty because they worked their magic and help came from a most unlikely source. In my headlong flight, I plowed right into a squadron of bushido bandits. It was a double rarity. The first rarity was that they were standing still and the second was that they didn't stomp me into mush for slamming into one of their sleds. I was looking over my shoulder at Saqqara's men and the next thing I knew, I was draped over the rear of a tiger-striped sled with the wind knocked out of me. A tiger-striped helmet with a long black crest and a dark visor gazed down at me while I fought to get my breath back. Somehow, I managed to gasp out, "Help me! They're trying to kill me!"

The dark visor stared down at me and an amplified basso reverb voice that sounded like a demon from hell came through the vocoder speaker in the helmet. "*Hai*, zen. Hang tight."

Knowing what was coming, I hung on for all I was worth. I take that back. I had *no idea* what was coming. As the black lycra-suited bandit with the tiger-striped helmet hit the starter button and the whine of the plastic-covered engine climbed quickly to a howl, Saqqara's men turned the corner. The sleds started to lift with a sound like wailing banshees and one of Saqqara's boys made a bad mistake. He pulled out his gun and started shooting.

His first couple of shots went wild, but his third one hit a bandit just beside us as he lifted and inadvertently got into the line of fire. His scooter spun wildly, gyroscoping sideways, slammed into the side of a building, and burst into a ball of flame as the fuel tanks exploded.

The bandit whose sled I was hanging onto screamed with rage. Amplified and processed through the vocoder in the helmet, the scream sounded like the bellow of a wounded dinosaur. Our sled shot straight up into the air, banked sharply, and came down in a screaming full throttle dive right at Saqqara's men. I quickly slipped my feet into the snap-bindings, clamped my fingers around the grab rail, and squinted my eyes against the sudden rush of wind.

Saqqara's men fired wildly, then broke and scattered as the bandits zoomed down at them. Tiger-stripe controlled the scooter with one metal-studded leather hand and reached down to his waist with the other, plucking loose one of the ornamental metal conchas on his belt. Only it wasn't an ornamental concha. It was a buzz disc. His thumb pressed the raised stud in the center and tiny serrated blades snikked out all around it. With a quick flick of the wrist, he threw the devilish device and as the stud was released, the little serrated blades started whirring around. His aim was uncannily accurate. The result was uncannily messy. We pulled out of our power dive at the last possible instant, inches above street level, and Tiger-stripe stood the scooter on its tail, his feet secured in the snap-bindings as he hung off the side of it, climbing fast and banking in one smoothly graceful motion. If I had eaten lunch, I would've lost it.

The bandits broke formation and chased down what was left of Saqqara's men, zooming low over the heads of pedestrians who threw themselves flat and strafing their quarry with plastic zip guns that fired nasty little metal needles with a sound that went something like *zzzzp-wheeeeew*, high-pitched and audible even over the whine of the scooter engines. It was mayhem.

One of Saqqara's boys had the sense to get out of the street and go sprinting down an alleyway, but Tiger-stripe spotted him, threw his body sideways, hanging off the sled and banking it in a full power dive right into the mouth of the alley after him. The man heard the sound of the scooter's engine behind him and broke to his right, into a passageway between two buildings that was little more than shoulder-width. We made an almost perfect right-angle turn and zoomed after him. It was a cul-de-sac.

The man came to a stop almost at the wall and turned, the desperate animal at bay. He leveled his pistol at us, but the one shot he had time for never even came close. At the speed with which we were moving, there was no way in hell to stop before we hit the wall. I flashed ahead about one second and saw us finishing off in a blaze of kamikaze glory as a fireball against that wall. I shut my eyes, heard a dull *klunck* as we hit the gunman, and then felt the scooter, still under full throttle, go up and *over*, flying upside down back the way we came. Tiger-stripe did a half roll and got us rightside up again, then threw his body sideways making that impossible near-ninety-degree turn and we were zooming up out of the alley, high above the Ginza Strip. The other bandits fell into V formation behind us. We headed downtown, toward the limits of the Strip and a wonky neighborhood known as the Combat Zone.

Years ago, the Zone was an industrial sector, but now it was a no-man's-land of psychopathic derelicts and screamers. All efforts to clean it out had failed, so they had given up, turned everything off, and rebuilt around it, walling in as much of it as possible. In the Zone, no one ever saw the sky. I had never been in the Zone and I wasn't enthusiastic about visiting it, but you don't just step off a skimmer sled when it's flying above the streets fast enough to make your eyes water.

We approached a narrow breach high up in the wall outside the Zone and Tiger-stripe made a wide, banking turn with the other bandits following and falling into single-file formation, like a swarm of bees entering a hive, and then we flew through the fissure one by one, headlamps stabbing through the darkness.

It was like being in a giant mausoleum. We were inside some huge, cavernous building. In the illumination of the headlamps, I could make out ancient machinery and some kind of hoists and tracks overhead. It must have been a factory at one time. I saw what looked like several primitive robotic assembly lines and pieces of what seemed to be the once-manufactured product hanging from various hoist tracks, metal frameworks of square tubing with engines bolted into them. We passed stacks of large crates that had been broken into and on one of the more or less intact ones, I read the word "Honda." It meant nothing to me.

We came out of the building, crossed a littered street, and entered what was probably once a large warehouse. It was tiered into several levels at the back. There must have been power from portable generators, because there was some light back there. I noticed armed bandits posted as we entered and, moments later, the scooters settled with a diminishing whine on the highest of the tiered decks. My ears were ringing and my eyes were red and sore from windblast. The bandits dismounted and started undoing their helmets. I discovered that my hands were white-knuckled and frozen to the grab rail. Tiger-stripe got off while I sat there, trying to will my hands to open. They didn't seem to want to listen. I took a deep breath and let it out slowly and my fingers finally let go. I looked up at the dark visor of Tiger-stripe's crested helmet.

"*Domo arigato,*" I said. "Thank you for saving my life. This zen's very grateful." I looked around uneasily. "I think."

The helmet opened like a clamshell from the back and I

stared as I saw that the long black crest was not a crest at all, but hair that had been pulled through a slit in the helmet's top. If I hadn't been so preoccupied earlier, I might have noticed from the skintight black lycra suit that Tiger-stripe was not a male.

She would have been breathtakingly beautiful if it wasn't for the ugly, jagged scar that ran all the way down the left side of her face. Without the scar, it would have been the face of a kokeshi doll, except that her features were too sharp and her mouth and eyes were hard. Very, very hard.

She had one of those small, bittersweet sort of smiles, the kind where the mouth barely moves and the lips curl down slightly at the corners. Her natural, unvocodered voice was soft and slightly breathy, incongruously like a little girl's.

Only little girls don't drill you with gunfighter eyes and say, "Fuck me."

And if she was a little girl, I wouldn't have.

We lay side by side on a bare bedpad on the floor behind some crates with a candle guttering in a holder made out of some old scooter engine part. She had her long bare leg hooked over mine and her elbow bent, head propped up on her fist as she stared down at me thoughtfully. I ran my index finger down the length of her scar.

"How did that happen?"

She shrugged. "Fight."

"I still don't know your name."

"Kami."

I smiled. A *kami* was a spirit being of unusual power, from the old Shinto myths. "My name's O'Toole. Arkady O'Toole."

She nodded once.

"I'm sorry about your friend," I said.

She shrugged.

"You're not much for conversation, are you?"

She shook her head. Her gaze was so incredibly direct and penetrating that I couldn't help looking away.

"I don't understand, Kami. Why me?"

"Don't know," she said. Then she reached across me and pinched out the candle flame.

-TWO-

There's an old Japanese belief to the effect that if you save somebody's life, you become responsible for it. No one in modern Japan followed the old ways anymore, but Kami was not exactly a modern Japanese. I'm not sure what the hell she was, but after a few days, I started to think about staying there with her.

It would have been a very foolish thing to do. My life expectancy as a bushido bandit wouldn't have been much greater than it was already and I was looking to increase it. Besides, I couldn't really see myself decked out in lycras and studded leather, zooming around the city on a hot scooter and terrorizing the "zens." It would not have been an equal partnership. I had nothing to contribute to her world and she had very little to contribute to mine, but what little she had to contribute would stay with me for a long time and as unselfconsciously—or unconsciously—as she gave it, it was nevertheless something to be valued.

She didn't ask anything at all of life, but within the narrow spectrum of the world she lived in, she took all it had to offer. And if it didn't offer, she took it anyway. You could make a lot of superficial observations about someone like Kami. You could say that she was self-destructive, that she was irresponsible, that she was a social misfit, that she was violent and immoral and confused and all of those things would have been true, at least to some extent, but they would nevertheless be superficial observations.

Sean O'Toole had taught me, by example if not by words, that people are rarely simple creatures. It's easy to make snap judgments, stick on labels, make a decision based on that and move on to the next thing. Lots of people do it and manage to get through life and their various relationships more or less okay, but they seldom learn much. Life is infinitely complicated and people are a part of life.

Kami wasn't my true love and I sure wasn't hers, but there was something there and that something wasn't merely lust. It was a surprise for both of us. I watched Kami try to work her way around it, fail to find a category that would conveniently fit, and then just shrug and go with it. I admired her for that.

It wasn't that I was a great lover or that I overwhelmed her with my terrific personality. I don't think the man's been born who would be capable of overwhelming that young woman with *anything*. She wasn't shogun of that bandit squadron for nothing. No, what it was, I think, is that we were just two very different people who, for some unfathomable reason, were able to create something together that made us feel warm, secure, and more of whatever it is we were in the first place. It would be nice if that were enough. Many people make the mistake of thinking that it is, but we've become too civilized for such simplicity.

For the other bandits, who had given up trying to understand life or were too busy burning it up to bother trying, our relationship was not something to puzzle over greatly. I was just something on a plate life had served up and Kami had decided to sample it. Period. Acceptance. I was with Kami until Kami decided I wasn't with her anymore and they would figure out how to deal with that when it came around, if it turned out to be something that required dealing with. For Kami, it wasn't quite so simple and for me, it was even less so.

We didn't have anything in common except an intense emotional attraction. The physical aspect of it was merely the catalyst. It was a fire that burned intensely when first lit and then died down to a comfortable glow in which we both found a very special warmth. We spent a lot of time basking in that warmth, simply lying there together, bodies touching. She didn't talk much and I talked a great deal, not only to fill the silence, but because she listened and she didn't judge or comment. She just accepted, with that characteristic shrug of hers—a shrug that did not dismiss, but recognized with its own peculiar eloquence that life was that way sometimes. She took it all in with those hard, dark Asian eyes of hers, eyes that always seemed to have little crosshairs in them. Except for those special moments in that filthy corner back behind the crates, when they would look at me with more affection than I would have thought possible from such a wild creature.

I was with the bandits for five days. I didn't ride with them. I preferred to stay behind and keep company with myself. I had a lot of sorting out to do and I needed the time alone.

I wondered what might have happened if I were twenty-six again, but I didn't wonder about that for very long, because it was utterly pointless. I wouldn't have been the same person. I wasn't even the same person who ran into Kami's scooter and uttered a desperate plea for help. She had given it to me, no questions asked and no conditions imposed, and it wasn't only a matter of having saved my life. In her instinctive, inarticulate way, she gave me a leg up, a leg up I needed badly. She was exactly what I needed at exactly the right time and somehow we knew that if we took it any further, it would sour for both of us. Five days is only an eyeblink, but under the right circumstances, a moment can seem like an eternity.

It was no great feat to recognize that I had made a mess of things. It was pointless to regret anything that happened. The cards were dealt and I had played them and it had been my decision to sit down at the table. The game wasn't over yet, but it was past time for a new deck.

Before I left, I cleared up a few final matters. I talked it over with the bandits and after laughing like hell about it, they decided it was a marvelous idea. I never would have dared to contemplate anything like that before, but Saqqara was correct in thinking me too dangerous now that I had nothing left to lose. Kami had shown me how to hang it out over the edge and just accept whatever happened.

It would have required major excavations of some labyrinthine corporate mazes to trace down the ownership of Saq-qara's Ginza holdings and the trail would have led to me, not to Saqqara. As the nominal controlling interest of Saqqara's Ginza operations—his tame insurance policy against being embarrassed now that he had risen to more reputable heights—I had never actually controlled a thing, although legally I was entitled to. It took some interesting maneuvering and a lawyer with a kinky sense of theater, but I succeeded in transferring my controlling interest to the bandits—as a corporate entity. The thought of being a corporation sent them into hysterics. I didn't think it would hurt Saqqara very much, but it would hit him where he lived and, not coincidentally, sever all ties I had with the Ginza. I never suspected what it would lead to.

I had nowhere to go and no money to go there. And staying in Tokyo would have been decidedly unhealthy. On the other hand, Psychodrome owed me a grand prize.

It was both the longest and the shortest five days of my life. At the end of it, I had only two days left in which to claim my prize. The bandits gave me an escort to the shuttle and we said brief good-byes. Kami never removed her helmet. I watched them as they zoomed off until they were out of sight.

She never looked back.

Every now and then, Psychodrome ran a game round in which a rank beginner, a lottery winner, was partnered with several of the psycho superstars. The whole thing was a massive multimedia public relations event in which the preparatory stages to game initiation were broadcast and the home audience got to follow the lucky winner through every step of the initiation process in addition to the gaming round itself. The idea was to stimulate sales in the lottery. The company decided I was the perfect candidate for one of these extravanganzas.

I wasn't aware of the extent to which public curiosity had built up around me. It was rare for a lottery winner not to contact Psychodrome within hours, if not moments, of the announcement of the prize. Five days had gone by without any word from me. I had become something of a mystery man.

In most large cities, there are certain members of the news media who specialize in covering crime. These people take great pride in their contacts and their knowledge of the underworld. In Tokyo, however, and especially on the Ginza, things didn't really work that way. On the Ginza, nobody, but *nobody*, talked to reporters. The Yakuza was treated with the same respect that ancient peasant farmers used to give the samurai, and with good reason. A reporter's not going to yank your heart out of your chest and show it to you before you die.

As a result, no one knew about my connection with Saqqara and his Ginza holdings. Saqqara wanted to make sure it remained that way. Ironically, so did I, in spite of the fact that he had tried to have me killed. Psychodrome represented a way out and I didn't want to give them any reason to disqualify me. I'm sure Saqqara understood that, but he was not the sort of man to leave loose ends lying around. I was a very loose end. No one knew anything about me and no one had any idea where I was, so speculation was running high. It made for great news and great drama and the effect had not been lost on Psychodrome. I had flashed them by screen to arrange passage on the shuttle to New York and have somebody meet me when I landed. I had no idea what a circus they'd have waiting.

The first thing they had done was inform the media of my arrival, so the reporters were out in force. The second thing was to orchestrate a scene guaranteed to get me maximum exposure and deny the reporters access to me as I got off the shuttle. Their timing was perfect. They hustled me into the limo just slowly enough to make sure there was sufficient coverage, but too quickly and efficiently to allow anyone to get close.

I hadn't expected it, so I was a little stunned. The first thing that registered clearly was the guy sitting across from me in back of the limo, telling me not to say anything to anybody until they "had the angles right."

"You looked confused back there," he said, "that was great. Just keep right on looking that way. 'What *is* all this? What's happening to me? Why has my life suddenly been turned all upside down?' It's perfect, perfect. That's just the way we're going to play it, an ordinary guy overwhelmed by an extraordinary event. We'll keep them on the hook until we get the press conference straight and then we'll feed it to them exactly the right way. Meanwhile, we keep them in suspense. What's the story, anyway? Where *were* you for five days?"

I blinked at him. "I don't know," I said. "I'm all confused.

I keep asking myself, what *is* all this? What's happening to me? Why has my life suddenly been turned all upside down?''

He stared at me. "You trying to be funny?"

"I'm only trying to be cooperative. Where are we going?"

"To your hotel. The word is to lock you up tight until we're ready to get the ball rolling. Arkaydee, old buddy, you've got no idea what we've got set up for you!"

I was never fond of people who called me by my first name when I didn't even know them and I liked it even less when they mispronounced it. The way he said it, it rhymed with ar-cade, and it doesn't. It's not "Ar-kay-dee," it's "Ar-kah-dee," with the accent on the second syllable. This character had his accents wrong all over the place. He was wearing shiny blue pants with a zoomy orange jacket, a diaphanous red scarf draped around his neck just so, and he had one of those geometric haircuts every young bandit in Tokyo was wearing about three years earlier, which probably meant he was *au courant* with New York style.

I had never been to New York, but I had met New Yorkers on my home ground and the problem with New Yorkers is that they never seem to realize they're not on *their* home ground when they go somewhere else. That's unfortunate, because if you fail to pick up your cues, people might think you're ill-mannered. However, I was on their home ground now, so I had to adjust my timing suitably.

"First of all," I said, "who *are* you?"

"Bob Stiers, Media Relations."

"Okay, Bob, now here's the way it is. Things have been moving just a bit too fast for me lately. I'm feeling edgy and tired and I haven't had a chance to absorb any of this yet, if you know what I mean. I appreciate your meeting me and I appreciate your getting me a room and I appreciate Psycho-drome going to all this trouble, but right now, all I want to do is get somewhere quiet, wash up, and shut my eyes for a few hours. I'm not going to be much use to you or anybody else until I've had a chance to do that, so if you don't mind, I'd really like to hold the conversation for a while."

He stared at me for a moment, then gave a little snort and shook his head. "Yeah. Yeah, sure, what the hell. First time in the big city, right? You want a drink?"

"No thanks."

"You don't mind if I do?" The question might have been

polite had the tone not been sarcastic.

"It's your party."

"Right. You might want to think about that."

I leaned back and closed my eyes. I was aware of his gaze for several moments, then the awareness went away. I opened one eye and saw him sitting sideways, talking to a screen with the speaker switched off and the remote set's receiver up close to his face, privacy shield hiding his mouth. I guessed the company was being informed that I might be a little troublesome.

I didn't want to be particularly troublesome, but Bob Stiers, Media Relations, had rubbed me the wrong way. I was tired of being treated as a commodity. I had used those five days in the Zone to think about who I was and what I had become and where I was going. It's not easy to consider things like that sometimes, especially if you're honest with yourself. I had been about as honest with myself as I knew how to be and I hadn't liked any of the answers very much.

Guilt can do savage things to you. It can tear you apart or it can be a potent driving force. The trouble with guilt as a driving force is that often you don't know what it is that's driving you. You think you've got it all under control; you've shoved the guilt back into a convenient dark little corner of your mind and your iron will isn't going to let it get to you, but the subconscious has a lot of leprechaun in it. It has a tendency to wait until you least expect it, then open little trap doors in your brain out of which spring nasty things that yell, "Surprise!"

In my case, what had leaped out was Sean O'Toole, all six-feet-six and two hundred eighty pounds of him, saying, "Fucked up again, huh?" We had a long talk, his shade and I. We discussed the one thing I had always wanted to do more than anything else and couldn't and that was to live up to him. The trouble was, there wasn't enough of me to do that. Sean had agreed in his amiable way and then he had said a most unexpected thing. He asked me why I bothered.

He never said anything of the sort while he had been alive. He was much too busy being Sean O'Toole. But as a ghost he was much more amenable. I didn't start to stutter at the mere thought of talking to him. He died about three years after I arrived in Tokyo, never knowing what his baby boy had got into, but it wasn't until we had our little conversation back inside my brain that I stopped being intimidated by him. Time, experience, and the impenetrable veil had helped take care of that. We had the sort of conversation I always wished we could have had while he had been alive, but I had been too young to know the right questions to ask and he had never had the time for giving answers. In reanimating him inside the bandits' warehouse, I suddenly saw him in a different light. I understood his limitations and I thought I understood why he had them. In his own way, the s.o.b. had loved me. But he hadn't known how to go about it very well. He was a winner in all the games he played except the most important one.

I had finally become a winner too, and not only because I won the lottery. I had won back myself, the self I gambled away to Saqqara when I made up my mind to make a life for myself and to succeed at it better than my father had, to grab onto everything I could get my hands on and hold on at all costs. It wasn't worth it. Nothing's worth losing yourself. I wound up with nothing, but Kami helped me realize that nothing wasn't such a bad thing to have if it was yours, free and clear.

New York did not look all that much different from Tokyo to me. It was more spread out, but it was just as huge, just as dense, and just as congested. The tops of its towers were lost in a murky gray haze and the jumble of interlacing streets below made it impossible to see down to the lower levels, which was probably just as well. The city looked older than Tokyo and dirtier. The traffic was as thick, but it moved at a slower pace. There were not as many scooters and the ones there were behaved a lot more sensibly than their cousins in Japan.

Generations earlier, some ancestors of mine arrived by boat in New York Harbor and the first sight that greeted them was the Statue of Liberty. It must have been a very moving experience for them, just as the sight of the Bradbury Obelisk must have been a moving experience for their descendents generations later when they arrived on Mars. Miss Liberty no longer looked out over the harbor. After she had been rebuilt and refurbished several times at great expense, it was decided to shield her from a hostile environment and she now lifted her torch over the lobby of Liberty Towers, one of the city's more exclusive neighborhoods, connected to Manhattan Island by a multilevel causeway.

I learned this from a tourist tape Bob Stiers, Media Relations, had punched up on the set. It provided a convenient excuse for us to avoid having a conversation. Heaven forbid that we should have to suffer silence! I pretended a mild interest in the program until we reached our destination, the McDonald Plaza Hotel. The limo skimmed beneath the massive golden arches and there was a hotel shuttle waiting to whisk me away to my suite before the reporters could close in.

"I wonder how they knew I'd be here?" I said. "I thought the idea was to lock me up tight?"

Bob Stiers, Media Relations, gave me a funny look. "You mean we're talking now? You're some kind of character, you know that? Most people would give anything to be in your position, but you, what, this is just another day?"

"You should see some of my days."

"Tell me about it," Stiers said. "I'd really like to know."

"So you could figure out how to sell me to the media?"

"It's my job. But I'd also like to know what sort of man wins the Psychodrome lottery and acts like he couldn't care less. You're *really* not impressed by any of this, are you?"

"I'm impressed by the serendipity of it all," I said as we entered the suite. I looked around. "And I'm impressed by this room."

Stiers took off his jacket and threw it down on a couch big enough to sleep six. He had a matching orange shirt on underneath. "Are you impressed by Stone Winters?"

"Who?"

He stared at me. "Oh, come on! You're putting me on."

"Oh, right, she's one of your top-rated psychos, isn't she? I remember the name now."

"You *remember* the *name*? This is a joke, right?"

"How about putting it on hold while I try to find the shower in this place? I haven't washed in several days and you've been very diplomatic by not mentioning it."

"Christ, you really *are* a down-and-outer, aren't you?" Stiers said. "You don't even own a psy-fi set, do you?"

I didn't own anything except the clothes on my back. Still, I saw no reason to upset him by admitting that I used to own one, but never used it. I shook my head.

"Well, no *wonder!*" Stiers said. "You really have no idea what's happened to you, do you? You've never actually experienced the game. Hell, this is perfect, *perfect!*"

He started waving his arms around, working himself up into

some kind of public relations frenzy.

"Christ, I'm going to go to town with this! Here's a guy who's sunk about as low as you can sink, struggling and scratching for survival in one of the toughest, seediest places on the entire planet, beaten down by life, nothing to look forward to, not even a chance to escape his dreary existence for a while with a fantasy because he doesn't even own a psy-fi set! The man's got nothing, *nothing*, even his emotions have been deadened, and he takes a desperate gamble, a long shot, the only shot he's got to get out from under. He takes the last bit of money he's got left and buys a chance in the lottery; odds are a billion to one, no, a *trillion* to one against him and he *wins*! And he doesn't even realize what it is he's won! All he knows is that he's out of the garbage heap, somewhere where he can breathe for once in his miserable life and just for that, just for the chance to get out, he's willing to face whatever comes! Christ, it's made to order!"

I shook my head with disbelief. "I gather you're pretty good at your job," I said.

"*Good*?" he said. "*Good*? Arkaydee, old buddy, I'm the *best*. By the time I'm finished with you, you're going to be the hero of every down-and-out slob who can draw breath. You're going to be their reason for existing! You're going to be every man's role model, every woman's fantasy, the guy who clawed his way out of the stinking lower levels of society where you have to be a fucking animal just to survive and BAM!—fate lands you right in the big time! Arkaydee O'Toole, the man with nothing to lose and the universe to gain! *Damn*, the fucking ratings are going to zoom!"

I left him to his ravings and went to take a shower. Ironically, there was a lot of truth in what he said, but hearing it from him that way made me feel particularly dirty.

I took a long, hot shower and stretched out on a giant, comfortable bed. I had the door closed so I couldn't hear Bob Stiers, Media Relations, as he cranked up his publicity machine. It was a hell of a nice bed, but I found myself missing a certain hard and filthy bedpad in a certain dark and filthy warehouse back in the Combat Zone of Tokyo. I wondered what Kami was doing, if she had found herself another lover or if she had crashed and burned trying some insane maneuver on her tiger-striped scooter. I had no idea that even as I was lying there, she was performing an even more insane maneuver than anything I'd seen her do on her scooter, a move destined to make certain Saqqara never forgot about me as long as I lived.

I fell asleep at some point and dreamed about getting drunk back on the Ginza and waking up in Junktown, only in the dream, I woke up with Kami next to me. I told her that I blew it, that there was nothing left, that we were stuck in Junktown with no idea of where our next meal was going to come from. She looked at me and shrugged and suddenly it didn't matter.

The next several days were a blitzkreig. Stiers was like a turbocharger; the more energy he expended, the more power he generated. I was briefed and prepped and groomed and polished. Part of the process included getting a new wardrobe, but I appeared at the press conference in a faded, well-worn service uniform they found somewhere, one that made me look appropriately down-and-outish. In accordance with Bob Stiers's media plan, I was presented to the public as an ex-serviceman from "the wild outback" of Mars who had fallen on hard times. There wasn't a great deal of truth in the presentation, but I suppose it didn't really matter.

Stiers and his staff then laid on a presentation that described the gaming round I would participate in, teamed with Psychodrome's two hottest stars, Stone Winters and Rudiger Breck. It was to be a sort of scavenger hunt composed of a number of challenging scenarios designed by one of the game's most celebrated playermasters, Tolliver Mondago. I had no idea exactly how "challenging" those scenarios would be. Then Winters and Breck were introduced.

I had never seen either of them before, but I knew something about them from my talks with Stiers. Stone Winters was a dazzler, a dark and sultry young heiress, a member of the fast set for whom Psychodrome represented the fastest ride around. She was already a celebrity when she started playing Psychodrome, but, since turning full-time psycho, she had become a major cult figure. She was twenty-nine years old, smoky and vivacious, with a slightly raspy, whiskey baritone voice and smoldering eyes that sent out waves of raw, unadulterated sex. And she could turn it on and off like a flick of a switch. Stiers didn't like her and I suspected the reason was he had made a move and been shot down. He said she was "a jaded rich bitch" who bought into sybaritic rounds of Psychodrome until some perverse impulse made her attempt a high-risk scenario. Apparently, something clicked and she discovered she was a thrill junkie, one of those people who thrive on walking the blade edge.

"She'll melt your mind, Arkaydee," Stiers said, stubbornly mispronouncing my name despite numerous corrections. "But save yourself a lot of grief. I say this as a friend, okay? She's cold. She doesn't need men. Christ, she can get any man she wants, what can it mean to her? Her lover's Death, if you ask me. She cockteases the fucker."

Breck was another kind of creature altogether. He was the man home audiences loved to hate, the maverick who broke all the rules—not that there were a lot of rules to break in Psychodrome. His goal, said Stiers, was to accumulate enough experience points and prize money to become a playermaster.

"He used to be an SS commando," Stiers said. "Lost his right arm from the shoulder down and got a bionic replacement. Designed it himself. It's an interesting piece of work. He's a top-notch player, but he's a freak. You don't believe me, check out his eyes."

I had the distinct impression Stiers didn't care much for any of the players, which made me wonder why he was being so solicitous of me. In Breck's case, he also seemed to have the same prejudice a lot of people had against those who had been bio-engineered. I didn't share it, but I could understand it. Superior abilities can breed resentment. I did check out Breck's eyes and what Stiers had been referring to had nothing to do with bio-engineering. Breck was a bang smoker, a comparatively rare vice on Earth because it was prohibitively expensive and there was not a lot of call for it.

Smoking in public was against the law in most countries, a holdover from the days when tobacco was still carcinogenic. Before the tobacco companies all went out of business, they'd been scrambling madly to develop a genetically engineered strain of tobacco that was not a health hazard. They finally succeeded, but by then smoking had become so socially unacceptable that there was no real market for it. On some of the colony worlds, the new strain of tobacco had taken hold and some people smoked it, but on Caribbia, some enterprising farmer had developed a hybrid of the mutated tobacco and a local plant called bangalla. The result was a potent stimulant. Smoking it had the effect of increasing adrenaline production, heightening visual acuity and tactile perceptions to an astonishing degree. This made bang very popular for use in sex, but it was highly addictive and there were serious problems associated with having super-amplified senses. It had a curious side effect which made it easy to spot an addict. Prolonged and heavy use of bang did something funny to the eyes. It made them glitter and become lambent like a cat's eyes when the light hit them just right.

With the already striking aspect of Breck's ice-blue eyes, the effect was unusually pronounced. He was tall and large framed, very muscular, with Aryan blond hair and angular, cruel-looking features. There was a cool, soft-spoken, clipped Teutonic aloofness about him and he moved with the subtle, hair-trigger manner of the born soldier. He was the sort of man you couldn't help but notice in a crowd, without really knowing why. I knew why. It was because he was a wolf among the sheep.

While the cameras were on, it was all good camaraderie, but the moment the press conference was over, the atmosphere became a little strained. During the press conference, Stone Winters had radiated an irresistible vivaciousness and sensuality. Her smile was infectious and her humor earthy and laced with *double entendre*, but later I saw what Stiers meant when he told me she was cold. It was as if a shield had slid down into place. She was totally indifferent to me. I think I would have preferred an obvious dislike to such casual disregard.

Breck, on the other hand, seemed outgoing and friendly, despite his predatory manner. It made me wonder why the game's most celebrated bad guy was being so nice to me, taking me under his wing and giving me friendly advice.

"So you were in the service," he said. "See any action?"

I shook my head. "The only action I saw was in boot camp. I spent most of my hitch in the supply corps."

"Nothing to be ashamed of," he said. "The supply corps is the backbone of the service. They were able to procure an arm for me when I lost my own in the Belter Uprising." He held up a normal-looking, black-gloved hand.

"Stiers said you designed it."

"This one, yes. I have since replaced the original prosthetic. I found it inadequate to my needs."

"What do you think of Stiers?"

"A loudmouthed, loutish bigot," Breck said. "He's never played the game. He's the sort who dreams of accomplishing great things, but lacks the courage to make the attempt, so he resents all those who do. He's reached his level and there he will remain, forever a secondary talent and a superficial human being. He will act the part of your best friend and then denigrate you when your back is turned. I find him altogether too insignificant to bother with."

I smiled at the neat and dispassionate summation. "And what about Stone Winters?"

He smiled back. "A work in progress."

"What does that mean?"

"It isn't easy to rearrange your priorities and world view at her age, yet that is precisely what she's doing, and in a very conscious, very deliberate way. The adventure scenarios have changed her totally. I've seen the phenomenon before in combat. A pampered, directionless young person who has never had to struggle to achieve a thing suddenly finds meaning in the highly charged atmosphere of combat. Life becomes pure, reduced to bare essentials. Choices become simple and vital. Stone is a young woman who's only recently discovered that all her life, she has been nothing but a construct. She doesn't give a damn about the voyeur/exhibitionist element of Psychodrome, at least not anymore. She tunes it out. She needs neither the money nor the fame. She needs the constant challenge to help her find out who she is. She doesn't like me, but I can respect her reasons."

"And they are?"

"Her reasons," Breck said. "If she chooses to share them with you, that is her business."

I nodded. "And what do you think of me?"

"You seem a pleasant enough young man, but I am not enthusiastic about being partnered with a newcomer. Tolliver Mondago designs highly dangerous scenarios. He's tried to kill me several times. He'll try to kill all three of us. It's something that amuses him."

"I see," I said. "What are the odds of a newcomer surviving his scenarios?"

"Not very good," said Breck, as casually as if he were commenting on the weather.

I shrugged. "Well, I'm a gambler. I like to bet long odds."

He raised his eyebrows. "Indeed? And are you prepared to lose?"

"No. I guess that means I'd better win."

Breck smiled. "Excuse me, but somehow you do not strike me as a very successful gambler. What is your game?"

"Most anything, but I like poker best."

"You have the face for it. We shall have to play someday. Do you play chess?"

"Yes, but not with you."

"And why not with me?"

"Because we may play poker someday."

Breck frowned. "I don't understand."

"A good chess player can tell a lot about how his opponent thinks from the way he plays. You don't strike me as the sort to go in for a 'friendly' game. You like to win. And, as I said, I'm not prepared to lose."

Breck smiled again. "I may have underestimated you. This may prove to be an interesting game."

"With partners who don't seem to like each other very much," I said.

"Did I give you the impression I don't like you?" Breck said. His voice took on a slight edge. "Or is it the other way around, perhaps?"

I shook my head. "I'm not threatened by superior abilities, Breck. I respect them. But I don't enjoy being sized up and categorized. Maybe it's our fault, all those of us who were born the old-fashioned way, but I've observed a certain attitude of 'us and them' among genetic hybreeds. I don't like being condescended to and I don't like being manipulated. We've been teamed for this game and you've already decided I'm a handicap. Now you're trying to get a fix on how much of a handicap. I suppose I can understand that, but I don't have to like it."

Breck grinned. "Well done, O'Toole. I've been properly chastised. But it occurs to me that I'm not the only one who's been 'sizing up and categorizing.' If it will make you feel any better, or any more secure, I'll authorize access to my psychological database for you. Cards on the table, as you gamblers say."

"Meaning, of course, that I'll have to reciprocate with access to my own file once it's been compiled, is that it?"

"You would object?"

"Yes, I would. But you already knew that, which was why you made the offer. I think I'd prefer to have that game of poker. But only if you wear short sleeves."

Breck chuckled and put a hand on my shoulder, giving it a friendly squeeze. He used his natural hand, but the strength of his grip could have fooled me. "I like you, O'Toole. You are refreshingly free of artifice. Unfortunately, you may find that a hindrance in this game."

It was the last chance I had to speak with him before game initiation. After the press conference, I was taken back to my hotel room, where I changed and packed the new clothes the company had been kind enough to buy for me, and then began the coverage of the lottery winner's preparation for the game. I had time to myself only when I slept and went to the bathroom.

We left the hotel and took a limo to the corporation headquarters in midtown Manhattan. I completed all the necessary paperwork, shook hands with the appropriate dignitaries, taped a pitch for the lottery—"It happened to me, it can happen to you!"—and then it was back to the limo and off to Brooklyn, to the Downstate Medical Center, for the medical and psychological stages of game preparation. The physical was routine, but exhaustive, and I was pronounced healthy, in excellent condition. Then followed hours of conversations with psychiatrists, several batteries of tests, and more talks with the shrinks.

I've always had my doubts about psychiatry. I had gone through similar sessions during my enlistment processing, though none quite so exhaustive, so it wasn't entirely new. The thing about psychiatrists that bothers me is that they never turn it off. Analysis becomes like a disease with them and one of the symptoms that it manifests is the belief that they know all about people. As I said, I have my doubts. I suspect they know all about certain mechanistic processes and linkages that have to do with various neuroses and conditions, much as doctors recognize diseases by their symptoms, but that's a far cry from knowing the works of the human mind so well that you can reduce them to some sort of comprehensive schema. Yet I have never met a shrink who did not, at least in some respect, pretend to a sort of godlike omniscience.

Having the ability to understand people is not the same as

knowing what makes them tick. The first requires empathy. The second requires a very deep and intimate knowledge of another human being and you can't achieve that without risking involvement. And I sure as hell don't believe you can achieve it through scoring a test. Nevertheless, those test scores and evaluations of my sessions were all going into a confidential file, a database for access only by company physicians and playermasters, a dossier that purported to be "me," reduced to bare essentials. I told them what I thought of that and that went into the file, too.

Surgery came next. Needless to say, I didn't remember anything about it except going to sleep in the operating theater and waking up after it was over, bald and with a bandage on my head. The truly interesting part came when I learned how to use the biochip.

Actually, there wasn't much to learn, as it did not really require my doing anything. It merely required my getting used to it. The programmers started with fairly simple procedures, such as transmitting images to my mind which I was then asked to identify and describe in detail. Then the procedure was reversed, with me sitting in another room at a table piled with various objects, looking at them and handling them to see how well the reception worked. It apparently worked fine. Then we proceeded to telepathic communication and I found it both fascinating and somewhat disquieting to "hear" voices in my mind. I was informed that my reactions were excellent, as was my "adaptability quotient," whatever that was. It seems it was not unusual for people to lose their cool completely when strange voices started speaking in their brains. The most amazing and, to me, most pleasurable part of the procedure was the computer interface. It was like a form of sleep learning.

I was given a mild sedative and made comfortable on a reclining couch. This was also to be a test of tachyon broadcast and reception, though on an extremely short range. I was asked if I had any preference of learning programs for test transmission purposes and I selected something I had always wanted to learn. I fell asleep and woke up after a nap of about two hours, feeling relaxed, refreshed, and possessing a fluent knowledge of the Russian language. Now I could converse with my archbishops in their native tongue.

To me, this was worth everything I had gone through, including almost getting killed. I found that I could take a ten minute nap during computer interface and wake up having "read" all of *War and Peace*. I could interface with the computer and "study" engineering or world history or foreign languages. I could take half-hour "courses" in combat weaponry and wake up an expert on the subject. The purpose of the computer interface learning programs was to prepare me for the various game scenarios of Psychodrome, but so long as I played the game, I would have the option of buying time on the computer for my own use between the game scenarios. It wasn't cheap and having a biochip implanted on my own would have cost a fortune, but it was worth it. And I realized that so long as I would have that opportunity, I would make full use of it. My only disappointment came on learning that I could not simply interface indiscriminately. There was danger of what they called "cerebral overload." Too much of a good thing, I suppose. The mind needed time to recuperate and assimilate. Without that time, there was serious risk of psychosis. And my access time would be limited by psych tests to determine my "assimilation quotient." Everything seemed to be a "quotient" or a "factor." Accumulating knowledge, I was told, could be highly addictive and it was "necessary to protect people from knowing too much." I let that straight line pass to avoid having my rejoinder go into my file. I was learning.

On the last day of my preparation, my playermaster came to visit me. Tolliver Mondago was an old man with a somber, sepulchral voice and deeply set, penetrating dark eyes. He was tall and gaunt, with large, heavily veined hands and a long, mournful-looking face, deeply etched by age. I thought of Marley's ghost without the chains. He sat down beside my bed—I was required to rest for at least six hours after interface—and looked down at me with a fatherly indulgence.

"How are you feeling?" he said, after introducing himself. All sorts of associations sprang to mind upon hearing that deep, tomblike voice. Coleridge's Ancient Mariner. The ghost of Hamlet's father. Oedipus Rex tearing out his eyes.

"F-fine, Mr. Mondago. And yourself?"

"Well, thank you. I wanted to give you the chance to grow accustomed to my voice, so that it will not disorient you when I establish contact during the game. Are you nervous?"

"No, I don't think so."

"Good. Better to take things as they come. Have you any questions?"

"I guess I'd like to know what to expect."

"Expect the challenge of your lifetime, Mr. O'Toole."

"I was hoping for a somewhat more explicit answer," I said.

Mondago smiled. "Very well. Your first scenario will involve jungle combat. And that is all I will tell you for the moment." He stood and turned to leave, then hesitated and reached into his pocket. "Oh, I almost forgot. This message arrived for you this morning. Since you were indisposed, I took the liberty of signing for it."

I took the message. It consisted only of two words: "You're dead."

There was nothing to reveal who sent it, but I had an excellent idea. I glanced up at Mondago, but could not read his impassive, woebegone expression.

"Good luck, Mr. O'Toole," he said.

-THREE-

It took us barely two weeks to secure the first objective of our gaming round. I had been convinced it would take much longer. A combat decoration was a mark of status among mercenaries, usually awarded only for extraordinary courage under fire or action resulting in saving fellow soldiers' lives. I had succeeded in doing both, no thanks to my own courage or to Breck's assistance.

I was furious with him, but, fortunately, it took some time for the shock to wear off and for me to be able to stand up on my own without falling down. It was fortunate because if I *had* been able to stand up immediately after the action, I would've taken a swing at him and that would have been a very foolish thing to do. I'd have had as much chance against Breck in a fight as a three-year-old would have had against me.

It was an interesting two weeks, to say the least. It gave me an appreciation of just how easy my hitch in the supply corps had been. I had never seen ground combat during my stint in the service. During those two weeks in the jungle with the CDI mercenaries, I saw it every day. I came to appreciate both the complexities of limited corporate warfare and the unwritten rules of camaraderie among combat soldiers—and, perhaps not coincidentally, among Psychodrome professionals.

Corporate mercenaries did not have an easy time of it. In some respects, I suppose it was better for them than for soldiers of the past. Wearing combat armor could hardly be described as pleasant, yet it was a considerable improvement over having to slog through the jungle without it. The bugs would have eaten us alive, in some cases literally. Pesticides of any sort were out of the question, as were defoliants, because a comprehensive ecological profile of the planet had not yet been compiled and no one wanted to risk damaging the real estate. Weapons which would have shortened the conflict drastically were prohibited by treaties and the inhospitable environment rendered it necessary to preserve existing facilities wherever and whenever possible. Consequently, the conflict was reduced to a deadly game of touch-and-go between the forces of the rival multinationals and chances were it would continue until some sort of compromise was reached inside a boardroom or until one or the other decided further involvement wasn't cost-effective.

For the mercenaries, it was a day-to-day existence and there was absolutely nothing in it for them but the money. For some, perhaps, there was the thrill of combat, but there was not much glory to be had in fighting for a piece of rock that would belong to someone else. They had no patriotic or idealistic motives and they could not derive support from the knowledge that people back home were pulling for them, because nobody back home really cared. In a few cases, some had wives and families who prayed for their safe return. These were usually the desperate individuals who went in for corporate combat as a last resort and, pathetically, they were all too often among the first to die. The hardcore professionals had learned long ago that they could not hold on to wives or families. They were corporate mercenaries because it was all they knew. It was what they did best and they usually didn't do anything else very well at all. Most of them would serve their hitch and, if they survived, go somewhere to unwind, get drunk, drugged out, and fucked blind until their money was all gone and then they'd start looking for another war somewhere. It was a life, after a fashion. A lonely life in some respects and not a very noble one, perhaps, but it was all they had.

Their social relationships could be best described as idiosyncratic, but they seemed to fall into one of two general patterns. There were those who functioned on the basis of a sort of fatalistic, "what the hell, we're here today and gone tomorrow" camaraderie, which pattern Breck seemed to fall into quite easily, and then there were those who were standoffish, as if they were waiting to see if you could prove something to them, such as your ability to cope and to survive. When I began to understand that, I thought I began to understand Stone Winters.

She was the consummate chameleon, extremely skilled at reading people and situations so that she could find the perfect niche to fill. With the mercenaries, the role she chose to play was that of iceberg, the iron maiden who was just as hard as any of them. There were not many female mercenaries and she was the only woman in our group. What's more, she was a celebrity, which was both an advantage and a drawback. Having Breck there was a help, because he was a man they all respected, but she quickly made it plain that she could hold her own. Someone as stunningly attractive as she was had to have learned to handle men at a very early age, but unlike many beautiful women, she did not do it through manipulation—although I had seen how well she could play that game when the situation called for it. She did it by meeting them on their own level. Yet I couldn't help but feel that it was all an acting job—a skillful and realistic one, but a performance just the same. Method acting. While she was doing it, it was real to her and that was what she became, but the real Stone Winters, whoever that was, remained elusive, inaccessible behind a lot of walls and bridges. "A work in progress," Breck had said. It was an insightful comment. It made me wonder exactly how well they knew each other. It also made me just a little jealous.

I had the feeling that Breck knew her a lot better than either of them would admit and I found myself thinking about her a great deal. There was, of course, the obvious physical attraction, an inevitable consequence of her beauty and the baser instincts of my sex, but there was also the attraction generated by my own ancestral mix—the Irish weakness for romantic mystery and the Russian tendency toward introspection. I wanted to peel back the layers and find the personality within.

I was sufficiently recovered from the battle after a few days and we took a jump ship back to Earth. The game required us to touch base with headquarters after each scenario, at which time we would receive orientation for the next stage of the gaming round. There were a number of reasons for doing it this way. The rules called for us to take a specified period of "hiatus" determined by the playermaster, during which we could relax on our own time or make public appearances if the company scheduled any, while the playermaster reviewed our performance in the previous scenario and made any necessary preparations or modifications for the next. It was also necessary to go back between scenarios because the next scenario could be a hallucinact in which we would, unknowingly, never leave the corporate headquarters.

The hallucinact worried me the most of all. On one hand, I'd be physically safe under a programmed hallucination at game headquarters, but I was worried about what sort of nightmare Mondago might devise. I was anxious to avoid it. I could, of course, drop out of the game at any time between scenarios—because once a scenario was under way, it was too late for second thoughts—but that would constitute a forfeit and I would only be entitled to the bonus money my experience points had earned. For a lot of players, that was plenty, especially after experiencing a high-risk scenario, but with Saqqara on my tail, dropping out of the game would not offer much security. Still, I had hopes we could cut some kind of deal, hopes which were promptly dashed when I made that call to him the day we returned. It was Saqqara who told me what my last defiant gesture against him had amounted to.

I had thought that by pulling my paper shuffle and transferring my proprietary interests in his operations to the bandits, I would force him to negotiate with them to get those rights back, thereby getting them some money as a way of paying them back for their help. However, it seemed Kami had something else in mind.

On the day after they dropped me off at the shuttleport, the bandits paid a visit to the Pyramid Club and trashed it thoroughly. Saqqara had been furious and had summoned the police. The bandits were still there when the police arrived and they had all submitted to arrest without resistance, much to the surprise of the police. The reason became apparent quickly when their lawyer pointed out a pertinent fact or two. The bandits could hardly be charged with trespassing or with destruction of property when that property belonged to them.

Too late, Saqqara realized how he had left himself wide open, but there was nothing he could do. He made a try at salvaging the situation and offered substantial sums of money to the bandits for the return of the controlling interest in his properties. I had expected that. Saqqara was a man who knew when to cut his losses. What I had not expected was Kami's refusal to sell . . . at any price. Instead, *she* offered to buy *him* out and, adding insult to injury, made an offer so ridiculously low that Saqqara would have been humiliated by accepting it. Nor would she back off. Unknowingly, I had touched off a spark that erupted into gang war—the Yakuza versus the bushido bandits—and the bandit squadrons who had fought amongst themselves for years were now uniting to stomp a common enemy. The news reports confirmed it. The Ginza Strip had turned into a war zone. The Yakuza was not very happy with Saqqara and he had me to thank for it. It almost made me wish I had stayed in the jungle with the mercenaries.

I needed time and money and, most of all, I needed distance from Saqqara. That meant seeing the game through to the end. It made my Russian archbishops very happy. Now they had something to be depressed about. I never left my suite in the hotel. I was afraid to. But also there was something I had to know, something I could only learn by doing a thing I really didn't want to do. I went back and forth about it for a while, but I finally succumbed, plugged in, and punched up a rerun of our combat scenario. Only this time I experienced it as Rudy Breck.

Curiously, it was different this time. Not the scenario, but the plugging in. Having already been there, I found myself reacting differently to the situation. I wasn't focused on the vicarious experience itself, but on Breck's relation to it. I was quite literally tuning *him* in, not just his activities. It wasn't the experience of jungle combat I was seeking, but the experience of being Breck. It was, perhaps, a subtle difference, but it was an important one. I don't think I could have done it if I hadn't been there. The sensory input would have been too distracting.

When it was over, I understood why Rudy Breck was such a star. To the average person who tuned in, the experience itself would be the overwhelming factor, but Breck's perceptions of it would be the guiding influence behind the psychodroid's vicarious fantasy. He would enable fans to be something for a while that they could never be themselves. Most of it, I realized, would be subliminal. They'd never consciously realize what specific factors were involved—his security of ego, his self-centeredness, his sense of natural superiority, and, at least from my perceptions, his apparent total lack of fear. I realized that some highly creative editing was done at Psychodrome, but I didn't think that even they could be that subtle. Breck was quite literally a swashbuckler, a personality throwback to another age. If that was a result of the way his genes were engineered, I could see why the commandos of the Special Service existed in so rarified an atmosphere. Danger was not so much a thrill as it was a game, not to be taken very seriously. While I had been experiencing my emotions at peak levels, Breck was merely *playing*. A very adult form of play, to be sure, but play nevertheless. It occurred to me that the most emotionally mouselike fan could tune him in and get a taste, if only for a little while, of what it felt like to have power in his world. And if that was what Psychodrome could do, then I had overlooked its potentially therapeutic value by considering only its more superficial aspects and I may have misjudged it, as I had misjudged Breck.

That night, Mondago appeared to me in a dream. In the dream, I woke up in my bedroom, not knowing why I had awakened. I sat up in bed. The room was dark. There was a knock at my door.

The door opened, but there was no one there. Then a silvery, luminous fog started to roll in through the open doorway. Through the billowing mist came Mondago, walking slowly, looking like a specter from beyond, dressed all in black with the gleaming blood ruby amulet of the playermaster worn around his neck on a gold chain.

"Congratulations," he said. "Your team is the first to complete the requirements of the combat scenario. The next stage of the gaming round will take you to Draconis 9. Orientation program broadcast will commence at O-six hundred hours. Your objective for this next scenario will be to secure a fire crystal gem and bring it back with you. Good luck."

I woke up. The room was dark. I sat up in bed, feeling a strange sense of *déjà vu*. It was two o'clock in the morning and someone was knocking on my door. I got out of bed, threw on a robe, and went to the door.

"Who is it?"

"Stone."

I opened the door. She was standing barefoot in the hall, dressed only in a long black silk robe.

She smiled and walked in as I closed the door behind her. "You were asleep?" she said.

"I was."

"Then you dreamed him. I suppose it was something dramatic."

She sat down in an armchair, leaned back and crossed her legs. They were very long and very lovely legs. It was a hell of a distracting sight.

"I guess you could call it dramatic. You had the same dream?"

She shook her head. "I was awake, waiting for it. I don't like him in my dreams."

"Can I get you anything?" I said. "A drink? Some coffee?"

She shook her head. "What did you do tonight?"

"Nothing much. Relaxed. Took a bath . . ."

"You plugged in to watch a rerun, didn't you?" she said.

I was embarrassed to admit I had. "I hadn't wanted to," I said, "but I found myself unable to resist. I had to know."

She nodded.

"I misjudged him," I said. "His jets really did malfunction. I think I owe Rudy an apology."

A strange look came over her face. "You tuned in Breck? Was that the only reason you plugged in? To find out if Rudy set us up?"

"I'm not proud to admit it, but yes. Why?"

She was silent for a moment. "They don't broadcast everything, you know."

"Well, sure, of course they have to edit. But I don't—"

"How do you know Rudy didn't sabotage his jets before the battle?"

I stared at her. "Would he really . . . no." I shook my head. "I was tuned in to him. I would've known if he knew—"

"Not necessarily," she said. "It isn't actually complete telepathy. It's more of an empathic interface. And when you've been a psycho long enough, you learn how to block what you don't want coming through. For Breck, it would be easy. He has superior powers of concentration. Greater mental discipline.''

"Still, that doesn't mean he did it."

She shook her head. "No, it doesn't. But don't be too quick to apologize. Breck wants to win and he doesn't much care how he does it. He can be quite compelling in his way, but everything he does is motivated by self-interest. If you don't believe me, ask him. He'll admit it. He's an unusual man." She paused. "But that isn't what I came to talk to you about." She looked down, then looked up at me again. "You didn't tune me in?"

"No."

"Weren't you even tempted to?"

"No. Not with you."

"Really?"

"You don't believe me?"

She shook her head. "No, I do believe you. And maybe I know why." She licked her lips. "I plugged in to a rerun, too. I tuned you in."

"I see."

"That makes you uncomfortable," she said.

"Maybe it shouldn't, considering how many other people were doing the same thing, but yes, I guess it does."

"I think maybe I will take that drink," she said.

"Name your poison," I said. "The bar's pretty well stocked here."

"Vodka. Neat."

I went to the bar to pour the drink.

"When you're teamed with someone," she said, "it's almost impossible to resist the temptation of tuning in a rerun of your last scenario to experience it from your teammate's point of view."

"I guess I can understand that," I said, my back to her.

"I know I haven't exactly been very friendly toward you," she said.

I turned around and almost dropped the drink. Her robe was completely open.

"I'd like to make it up to you," she said, her husky voice even huskier than usual.

I started to ask her why and found my voice cracking, so I had to clear my throat and start again. "Why?"

She didn't move from the armchair. She simply sat there, staring at me darkly, her lush body exposed and framed by folds of black silk.

She smiled. "Because you have a very sexy mind."

"I'm serious."

"So am I," she said, getting up and coming toward me, losing the robe along the way.

I shoved the drink at her. She took it and tossed it back in one swallow, then dropped the glass on the carpet and put her hands on my chest, sliding them to the lapels of my robe, pushing them back and pulling the robe off my shoulders. I gently but firmly pushed her away.

"Stone . . . please."

"What's wrong?" she looked puzzled, suddenly unsure of her ground.

"What's wrong is that I've just used up the last bit of will-power I had left and I'd really like to know why this is happening before I let it happen."

She backed off. "Oh." She sighed. "I guess I picked the wrong approach, huh? I thought maybe if I made it easy for you, we could . . . oh, the hell with it. Can we start again?" She bent down and picked up the glass. "How about a refill?"

"Only if you put your robe back on."

She gave me another, even more deadly, smile, handed me the glass, and went back to the chair to get her robe. And then the door burst into splinters and a body came flying backwards into the room.

He was dressed all in black, with a hood and mask covering his face so that only his eyes were showing. He rolled as he hit the floor and I heard Breck yell, "*Get down, O'Toole!*" and then I was on the floor as Stone hit me with a flying tackle.

Something whirred over my head with a buzzing sound and thunked into the wall behind me. I saw the black-garbed body flying across the room, feet extended, to deliver a devastating kick to Breck's chest and send him staggering back to smash into the wall. Breck blocked the next three kicks which came like a blur in almost one motion, trapped his opponent's foot on the last attempt, and flipped him backwards. The assassin back-somersaulted and landed on his feet. Breck's glove was off and he held his nysteel hand in front of him, fingers rigid and spread wide apart. There was a pneumatic hissing sort of sound and five razor-sharp, six-inch blades slid like stilettos out of the ends of his fingers.

The assassin saw them too late. Breck laid his face open as if it had gone through an egg slicer. The man screamed, involuntarily bringing his hands up to his face. Breck finished it by plunging all five blades deep into his chest and giving a savage twist. The scream was cut off abruptly.

Breck used his normal arm to push the dead body off his knife-edged fingers and it crumpled to the floor. Blood dripped from the five blades, which made me think insanely of the long fingernails of some ancient Chinese mandarin.

"Good evening, O'Toole. Have you got a towel?" said Breck, holding up his dripping blade-edged hand. He looked down at the two of us, Stone stark naked, still on top of me. "Oh, I beg your pardon. Am I interrupting anything?"

"Lord, Rudy, you're sick, you know that?" Stone said, getting up and belting her robe around her.

"Never mind, I'll get it myself," said Breck, going into the bathroom. From inside the bathroom, he said, "Stone, you'd better call the police. And then—"

We all heard it in our minds at the same time. Mondago's voice coming through the interface. *"The police are already on their way. All three of you please stay where you are. Stiers is en route. He'll handle this."*

"Mondago, if you broadcast any of this, I'll sue the company for invasion of privacy," said Stone. "We were on our own time."

"I quite understand, Miss Winters," said Mondago. *"You need have no concerns on that account. I would advise you to be circumspect with the police until Stiers arrives."*

Breck came out of the bathroom, wiping his knives on a towel. He looked down at the corpse. "I've heard of ninjas, but this is the first time I have encountered one. Before the police arrive, O'Toole, do you have anything you'd like to tell me?"

He dropped the towel and looked down at his hand. I didn't see him do anything, but there was a soft hissing and chunking noise as the blades retracted quickly one by one somewhere into the front part of his forearm. He flexed his gleaming nysteel fingers. There was some noise out in the hall and people were looking in through the doorway. There was no longer any door to shut.

"On second thought, perhaps we'd better wait for any explanations," Breck said.

"All right, nobody move!"

Several policemen came into the room, their pistols drawn.

"You three, get your hands up and leave them there."

The policeman who spoke walked over to the corpse and looked down at it while the others kept us covered. He gave a low whistle. "What the hell kind of weapon made that wound?"

"If your men will avoid overreacting, I will show you," Breck said.

"Okay. Let's see it, nice and easy."

Still holding up his hands, Breck snikked out his blades.

The policeman's eyes grew wide. "Sweet Mother of God," he said. He swallowed hard. "Put 'em back."

Breck retracted the knives.

"What the hell are you, some kind of cyborg?"

"Wait a minute, Lieutenant," one of the other policemen said. "I know this guy. That's Rudy Breck, the Psychodrome star."

The lieutenant looked at Breck again, then at Stone and me. He nodded. "I thought you looked familiar. Okay, you can put your hands down. What happened here?"

"Breck, don't answer that!"

Stiers pushed his way into the room. There was another man with him, a white-haired, very well dressed older man.

"Hold it!" the lieutenant said. "Who the hell are you?"

"Bob Stiers, Psychodrome Media Relations, and this is our attorney, Delevan Smith. These people aren't answering any questions without benefit of legal counsel."

The lieutenant nodded. "I'm well acquainted with Mr. Smith's reputation," he said. "You don't waste any time, do you?"

An officer came in out of the hall. "Lieutenant, I think you'd better take a look at this. I found it outside in the hallway."

He held out a zip gun, wrapped in a handkerchief.

"It belonged to the perpetrator," Breck said. "I managed to disarm him in the hallway."

"That will do, Mr. Breck," said Smith. "Lieutenant, are my clients being charged with anything?"

The lieutenant sighed. "Why me? Why on *my* shift? Mr. Smith, at the moment, we're just attempting to ascertain what happened here. I'd like to proceed with that, if you have no objection. No one's being charged with anything, except possibly a concealed weapons charge against Mr. Breck here."

"My weapons are registered. I have a permit to go armed," said Breck, smirking.

"Cute," said the lieutenant. "We'll check on that, if it's all the same to you."

"Lieutenant, may I have a moment to confer with my clients in private?" Smith said.

"No, Mr. Smith, you may not. No one has been formally charged here. You are, of course, entitled to be present and to advise your clients. Now could we please get on with this?"

Smith nodded and sat down in an armchair. The lieutenant beckoned us to the couch, then turned and pointed to Stiers. "*You*, I don't have to put up with. Out."

"Now just a minute—"

"Go ahead, Bob," Smith said, "I'll handle this."

Stiers left, but he didn't look happy about it.

"Now," said the lieutenant, "my name is Lieutenant Wilkerson. Mr. Breck and Miss Winters, I already know." He looked at me. "You are?"

"Arkady O'Toole."

"The lottery winner?"

I nodded.

"Whose room is this?"

"Mine," I said.

"You want to tell me what happened?"

"I'm sorry, Lieutenant Wilkerson," said Smith, "but would you mind asking specific questions?"

Wilkerson gave Smith an irritated look. "Right, counselor. Mr. O'Toole, were you alone in here or were any of these people present in the room with you at the time of the occurrence?"

"I was here," said Stone.

"Mr. Breck?"

"No," I said.

"I see. Were you awake?"

"I'm sorry, Lieutenant," said Smith, "that's immaterial."

"For Christ's sake, Smith—"

"We were talking," I said. "About to have a drink."

Smith glanced at me and shrugged.

"Mr. Breck, where were you at this time?"

"I was on my way down from my own room to join them," said Breck. "I wanted to discuss some aspects of our next game scenario."

"I see. And you encountered the alleged perpetrator in the hallway?"

"He was in the process of climbing through the window at the far end of the hall when I got off the lift," said Breck.

Wilkerson frowned. "Are you suggesting he climbed up a sheer wall to the *thirty-fifth* floor?"

"You'll find where he cut through the window," Breck said. "The man was a ninja."

"Locker, check the window," Wilkerson said to one of the other policemen. "What the hell is a ninja?"

"A genetically engineered and bio-modified professional assassin," Breck said. "An autopsy of the deceased will bear me out."

"What happened when you saw him coming through the window?"

"He threw down on me," said Breck.

"Could you be more specific?"

"He attempted to shoot me with his pistol. The one the other officer found out in the hallway."

"And did he, in fact, fire?"

"Three times," said Breck.

Wilkerson raised his eyebrows. "*Three* times? And this professional assassin missed you all three times?"

"I took evasive action," said Breck.

"What does that mean?"

"I ducked."

"Do you expect me to believe that—"

"Lieutenant, I believe my client has already answered that question," Smith said. "Mr. Breck is a former officer in the Special Service. He possesses physical reactions at least three times as fast as those of ordinary people."

"Yes, I was aware of that," said Wilkerson, "but, really!"

"Is that a question, Lieutenant?" said Smith.

"Okay, okay," said Wilkerson. "So he fired at you and missed. What happened then?"

"We grappled," Breck said.

"Where was this, specifically?"

"Approximately halfway between the lift tube and the hallway window," Breck said.

"That was when you disarmed him of the weapon?" Wilkerson said.

"That's correct. He was pretty good. Strong. Very quick."

"How did he wind up inside this room?"

"He crashed through the door when I threw him off me," Breck said.

"And you pursued him in here?"

"That's correct. I knew this was O'Toole's room and I was afraid he might be hurt."

"And that was when you . . . produced your weapon?"

"Ninjas are walking lethal weapons, Lieutenant. You don't want to take any chances with them. He had already fired at me several times and he threw a buzz disk at me. You'll find it embedded in the wall there. I wasn't about to give him a chance to produce another weapon. I expect you will find a few on his body."

"You've encountered these ninjas before?"

"No, but I had heard about them. In the SS, we always used to wonder if they were as good as we were."

"And are they?"

"I'm alive. He's dead."

Wilkerson nodded. "Why do you think such an unusual professional assassin would be after you, Mr. O'Toole?"

Smith jumped in quickly. "Excuse me, Lieutenant, but there is nothing to indicate that Mr. O'Toole was this assassin's target. Breck encountered him coming through the window and was attacked. The assassin happened to be thrown through Mr. O'Toole's door during the struggle. His target could have been anyone on this floor, or even someone on another floor to which the assassin intended to have access by means of this one."

"And I suppose it's just a coincidence that Mr. O'Toole is from Japan and the assassin was a ninja?" said Wilkerson.

"I thought you didn't know what a ninja was, Lieutenant," said Breck.

Smith interrupted. "As it happens, Mr. O'Toole is not from Japan, he is from Mars. Bradbury City, to be specific. It's true he spent some time in Japan, but you will find the same is true for a lot of servicemen. It appears to me that what we have here is a case of breaking and entering, assault with a deadly weapon, and attempted murder. Mr. Breck surprised the perpetrator and was attacked. He merely acted in self-defense and, considering his attacker, he did not employ excessive force. It appears to me that this situation has been amply clarified. My clients were merely innocent bystanders and Mr. Breck probably foiled an assassination attempt against someone in this hotel.''

Wilkerson gave Smith a long look. ''I see your reputation is well deserved, counselor. I trust your clients will remain available for further questioning?''

''My clients are show business personalities whose work frequently takes them out of the country and off-planet,'' Smith said. ''I see no reasonable grounds to enjoin them against pursuing their careers. If you have any further questions at any time, my office will be at your disposal. Now, if you don't mind, I'm sure my clients would like to recover from this ordeal.''

Wilkerson gave us all a long look. ''Right,'' he said. ''You'll have to make arrangements with the hotel for another suite, Mr. O'Toole. I'm afraid we have work to do in here.''

''He can stay with me tonight,'' said Breck.

''Okay, no further questions. Mr. O'Toole, you can return in the morning to pick up your possessions. I'll post an officer outside, meanwhile. Counselor . . . it's been educational. Good night.''

Stiers was waiting for us outside. ''What in God's name happened?'' he said.

''Mr. Breck, do you mind if we use your room for a few moments?'' Smith said.

''Not at all.''

We took the lift tube up one floor to Breck's suite.

''The hotel's not going to be happy about this,'' said Stiers. ''I need to tell them something.''

''Thank you, Bob, we're all fine,'' said Stone. ''Nobody was hurt. We appreciate your concern.''

''Back off, Stone,'' said Stiers. ''I can see you're all fine and I'm glad no one was hurt, but I've got to know how to handle this thing.''

''It should be fairly simple, Bob,'' Smith said. ''The hotel should be grateful to Mr. Breck for surprising a professional assassin and foiling an assassination attempt against one of their guests. Needless to say, we don't know who the ninja's target was. Considering what the luxury suites in this hotel cost, I'm certain there are any number of likely possibilities in residence, although I would caution you against making any literal suggestions as to who that target may have been. However, just between us, what really did happen?''

"Exactly what I told the police," said Breck.

"So we really don't know if one of you three was the intended target?" Smith said.

I was about to say something, but saw Breck shake his head minutely.

"Well, it's not my job to speculate about that," Smith said. "Bob, I think we're finished here. We can discuss what you tell the press tomorrow while you take me home. I'd like to get some sleep."

Stone waited until they left, then said, "Mondago, are you tuned in?"

There was no response. At least not in my mind.

"Mondago!" she said again. "Mondago, damn it, I want to talk to you right now!"

This time, he replied. He sounded—or rather, felt—a little tired. *"Yes, Miss Winters?"*

"Why didn't you answer the first time?" she said out loud.

"Because I had gone back to sleep, Miss Winters. It is the middle of the night, you know."

"The police were awful quick arriving," she said. "So were Stiers and Smith. Why is that, I wonder?"

"I was not eavesdropping on your private time, if that is what concerns you," Mondago's voice came through. I wondered if he was actually speaking or just thinking it. *"My computer alerted me that Breck's bio-readings indicated physical combat and I interfaced immediately, perceived what was happening, and made the necessary calls. I am pleased they were so prompt. The moment the situation was in hand, I disengaged and went back to sleep. The computer woke me when it registered that you wished to interface. Now was there any other purpose for this contact or may I go back to sleep?"*

"If I find out you're turning me in while I'm on my own time, Mondago, you'll be one sorry son of a bitch," she said.

"Really, Miss Winters, after all this time, do you honestly think I need to interface with you clandestinely for some

vicarious entertainment? What would be the point? Besides, if that was what I wished, I could merely punch up a rerun of any one of dozens of your old lust channel experiences. I understand some of them were quite exotic. However, if you must know, I prefer to find my entertainment in a good book. I find that sufficiently stimulating. Now, if you don't mind, I am going back to sleep. We will reschedule your orientation session for noon tomorrow. I will adjust the required hiatus period for the other teams so that you will not lose the advantage you have earned. Good night."

I felt embarrassed for her. Or perhaps I felt embarrassed for myself; I wasn't sure exactly which. There was no need for all three of us to have been interfaced—Mondago could just as easily have interfaced with her in private. In the brief moment of silence that followed, a lot was said, though never stated. And we didn't need an interface.

"I need a drink," said Stone.

"It's quite late," said Breck, "but at the moment, I'm feeling a bit keyed up. Understandable under the circumstances, I should think. Anyway, I feel the need to dispose of some excess energy, otherwise I shall never get to sleep. I will be back in about an hour, O'Toole, if you are still awake and feel like talking. You realize, of course, the ninja was after you. I came upon him drawing his pistol directly outside your door. Had I been a moment later, I would have been deprived of both my teammates. I wonder if Mondago would have considered that a forfeit?"

Stone watched him from behind the bar as he left, then looked at me and raised her glass. "That was his rather clumsy, heavy-handed way of giving us some privacy," she said. "As if privacy was something we could ever really have. You want a drink?"

"No, thank you. I don't drink very well, so it's probably best that I don't drink at all."

"I drink very well, indeed," she said, tossing back a healthy slug of booze and refilling her glass. "Well. The evening didn't go exactly as I planned."

"You want to talk about it?"

"Do *I* want to talk about it? You almost got killed tonight and *you're* asking *me* if I want to talk about it?"

"You were there, too," I reminded her. "If Breck hadn't shown up, you would have been killed as well. It would have been my fault. I thought, under the circumstances, you might not feel much like talking to me right now."

"Aren't we something?" she said. "We allow everyone to use our minds and bodies, yet look how awkward we are around each other."

"Maybe that's why," I said.

"Why does somebody want to kill you, Arkady?"

"It's a long story."

She tossed back another drink. "Tell me later," she said. "Do you really want to sleep here tonight?"

"I find it a little hard to believe you'd want to pick up where we left off after what's happened."

"Especially after what's happened," she said.

"Wouldn't I make you feel a little vulnerable?"

"I'll tell you a secret, O'Toole," she said. "I always feel vulnerable. We don't have to do anything if you don't want to. I just want to be with you tonight. God damn it, I *know* you're attracted to me. I'm not used to throwing myself at men. Why are you putting me through this? Is it because of what Mondago said?"

I shook my head. "No, it isn't. And you're right, I am attracted to you. Very much so. I know my reasons, obviously. However, your reasons aren't obvious to me at all. Maybe it's peculiar, but I'd like to know what they are."

She downed another drink. She looked down when she spoke, avoiding my gaze. "That's one of them," she said. "Because you need a reason. Because my body turns you on, but that's not enough for you. You don't think with your cock. I know I'm being crude, but that's how most men are."

She looked up at me with a very strange, intense expression. "I know you don't like the game," she said, "but you're exactly the sort of person who should play it. I play it because it gives me something; I don't know exactly what it is, but it helps me feel alive. I guess a lot of that comes through and it makes the fans feel alive as well. Maybe that's why I'm so popular. But you . . . you bring something very different to it. I felt it the moment I tuned you in. Those of us who play the game get more out of it when we tune into another player. We . . . fixate more strongly. I picked up on a lot of what you felt about me. I suppose a lot of other people probably did too, but that doesn't bother me. Do you know why? Because you think about things in a special sort of way and because you feel about people and a lot of that comes through the interface. It makes for pretty strong stuff. You're a very emotional man, Arkady. People need to feel about things the way you do. People need to care. And for once in my damn life, I'd like to be with a man who really cares. I don't know what it's like.''

I exhaled heavily. "Wow. And to think somebody told me you were cold." Now I couldn't meet her gaze. "I . . . I really don't know what to say."

"Well, for God's sake, say *something*," she said.

I took a deep breath and let it out slowly, knowing that no matter what I said, it would probably come out sounding foolish. "Are you sure it was *me* you were tuned into?" I winced. "I'm sorry, that was a pretty stupid thing to say. I guess I'm not handling this very well."

She came around from behind the bar and stood very close to me, forcing me to look at her. "There's no need to feel embarrassed," she said softly. "Don't you realize that, in a way, you've already made love to me?"

She was so close that there was nothing else to do but kiss her. And it was just the right response. And she wasn't cold at all.

"It's late," she whispered. "Let's go to bed."

-FOUR-

It's hard to deal with the fact that you've got some powerful feelings about someone when you know those feelings have been broadcast to several billion people. I don't know why I hadn't expected that, but even if I had, what could I have done about it? I guess that was what Stone meant about us not ever having any real privacy. We could have private moments on our own time, which made it that much more valuable, but we were public figures—public *minds*—and knowing that made me feel I'd never really know privacy again. It made me feel a tremendous sense of loss. It also made me feel self-conscious.

"It doesn't matter," Stone said, lying naked next to me. "For God's sake, somebody just tried to kill you. That could tend to put a damper on romance. But don't worry, you're safe with me. I'll protect you." She reached beneath her pillow and pulled out a plasma pistol. She saw the expression on my face and stopped smiling. "Look, will you stop worrying about it? I told you, it really doesn't matter. There's more

67

to two people caring about each other than simply sex. At least that's what I hear."

"I didn't mean that," I said. "I'm a bit upset about it, but my ego isn't on the line here. I know exactly why it happened. On the other hand, maybe my ego *is* on the line. Maybe it isn't even *my* ego anymore. But I have the feeling that as we're lying here, several billion people are looking in."

"They damn well better not be or the company's going to have a hell of a lawsuit on its hands for accessing our personal time," said Stone.

"I didn't mean literally," I said.

"I know," she said. She took a deep breath and let it out in a sigh. "I suppose making jokes about it isn't going to help much." She sat up in bed and pulled her legs up under her. "So we talk. What the hell, I wasn't feeling sleepy anyway."

I bunched the pillow up behind me and propped myself up. "It *really* doesn't bother you?"

"Silly question," she said. "Remember who you're talking to? I used to be queen of the lust channels."

"I know. I guess I don't understand."

"There isn't all that much to understand," she said, resting her chin on her knees and hugging them to her. "My family's fabulously wealthy and I've always had everything I ever wanted. They didn't believe in saying no because it would have meant explaining why and they didn't really care anyway. It was a lot easier to simply say yes. I took up less time that way. I grew up knowing I could have anything I wanted, do anything I wanted, and so I wanted more and more. There was no such thing as enough. Everything came easy and nothing meant very much. Especially sex. So I looked for a way to have it mean something."

"Isn't that what they call love?" I said.

"You really are a romantic, aren't you?" she said. "Listen, love is love and sex is sex. I suppose they're kind of nice together, but you can have love without sex and you sure as hell can have sex without love. I didn't know what love was, but I knew all about sex. When you have a lot of money and you look the way I do, it's an easy education to come by. I learned early. I was precocious. But as soon as the novelty wore off, so did the thrill. At first, I thought it was just a matter of finding someone who knew how to push the right buttons. Then I started thinking there might be something wrong with my buttons. And finally I decided that maybe I was one of those people whose buttons needed a real hard push, you know? So if one won't do the trick, try two. If two won't do it, try three. Only it can get a little tiring if you keep escalating things that way. With Psychodrome, I discovered that by buying into lust scenarios, I could have a billion people all at once, without having to deal with the sweaty reality of all those bodies. It was a real ego thing. I was turning on all those people . . ."

"And turning yourself off," I said.

She nodded. "I didn't have much of a self-image to begin with. Being a mindfuck didn't improve it any. It got so I didn't know who the hell I was anymore. It wasn't until someone suggested I try one of the high-risk scenarios—"

I took a wild stab. "Breck?"

She glanced at me with surprise. "Yes, actually, it was Rudy." She pursed her lips. "He told you?"

"No. It was just a guess. I had a feeling there was something between you two once. He said you didn't like him, but that he could respect your reasons. He said it was up to you if you wanted to tell me what they were."

She made a wry face. "That sounds like Rudy all right." She thought a moment, then shook her head. "I'd rather not talk about it." She looked at me. "Does that bother you?"

"Yes, but I think I can live with it. You're entitled."

"Boy, you aren't even the least bit insecure, are you?"

"Don't kid yourself. Of course I'm insecure. Most everybody is in one way or another. I try not to expect more of anybody else than I'd expect of myself. Too many people get involved and then try to rip each other's brains to pieces, wanting to find out everything at once. It's like you and the sex thing. Nothing means much if it's easy. Quality takes a little time."

She smiled. "Where were you when I was fourteen?"

"I think I was dating older women."

"And I was fucking older men. Sounds like we're made for each other. Want to get married?"

I raised my eyebrows. "Aren't you rushing this a little?"

She took on a mock serious look. "Oh, no. By all means, take your time. I wouldn't want you to be easy."

"You're in serious danger of being belted with a pillow."

"Don't forget," she said, "I've got a gun."

She leaned forward and kissed me. "Don't let this throw you, but I'm not entirely sure I was only kidding. I'm joking about it because it makes me nervous, but, at the same time, it really doesn't bother me that you broadcast all those feelings about me. They were good feelings about *me*, not just my body. About wanting to know me, about wanting to understand how I feel and think about things. Most people keep a tight rein on their emotions, especially me. Half the time, *I'm* not even sure what they are. Maybe I'm burned out in some ways. But you don't hold back at all. You have no idea how sexy that can be. That interface with you was very powerful. I can't help but wonder how people will react to that. If they react anything like I did, you're going to be very popular with the female audience." She grinned. "Maybe I should snap you up before somebody else does."

"I'd say you have the inside track," I said.

"You know, all kidding aside, I think I could get very serious about you," she said. "Could be I already am, but I'm honestly not sure. Something happened when I tuned you in. Maybe the interface made me fall in love with you, but I don't know if this is really love. I'd hate to think it was and then find out it was only some kind of self-gratifying reaction to being me experiencing you thinking about me. It would be unfair to you if this was no more than an ego thing on my part. I've had a lousy track record and I don't trust my instincts."

"I think I can trust mine," I said.

"And what are they telling you?"

"They're telling me not to expect more than you can give. And you're not even sure how much that is. You don't seem to have had much experience with giving. It sounds as if you've been a taker all your life. I don't mean this to be unkind, Stone, but I don't think you know how to lay down all the cards."

"You may be right," she said. She kissed me and burrowed into my shoulder. "But you may not be right for long. This could turn into something really special."

"Why don't we just leave it at that?" I said.

"Why don't we," she said. She turned out the light.

Breck knew where I had spent the night, but nothing in his speech or his demeanor alluded to it in the slightest. If he was a bastard, he was at least a gentlemanly one. Or maybe he just didn't care. Even after I had tuned him in, he remained elusive, difficult to read. Unlike somebody else I knew real well. If he was curious about Stone and me, he didn't show it. He was much more curious about the attempt on my life the preceeding night. We took a limo from the hotel to corporate headquarters and had a late breakfast in the executives' lounge, where I told him why a former down-and-outer had a ninja try to kill him. Stone already knew. I had told her the night before.

"What I can't understand is Mondago's reaction to it all," I said. "Or maybe I should say his lack of reaction."

"Simple," Breck said. "Mondago knew there was a contract out on you. That message you received—he must have tracked it down and found out it came from Tokyo. The rest he most likely got from you."

"From *me*?"

"It's the logical assumption," Breck said. "Mondago is the oldest and by far the most experienced playermaster. He used the biochip to probe your memories."

"But I thought that was illegal!" I said.

"So what?" said Breck. "Can you prove he did it? You're still fairly new at this, O'Toole. Someone with my knowledge and experience would detect a memory probe and be able to guard against it, at least to some extent. But with someone as experienced as Tolliver Mondago, you probably didn't even realize it was happening. Besides, some people are better broadcasters than others, more naturally empathic. You might think of it as the psionic equivalent of wearing your heart on your sleeve."

Stone gave me a sidelong look.

"You're saying he knew about it and did nothing?" I said.

Breck shrugged. "What could he do? Admitting he knew would be tantamount to admitting he had probed your mind. You'd have lawyers coming out of your ears, eager to sue Psychodrome on your behalf and retire on the contingency fee. Besides, why should he do anything about it? Suppose that ninja had succeeded in terminating you. It would have been a hell of a news story and the company would have owned the exclusive broadcast rights. Think of the publicity."

"Some company we work for."

"No better and no worse than any other," Breck said. "You can always count on people to look out for their own interests first. Why should corporations be any different? However, that is beside the point. The question is what to do about your current situation. Ninjas are the highest priced assassins in the world, but if your friend Saqqara is a warlord of the Yakuza, he can afford to throw them at you by the dozens. Calling him from the hotel was stupid. That was how he located you. Next time, and I think we can safely assume that there will be a next time, he may well send more than just one ninja. I would not be anxious to face two or three of them. Besides, I have no intention of becoming your bodyguard for the rest of your life."

"I had no intention of asking you to," I said. "I wouldn't expect you to jeopardize your life for mine. The trouble is, I don't see what can be done. Sooner or later, they're bound to get me."

"Oh, that's just great," said Stone. "That's a terrific attitude. Give up without a fight."

"He's right," said Breck. "There's no real defense against assassination. If you're a target, eventually someone has to hit you. But that doesn't mean giving up without a fight. There is a virtually limitless supply of assassins if the price is right. However, in this case, there is only one contractor. Your only option is to kill Saqqara before he kills you."

"You expect *me* to try killing a warlord of the Yakuza?" I said.

"I don't expect you to do anything," Breck said. "What you do or do not do is entirely your business. I am merely pointing out what seems to be your only possible alternative to getting killed. Assuming, of course, that you survive the next scenario."

I sighed. "So if Psychodrome doesn't kill me, Saqqara will. Ain't life just wonderful?"

"I find it preferable to death," said Breck. "Either way, there is nothing you can do until the next scenario has been completed. Unless, of course, you choose to drop out of the game. Compared to what we can expect on Draconis 9, our last scenario was like a holiday at a beach resort."

"What *can* we expect on Draconis 9?" I said. "After a hitch in the supply corps, you'd think I'd know. Seems to me I've heard the name, but I'm drawing a blank. Where is it?"

"It's a small planet in the system of 61 Cygni," said Breck.

"It was the ninth new planetary body discovered by Florescu Draconis during the last century, hence its name. It had an atmosphere capable of supporting human life, though it was on the thin side, similar to what you might find at the highest elevations of the Andes. Preliminary probe reports indicated that with only minimum modifications to its ecosystem, Draconis 9 could comfortably support a human colony. The EuroCon consortium undertook development, but they gave up and wrote it off after suffering substantial losses. After their experience, no one was anxious to attempt colonial development and Draconis 9 has essentially remained undeveloped real estate ever since."

"Why?" said Stone. "What happened?"

"A rather serious error in judgment," Breck said. "There was already a sentient race on Draconis 9, only no one noticed. They didn't notice because the Draconians did not fit any of the established criteria for sentience. They did not construct shelters or use tools, for example, but most important, they were not even remotely humanoid. We—meaning humans—mistook them for animals. And by the time we realized our error, it was too late. The contamination was irreversible."

"What kind of contamination?" I said.

"The worst kind there is," said Breck wryly. "The contamination of human arrogance and conceit. *We* contaminated *them*."

He finished off his coffee, lit up a bang stick, and signaled for another cup. "The Draconians are a race of ambimorphs."

"Good God!" I said. "Shapechangers. Now I remember where I heard the name."

Breck nodded, inhaling the pungent bang smoke deeply. "What the EuroCon people mistakenly thought were herds of animals were actually primitive tribes. Primitive by our standards, at any rate, and Draconis 9 proved quite an education in the fallacy of applying our standards to extraterrestrial life forms. They looked like animals, they lived like animals, they behaved like animals, ergo, they *were* animals. And since they were animals and reasonably numerous, it seemed equally reasonable to consider them a potential food source. The people of the development team hunted them, cooked them, and ate them. Apparently, they were quite tasty. Supposedly, the taste was not very unlike beef, though quite tough and a little on the gamey side—"

"Rudy, for God's sake," Stone said.

Breck shrugged. "However much we may have evolved," he said, "we are and always have been a predatory species. We tend to export our baser instincts along with our more noble ones. Something the Draconians evidently didn't understand."

He took a long pull on the bang stick and held the smoke a moment. His eyes were beginning to shine. "The particular mammalian form they apparently chose most often was useful to them until a predator that was not intimidated by it arrived. Humans, in other words. Humans confused them. The Draconians are telepathic. Or perhaps empathic would be the more accurate term, since they do not send. Their method of communication is to read each other's minds. They read the minds of the humans and realized they were sentient beings who—at the outset, at least—meant them no harm. They also realized that the humans were curious about them, so they tried to accommodate them by remaining in the shape the humans were so curious about and being accessible. It must have been quite a shock to them when these harmless new arrivals experienced a change in attitude and decided to try adding them to their diet.

"Their sentience was a very different form of sentience from anything we're used to," Breck continued. "They seemed a very placid, peaceful sort of creature, accommodating and not terribly curious. Well, they didn't *seem* curious, but in fact they were learning about humans all the time. Being shapechangers, they were also highly imitative. Perhaps shapechanging was a defensive response and they didn't do it in the absence of an overt threat. No one knows for certain. There are still a lot of unanswered questions about the Draconians, but once they learned to fear humans, their instinct for self-preservation lead them to imitate humans. They not only learned to imitate human shape, but, being empaths, they began to think like humans, too. They incorporated what they learned about us into their own experience and essentially mutated.

"At first, the EuroCon people were puzzled by the disappearance of the herds, but soon after that, there was a great

deal more to puzzle them. The Draconians began to infiltrate
the EuroCon development team. Being able to read human
thoughts made it easy for them. A Draconian could duplicate
your shape, your voice, your mannerisms and memories and
be virtually indistinguishable from you. So how do you tell the
original from the imposter?"

"How *did* they tell?" said Stone.

Breck shrugged. "They didn't. That is, they couldn't, so the
Special Service was called in. I was very young then and it was
one of my first combat assignments. Mondago knows that, of
course. I'm sure that's why he selected this particular scenario.
It isn't one of my more pleasant memories. We were able to
avoid being infiltrated by wearing transceivers with coded
signals that the shapechangers couldn't duplicate. But that did
not assist us in telling the humans who were already there from
the Draconians. We killed a large number of Draconians, but
we also killed many of the humans by mistake. There was no
way of telling because the Draconians did not automatically
revert to their natural form upon death. They seem able to
alter their molecular structure somehow, to literally become
the life forms they are imitating."

He stared into his coffee for a long moment, his eyes glittering like strobe lights. "There was talk of wiping them out
completely, but there didn't seem to be any way of doing it
short of severely damaging the planet with strategic weapons.
How do you fight creatures that can assume any shape in their
environment? Besides, there was also the moral question to
consider. Did we have the right to commit genocide upon a
sentient race that, because of us, had become more like us? So
Draconis 9 was written off and the surviving members of the
EuroCon development team were left behind. Marooned."

"You mean you just *left* them there?" said Stone. "Several
thousand people?"

"How would we know whom we were taking back with
us?" Breck said. "Orders were quite specific on that point. No
shapechangers were to leave Draconis 9 under any circumstances. A quarantine of sorts was imposed. The service main-
tains a base in orbit above Draconis 9. The base personnel are
all SS, for a number of very good reasons. A number of independent concerns have since taken over the habitats EuroCon
originally established for the terraforming of Draconis 9.
These habitats are all governed by the military base." He

grimaced. "Governed is, in this case, a somewhat loose term. The authority of the SS in the 61 Cygni sector is absolute, but they're chiefly concerned with maintaining the quarantine and in that, their measures are . . . well, draconian, if you will excuse the pun. As to what happens on the habitats themselves, they're not terribly concerned. Humans are allowed to visit the surface of Draconis 9, but they do so at their own risk, the risk being that they may never get off the planet again if their humanity cannot be proved. Assuming they survive down there in the first place—human contamination has made the Draconians a great deal less placid and peaceful than they were originally."

"Who the hell would want to go there?" Stone said.

"Crystal hunters," Breck said.

"Fire crystals?" said Stone.

Breck nodded. "The rarest and most treasured gems in the known universe. They are impossible to synthesize and a flawless one is worth a king's ransom."

"I know," she said. "My mother had one. I knew they came from one of the outsystem worlds, but I never knew which one. I always wanted one for myself, but it's the one thing they wouldn't give me."

"I doubt that even your family could have afforded more than one," Breck said. "They are found only on Draconis 9 and very few of them ever make it all the way to Earth. They're usually snapped up by bidders in the colonies and the ones that do make it increase in value exponentially. The habitats around Draconis Base are populated by crystal hunters and those who cater to their needs. If you can imagine the Barataria Bay pirate colony or the opal mining camps of the Australian outback in the nineteenth century, you'll have some idea of what life is like out there. Now *that's* where you have the animals, not down on Draconis. I'll tell you something, O'Toole, whether you have ninjas sniffing at your heels earthside or shapechangers and homicidal crystal hunters to deal with on Draconis 9, it's six of one or a half dozen of the other. Except there is a possibility of earning prize money on Draconis."

"Assuming we actually go to Draconis 9," I said. "The next scenario could be a hallucinact."

"What makes you think so?" Breck said.

"Well, the expense, for one thing," I said. "I mean, sending us all the way to 61 Cygni—"

"Considering what the ratings are likely to be, it would be well worth the expense," said Breck. "Besides, sponsors bear a large part of the costs. The company could also negotiate a contract with one of the larger multinationals that has precious mineral commodities as one of its diverse interests."

"Of course," I said. "They receive the fire crystal if we bring it back and get a corporate deduction for investment and advertising expenses. And if we fail to bring the gem back, they can take advantage of the extraterrestrial speculative capital exemption and write off a loss."

"That's right," said Breck. "I had forgotten you were a broker once."

"But it could still be a hallucinact," I said.

"It could be," said Breck, "but I suggest you try to forget all about hallucinacts. The way to get through a hallucinact is to convince yourself it's real. Psychos cannot afford to doubt the reality of their perceptions."

I tried to follow Breck's advice, but the first thing I thought of when I woke up from orientation was that I might still be asleep. Well, not exactly asleep, but not exactly awake, either. I had never experienced a hallucinact, but I knew that while a hallucinact was in progress, I would be conscious . . . well, maybe not exactly conscious, because I wouldn't be conscious of my actual surroundings or perceptions, but I *would* be conscious of the reality dictated by the hallucinact . . . well, maybe not exactly reality, more like subjective reality, reinforced by interface with Breck and Stone and interaction with other people involved in the hallucinact . . . well, maybe not exactly people, although some of them would be real, actually real, as opposed to subjectively real, except I wouldn't be conscious of their objective reality, only of their subjective reality as dictated by the hallucinact.

I know. I didn't understand it, either.

But then Breck explained it to me in a way that made all the technical jargon clear to the layman. If you wake up from it, it was an illusion. If you don't, it wasn't. I thought I could follow that.

It didn't seem like an illusion, but then that was the entire point. For all I knew, they had used our biochips to "keep us under," as they so quaintly called it, and loaded us onto a jump ship. On the other hand, maybe we were still "under." I had been preoccupied with much the same thoughts at the beginning of the first scenario, but once the fighting started, I didn't dwell a great deal on whether it was real or not. Your senses are all you have to go on and what they tell you is real is easily accepted as being real. Sensory deprivation can lead to insanity. So can sensory overstimulation. Whether your senses are being fed too much information or too little, it's impossible to ignore them. But what Breck had told me kept coming back to haunt me.

People who reject reality and construct their own are usually considered schizophrenic. Yet even mentally healthy people engage in vicarious denial of reality. People confronted with unfortunate situations have been known to respond with, "This can't be happening to me!" And how many otherwise perfectly normal people routinely practice actual reality denial, as in denying the reality of situations resulting from various personal problems? Could I really expect myself to be infallible? Could my mind, confronted with an unacceptable reality, resist the temptation to seek safety in denial?

In combat, with plasma rockets exploding all around me, a little voice in the back of my head had started reassuring me. Maybe it's not real, it said. Maybe you're really safe and this is all a psychodream. I managed to silence that little voice before it got me into trouble, but would I still be able to silence it if I was confronted with beings who could assume any shape at will? Beings who would be capable of reading my mind and finding out my secret terrors and becoming them? If it was a hallucinact, that voice saying "This can't be happening to me!" would be the voice of sanity. But if it wasn't a hallucinact, it could be the voice of doom.

I might be better off taking my chances with Saqqara. Only it was too late for second thoughts. Dream or reality, I was in the middle of it.

The way to get through a hallucinact is to convince yourself it's real, Breck had said. Well, so far, that didn't seem particularly difficult. The ship seemed real enough, the crew seemed real, even the latrine—or the head, as they called it on a ship, for some reason which totally escaped me—was in need of some deodorizing. Had I been this nervous on the first time out? Nervous, hell, had I been this scared? No, I hadn't been, because . . . well, because at that stage, it hadn't yet been "real" for me. I realized that if I didn't stop this line of thought soon, this scenario could become a major problem.

It was, from our standpoint, a very short trip. In fact, if it weren't for the slightly disorienting effects of "downtime," it would have seemed as if we had gone under for orientation programming and come out of it on board the ship scarcely a restful night's sleep later. Only we were already making the approach to Draconis Base, so we had been down for a considerably longer time than that. It was more cost-effective that way.

Downtime was a sort of biorhythmically controlled, cybernetic yogic trance state. Not quite the coldsleep of short-term cryogenics, but close. And for the regular passengers, of which there were none on this flight—you couldn't exactly call outbound crystal hunters and SS commandos "regular" passengers—short-term cryogenics was merely a no-frills option. They could, if they chose, remain awake during the entire voyage and enjoy it as a sort of luxury cruise, but that was considerably more expensive and only the very well-heeled with time on their hands took advantage of it. First Class accommodations were, as a result, extremely limited. Passengers who traveled Coach—another term which made absolutely no sense to me—were far less cumbersome.

It was hard to believe that only in the last century, space flight was a long-duration ordeal, done entirely under long-term coldsleep. Tachyon technology, or, as the media newspoke it, "Tach Hi-tech" (THT for short, as in Marietta-Hughes THT on the Big Board), had changed all that. It was the legendary "warp drive" of the classics come to life, only far less dramatic in reality. Unlike the FTL drives of "science fiction" writers, as the precursors of the modern neoclassicists were called, the tachyon drive "jump" was a very unglamorous phenomenon.

The starship captain did not issue a terse command to the astrogator to "Go to Warp Factor Five" or "Shift into Hyperdrive," mammoth starship engines did not fill the ship with a climbing howl of turbines or whatever, and the viewport did not suddenly fill with cracked prism dopplered starlight as the spacecraft ignored the Sisyphus Effect, achieved infinite mass, and then "exceeded" it to "break" the speed of light. Instead, it was all programmed into the ship's computers in advance and when Point of Departure was reached, the Particle Accelerator Drive was activated automatically, translating the ship and everything in it into tachyons. Einstein turned inside out in his grave and the jump was made via tachyon beam aimed through nonspace. No one aboard who was awake during the process even noticed it happen. How can you notice something that happens at multiples of light speed? It was probably the safest form of travel, because only two things could go wrong.

During the jump, there wasn't time for anything to go wrong, because the jump was made in nontime, but at any stage prior to jump, either the ship's programmer or the Earth orbital-based traffic controller could make an error. If the tachyon tracking beam wasn't aimed correctly, there was no telling where you might end up. However, that was so rare, what with the redundancies built into the system, it was almost unheard of. It was more common, though still exceedingly rare considering the consequences, for the ship's programmer to make an error and fail to have the ship properly "beam-tracked." If the ship got off the beam and made the jump, there was nothing to control the direction of the tachyon flow and all the little particles departed at multiples of light speed in billions upon billions of different directions. Still, if you had to go, it wasn't a bad way to die. You'd simply cease to exist without even noticing it. Either that, or you'd wind up existing everywhere at once, depending on which physicist you listened to. I try not to listen to physicists; I only get confused.

Draconis Base was smaller than most orbital military bases, housing only about eight thousand personnel, but another thousand or so commandos lived off-base in other habitats. The base itself resembled a sort of studded cylinder, with docking ports and work and observation stations dotting its exterior surface. A series of skyhooks connected it to a number of the other habitats in nearby synchronous orbit. The whole thing looked like some kind of exploded machine with wires still connecting the various pieces as they "dangled" in the sky.

As the ranking officer aboard, even though he was retired, Breck rated being piped aboard the base. It was an impressive display. Two squads of Special Service commandos lined up on either side of the entry hatch and stood at attention in their dress blues while the regimental sergeant-major piped the call on an ancient traditional instrument known as a bosun's whistle. Breck snapped to a crisp attention in front of the Officer of the Day, returned his salute, and said, "Permission to come aboard, sir." It was pure ritual, of course, though it would have been amusing if the OD had said, "No." I wondered if we would then have been required to turn around and go back home.

"Welcome aboard, Major Breck," said the OD.

"Thank you, Lieutenant," Breck said. "Please have the men stand at ease."

"Sir. At ease, gentlemen."

"I appreciate the courtesy, Lieutenant," Breck said. "However, I am a civilian now and would prefer to be treated as such during my stay here. I expect no deference to my former rank. Who is your base commander?"

"I understand, sir," the lieutenant agreed. "Colonel Renn is—"

"*Bill Renn?*"

"Yes, sir. I've been informed that you served together. The colonel wishes me to pay his compliments and ask if you and your party would join him in his quarters."

"I'll be damned," said Breck. "Yes, thank you, Lieutenant. We will. Please dismiss the men. I know they wouldn't be spared from their duties for something like this and I hate to cut into their off-duty time."

"They were all volunteers, sir. We had many more than we required. Your reputation precedes you. With your permission?"

"Please."

"Ten . . HUT!" It was one sharp crack, not a boot heel out of sync. The lieutenant saluted Breck. "Dismissed. Sergeant-Major Harris, please escort Mr. Breck and his party to the commander's quarters."

"Sir." The sergeant-major turned to Breck. "If you'll follow me, sir."

We took a track shuttle that whisked us through a tube at a brisk pace along the inside circumference of the cylinder. The curvature was gradual enough that it wasn't really noticeable unless you looked "up," toward the center of the cylinder. Directly overhead, at least from our perspective, was a cluster of modular buildings that were the living quarters of the base personnel. We traveled from one group of buildings designed along the Soleri Arcube plan, past the domed agricultural sector, where the food processing and recyling plants were also located. The "acres" were multiple-tiered, hydroponic gardens cultivated under controlled environment conditions. Humidity, water vapor, wind, circulation, temperature, and carbon dioxide concentration were all regulated within the various microclimate domes. Sergeant-Major Harris gave us a brief guided tour along the way, also pointing out areas we passed that were overhead.

"We're completely self-sufficient here," he said. "We don't really require any supply corps support, but occasionally we'll requisition something on the next incoming ship. Since we don't get too much traffic out here, obviously we need to rely upon ourselves for nearly all the essentials. Such things as ordnance and medical supplies we try to manufacture as best we can."

"You require much in the way of ordnance?" I said.

"Not really, sir. Sidearms, mostly. The civilians can be a bit unruly sometimes, but we never draw a weapon unless we're fired on first."

"Wouldn't it be simpler to disarm the civilians?" Stone said.

"It might be, ma'am," Harris said. "We could collect their weapons and store them until they went down to the planet surface or we could simply prohibit their owning any weapons at all and issue them whatever we felt they needed when they went down, then collect them when they came back up. Either way might work, but it would require time and effort. We'd have to watch out for people smuggling weapons in, conduct inspections, set up armories at every habitat for storage . . . it would be more trouble than it's worth. The point is, we don't really want to encourage people to come out here. Fire crystals are a pretty powerful incentive as it is. If you know you stand a good chance of getting killed either on the planet surface or in the habitats, you might think twice about getting rich off crystal hunting. We don't want people to think the habitats are safe. We get a pretty rough crowd. If they want to kill each other off, that's their business. We just keep them from getting too far out of hand."

"If killing each other is okay," I said, "what do you call getting out of hand?"

"Anything that threatens our control. Or anything that threatens the safety of the habitats themselves. Something like that is usually a judgment call. We're passing what we call the ranch,'' he said, segueing back into the guided tour as if talk of killing people was no more remarkable than pointing out various features of Draconis Base. Perhaps out here it wasn't.

"This is where we raise our meat. We maintain a small herd of miniature beefalo, as well as pigs and chickens. It's not very efficient food production, because they consume more weight in feed than they produce in edible protein, but it gives us a chance to have meat once in a while. Vegetarian personnel are exempt from ranch duty, but a lot of them do it anyway because they like working with the animals.

"We have fish as well. We've got a couple of ponds here stocked with trout, for personnel who like to go fishing every now and then, but most of our fish farming is done in the aquarium. Actually, we only call it the aquarium; there isn't any water in it. It's in a separate habitat we've constructed outside the base. A weightless environment with high humidity. The fish sort of float around and the absence of gravity keeps their gills from collapsing. We have a fish farm duty roster, but a lot of us like to go there even when we're off duty. It's quite pleasant and relaxing. We've even got some tropical fish. We don't eat those, of course, but they're pretty to look at and fun to float around with. Some people might consider this a hardship post, but it's not so bad at all."

"Ever go down to the planet surface?" I said.

"No, sir. Draconis 9 is off limits to military personnel, except for ground base duty. And we're prohibited from venturing outside the confines of the ground bases."

"Ever get curious about it, Sergeant-Major?" said Stone.

"We all do, ma'am. We've heard stories from the crystal hunters, but we have to get along with those people. The only thing that keeps the hunters from resenting our authority is the fact that we're not in competition with them. We are the one constant element out here, the only people the crystal hunters can really trust. They appreciate that. And there are certain compensations."

"What sort of compensations?" I said.

"Well, sir, a military posting is, to a large degree, what you make of it. You take an outpost base roughly similiar to this one—most people would regard that as a hardship posting. But if you can find ways to develop the introspective side of your personality, a posting like this can become quite pleas-

ant. You find ways to enjoy what might otherwise be op-
pressive. If you have a hard time doing that, then you spend
your off-duty hours working on ways to make your environment more pleasant. In our case, we constructed an aquarium
from a hollowed-out and sealed asteroid and now we have a
sort of fish park to visit when we're off duty. You'll notice
we've done a lot to make things more comfortable. But this
posting is a bit unusual in that we have the other habitats; the
Fire Islands, as we call them. There's a lot of money to be
made out here if you can handle the life-style and the people
who come here aren't all crystal hunters. In some ways, being
assigned to Draconis Base is like being posted to a frontier
liberty port. The locals are a rough lot and they tend to like
their entertainment on the wild side. Life in the Fire Islands is
expensive to begin with, even if you don't go in for that sort of
thing. But if you keep good relations with the locals, there can
be a lot of fringe benefits. We'll be getting off at the next
stop.''

The shuttle stopped at the cluster of modular buildings
where the base personnel lived and Harris led us to the of-
ficers' quarters. There was no segregation of married and
single personnel, primarily because there were no married personnel assigned to Draconis Base. Special Service commandos
did not often marry outside of their own elite circles, although
it was known to happen. They were mules, incapable of having children. The differences between them and "straights,"
as they called those who had been born the normal way, were
often significant enough to make the odds for a "mixed marriage" fairly poor, except in certain rare cases.

Pair bonding was a natural human tendency, but it was unusual in genetically engineered humans. They had a tendency
to think of their entire hybreed as an extended family unit.
The SS hybreed was the most unusual one in that the genetic
modifications were quite radical. It was not cloning as most
people understand the term. They did not all look the same.
They were not all derived from identical genetic material.
Rather, the augmenting genetic template was identical.

Beginning with normal human cells, donated from various
individuals, the genetic tailoring was accomplished *in vitro*,
working from a template assembled from various individuals
and races. Germanic and Nordic genetic material was com-
bined with African genetic material in order to select for those

coded elements which often resulted in large-framed and heavily boned mesomorphic body types. Depending upon the original genetic material of the donor, SS hybreeds could either come out looking very Aryan or with a sort of *café au lait*-colored complexion. They were bred for strength, high IQ, resiliency, quick reactions, and stability under pressure, traits which were not normally race-associated, so that portion of the template had been created from a wide and varied assortment of genetic material, including animal genetic material taken from such creatures as jaguars and black leopards. Someone once told me there was dolphin in there somewhere.

I suppose that was one of the reasons why a lot of people were prejudiced against hybreeds. The concept of the *übermensch* was bothersome to a lot of people and prejudice was facilitated by the fact that SS hybreeds in particular were not only a racial mixture, but were "part animal" as well. There was nothing about them that made them look like animals in any way and it was usually impossible to tell if a person was a hybreed or not. But reaction time was a dead giveaway and so was body movement. SS hybreeds could move with the grace and muscular dexterity of jungle cats. They looked like anybody else, but they were different largely because most straights chose to perceive them as being different.

They did not have the advantage of birth within a traditional family unit, so they developed a real closeness with each other. Most of them did not have a procreative urge, but some had a real longing for children, perhaps due to some carryover of a strong nurturing instinct in the original cell donor. These were the hybreeds who, upon retirement, pair bonded with straights who had children from previous marriages. Though not very common, these relationships were almost always very solid ones.

Hybreeds lacked a sexual drive, though they were quite capable of performing sexually. It was a matter of "dispassionate" choice with them and their choices were motivated by personality rather than by chemical considerations. That was another reason why I was curious about what had transpired between Stone and Rudy.

Colonel Renn's quarters were at the top level of the village, which was arranged in the style of a multitiered mall. It was an attractive living environment, with hydroponic gardens, sculptures, several aviaries, and a number of small fountains arranged pleasantly in the open spaces between the tiers. The architectural scheme was economical without being cluttered or claustrophobic.

The actual quarters were a sort of modular penthouse, with a large window looking out over the literally surrounding landscape. He and Breck greeted each other warmly, using the Roman handshake of the commandos—grasping each other's forearms.

"Breck, you old bastard, it's good to see you!"

"It's been a long time, Bill," said Breck.

"Too long. I couldn't believe it when I heard you were coming. Introduce me to your friends."

We shook hands all around. "Wild Bill" Renn was tall and large-framed, as were all Special Service hybreeds, with close-cropped graying hair and light blue eyes. His features were not as well defined as Breck's and his face was slightly narrower and longer, more Anglo-Saxon-looking. He was dressed in base fatigues, loose-fitting, comfortable, light blue trousers and tunic, bare of any decorations or insignia save his SS shoulder and breast patches and the eagles on his epaulets.

"So you got your birds," said Breck, referring to the colonel's eagles. "Congratulations. When did you become a base commander?"

"Five years ago," said Renn. "And they sent me to this paradise vacation spot."

"Looks pretty nice to me," said Breck. "I've seen lots worse."

"Wait 'til you see the other habitats," said Renn. "Don't judge the Fire Islands by Draconis Base. We generally don't allow civilians here. An exception was made in your case."

"Then don't show me anything you don't want civilians to see," said Breck. "Remember, we're psychos. They're liable to broadcast anything we see or hear."

"I had assumed that," Renn said. "There's no need for concern. Nothing on this base is classified. We just don't like civilians running around loose. But while we're on the subject of this broadcasting thing, what happens if you and I want to have a private conversation?"

"No problem," said Breck. "Action scenarios are sometimes broadcast live, but generally, they edit for maximum dramatic impact. In scenarios where we become involved with people in ways that could be construed as invasion of privacy, we're required to inform them that we're psychos. All that's necessary is for you to refuse access to your privacy."

"How do I do that?"

"Simple. You tell me anything you don't want broadcast. So far as your own personal privacy is concerned, you have the right to deny use of same."

"How about if I want to make sure something gets broadcast?"

"Again, all you have to do is specify that," said Breck, "but I can't guarantee you they'll use it."

"Okay, then I'd like this to go out to your audience," said Renn. "I'll address them directly through you, if I may. I'd like you home viewers to know that I consented to authorize Psychodrome's use of Draconis 9 for one of their adventures because I wanted people to have some idea of what it's really like out here . . . and down there on the planet surface. In the past couple of years, we've experienced some growth in the Fire Island habitats, growth we would frankly like to discourage. This is not Earth, nor is it a formally established colony. We have no laws here, except what I choose to have enforced, and we have no police.

"Some people have come out here hoping to get rich without having any idea what they're up against," Renn continued. "It's dangerous. It's also very expensive. And crystal hunters have a unique society of their own. They're not very tolerant of outsiders. It stands to reason. They don't like the competition and they have their own methods of dealing with it. Some of those methods are rather extreme.

"If anyone considers coming out here, they should know that they won't be made particularly welcome. It's not easy to get the crystal hunters to accept you. The mortality rate is very high. No one will protect you and no one will support you. An average meal costs the equivalent of what most people on Earth make in a week. And everything else costs a lot more. If you run out of money, you don't have a lot of choices. You can either try to get someone to support you—which amounts to slavery, because then you'll belong to them until you can buy out of whatever contract you make—or you can sign enlistment papers, which I'd be happy to arrange. That means the service pays your way out of here in return for a twenty-year enlistment with no options. You're sent wherever the service feels you're needed. Or you can take a short walk out the nearest airlock.

"As for what you can expect on the planet surface, I'll leave you to judge that for yourselves after you've experienced this so-called adventure. If you still want to come after that, it's up to you, but don't say I didn't warn you. And now I'd like to have that private conversation, so 'Cut,' or whatever it is you show business people say."

We all "heard" Mondago's voice in our minds at the same time. *"Mr. Breck, please inform Colonel Renn that his wishes will be complied with and that his remarks will be included in the broadcast as he specified. And please thank him on behalf of the company."*

"The playermaster says fine," said Breck. "Your remarks will go out as part of the broadcast and we're on our own time as of now, until you release us for broadcasting again. And I'm supposed to thank you on behalf of the company."

"Tell them they're welcome," Renn said.

"You just did," said Breck.

Renn shook his head. "Show business," he said sourly. "It's all a lot of crap if you ask me." He looked at Stone and me. "No offense, people, but why the hell would anybody in their right mind want to do this sort of thing?"

"Why don't you ask Breck?" I said.

"I know why *he* wants to do it," Renn said. "I never said anything about Breck being in his right mind."

Breck grinned. "Thanks, Bill."

"Don't mention it."

"You don't really want to know, do you, Colonel?" I said.

"No, Mr. O'Toole, not really. I'm sure you have your reasons. Besides, that's not why I wanted to see you people. Breck and I have some old times to talk about, but I did want to bring up a few important points about your stay here, so there won't be any misunderstandings. These people make their living hunting fire crystal. They risk their lives to do it. I just want to make sure you understand that no one's going to give you any special treatment. In fact, I've issued orders to those under my command to go out of their way to *make sure* no one thinks you're being treated any differently."

"Because of me?" said Breck.

"Because of you," said Renn. "You're something of a

celebrity already. They know you're a former officer in the SS who was stationed here once before. Your coming back now to hunt for fire crystal doesn't look very good at all. They'll be looking to push you, to see how my command reacts. The three of you can look forward to some unusual attention. Bet on it. Frankly, I don't give a damn what happens out there so long as none of my people are involved. You'll be completely on your own. Not a single SS commando will lift so much as a finger on your behalf against any of the hunters."

"I understand," said Breck.

"I knew you would," Renn said. He glanced at Stone and me. "If either of you can't handle that, now's the time to tell me. You won't get another chance."

"I wasn't expecting any special treatment," Stone said.

"No problem with me," I said.

"Okay, then. Sergeant-Major, why don't you take Miss Winters and Mr. O'Toole out to the aquarium. They and their audience might find it an interesting experience. Major Breck and I will see you back here in about one hour."

"Sir!" Harris snapped to attention and saluted.

Renn returned his salute. "Dismissed."

Harris turned to us. "You're in for a treat," he said. "You'll be the first civilians ever to visit the aquarium. Ever come face to snout with a great white shark?"

"A *what*?" I said. "You're joking."

Harris smiled. "Wait 'til you see the punch line," he said. "It's about sixty-five feet long."

-FIVE-

You don't live in Japan for five years without learning something about fish, so even though I had grown up on Mars, I knew what a shark was. I knew what a shark looked like and I knew what the meat tasted like—quite good, actually—and I knew that you could use the skin to make expensive boots and jackets that were practically indestructible. The reason they were practically indestructible is that a shark is practically indestructible. And just as people ate sharks, sharks also ate people. Only they were better at it.

I had never seen a great white, but I had heard some frightening stories. The shark was one of the oldest life forms in existence. They were around long before we were and they'll probably be around long after we are gone. In spite of everything we had done to our oceans, sharks survived. Sightings of great whites were pretty rare, but occasionally one of them would come up to the surface and eat a boat or something. The thought of a sixty-five-foot great white shark living inside a hollow asteroid in the system of 61 Cygni, about 65 trillion miles away from its natural habitat, was astonishing in itself. The thought that I would soon be in there with the damn thing was frankly terrifying.

We took a small shuttle from Draconis Base to the aquarium. From the outside, it looked nothing like an ordinary asteroid, even though it had started out as one. Most asteroids were potato-shaped and pockmarked with craters, but this one was spherical from the hollowing-out process, which involved using a solar mirror to bore a hole down to its center, placing water tanks within the asteroid's core, then spinning the asteroid and mirror-heating it to its melting point. As the asteroid softened and melted, the spinning action pulled it into a spherical shape while the tanks within the core slowly heated up, finally exploding from steam pressure. The resulting expansion created a much larger, hollow, spherical asteroid with a thin crust, the interior of which could be sealed with ferroplast. The result was a finished shell for a space colony, ready for interior construction.

Only in this case, the engineers of Draconis Base had used it to create a huge orbital humidarium and fish hatchery. Rather than leave the asteroid spinning to impart artificial gravity to it, the engineers despun it so that the environment inside would be zero G. The atmosphere within the "aquarium" was a breathable one, though quite high in humidity.

It was obvious that the SS commandos had invested a great deal of time and love in their project. It was practical as a food source, but it had its aesthetic side as well. The inner asteroid was divided into sectors; carefully controlled, pressurized environments, misty and ethereal. It was like swimming through a waterless sea. You could float, breathe, and talk without aid of any special apparatus and do it all side by side with schools of brilliantly colored fish. They floated everywhere, tumbling lazily end over end, "swimming" in their weightless, waterless ocean. Nutrients were misted into the air. Hydroponic plants undulated upon "reefs" made to resemble coral containing artificial caverns teeming with marine life. A sargasso of sculptured struts webbed the interior of the chambers; struts containing pipes to mist the air and release nutrient fog also doubled as hand- and footholds. It was like some sort of surreal, "undersea" children's monkey-bar jungle.

"My God," said Stone. "I've never seen anything so beautiful!"

Sergeant-Major Harris floated beside us, using a small, portable directional thruster to control his weightless flight. "We weren't allowed to go down to the world below," he said, "so we created our own out here. There's nothing else like it anywhere. It's taken years to get it like this. A lot of us spend almost all of our off-duty time in here. It may seem kind of strange, but to me, this feels like home."

I remembered what I had heard about there being genetic material from dolphins in the SS hybreed matrix and decided that it didn't seem that strange at all. Even I, whose genetic matrix had been dictated by eons of chance, felt spiritually moved in this spectacular environment, and oddly at peace. But then we had all come from the sea. Perhaps there was some vague, far-off echo of an instinct responding to a primeval call across the centuries.

"These fish are hybreeds," Harris said. "All designed to survive in fresh water . . . or maybe I should say fresh air." He grinned. "It's pretty moist air, though. Takes a lot of getting used to. Look over there," he said, pointing down, or at least "down" relative to where we were. Stone and I looked in the direction he indicated and saw an honest-to-God shipwreck on one of the larger reefs. The wood was rotting and there were gaping holes in the hull. A sheared-off smokestack was sticking out at a crazy angle and corrosion was turning the brass fittings green.

"I don't believe it," I said.

"That's my pet project," Harris said. "We call it the *Titanic*. A bunch of us have been working on it for almost a full year now. It's completely to scale. We've almost got it right." He waved to several people who were working on the "wreck." He led us through into another sector and it was like floating through a nautilus chamber. "You're about to meet our great white mascot," he said.

Stone glanced at him anxiously "You're sure this is safe?"

"You can never be sure of anything with sharks," said Harris. "But he should have been fed by now, so he probably won't be feeling very hungry."

"I heard somewhere that sharks were always hungry," I said.

"You heard that, too?" Harris said. "Well, maybe we shouldn't get too close then."

"He's putting us on," said Stone. "Isn't he?"

I reached out and grabbed her arm. At the same time, I used my thruster to immediately reverse my direction. The air was suddenly full of sharks. There were dozens of them, all different sizes, all different species. The sergeant-major was floating right into the thick of them.

"They don't seem to be bothering him," said Stone, swallowing hard.

"I don't care," I said. "I'm getting out of here right now."

"*I'm sure the audience would be disappointed if you went back now,*" Mondago's voice came to us both simultaneously on tachyon broadcast through the interface. "*How often would they have a chance to confront a sixty-five-foot-long extraterrestrial great white shark?*"

"How often would they want to?" I said.

"Let's go," said Stone, hitting her thruster and pulling me forward with her.

That little voice started speaking to me as we floated into the midst of all those sharks. This can't be real, it said. You can't actually be floating in midair with a school of sharks tumbling all around you. It's like some sort of macabre surrealistic painting; it can't possibly be real.

"Oh, my God!" said Stone as we floated through the school of sharks, following the sergeant-major down toward a reef . . . only it wasn't a reef. It was moving, floating in the mist like some giant zeppelin. Harris looked tiny floating beside it, like some remora fish. He waved us on.

"Meet Winslow," he said. He patted the monster. "Say hello, Winslow."

That huge maw opened wide and every last nerve fiber in my body went berserk. At the sight of that vivisectorium, primitive racial memories sent waves of stark, raving terror screaming up from deep within and it felt as if a giant fist had closed around my heart and started squeezing. I panicked and hit my thruster, accelerating back the way we came. I thought I screamed, but no sound came out. My mouth was open and, mentally, I *was* screaming, but my even my vocal chords had frozen with fear.

I slammed into one of the struts and rebounded off it, tumbling wildly end over end. I hit one of the smaller sharks and we both spun off into opposite directions. I kept tumbling until a couple of commandos on duty in the aquarium caught me. Harris was there almost at once, pulling Stone along with him.

"I'm sorry about that, sir," he said, sounding as if he truly meant it. "These sharks don't attack humans. We've bred it out of them. You're perfectly safe here."

"I feel like an utter fool," I said, humiliated in front of Stone.

"It's my fault, sir," Harris said. "We'd best be returning to the base."

"No," I said. I tried to avoid looking at Stone. "Not yet. I'm going back."

"Go on ahead, sir," Harris said. "We'll just wait here."

The man understood. You take centuries of civilization and all that it's accomplished and what you have, at best, is still a thin veneer. And it doesn't take much to wear away that surface. You never really know what will strip away the layers of control until something happens that triphammers the adrenalin and opens up the sluice gates, letting the primordial instincts gush forth out of the depths of your subconscious. There's nothing rational about it. I had simply reacted.

Now there was another primitive emotion at work, not quite as powerful or overwhelming, but equally undeniable. The man had shamed himself before the woman. The hunter, the protector, had deserted the keeper of the cave and the bearer of the children, leaving her to the mercy of the predator while he abandoned all responsibility and fled to save his own miserable skin. It made no difference that in the modern world, those simple roles and definitions made about as much sense as carrying a spear. Deep down inside, there was still a vestigial machismo that said, "Thou shalt not reveal thy yellow streak before the woman and fail to defend her from the scary monster." So maybe I was being foolish, maybe I didn't need to prove anything to Stone—who certainly did not require the likes of me to protect her—and maybe I was only putting on a false show of bravado for myself more than for anybody else. Now that I knew Winslow wouldn't eat me, I could go back and conquer my fear. It was all a lot of nonsense. But I had to do it anyway.

I took a deep breath and hit my thruster. I started drifting down toward that impossibly huge and terrifying fish, which didn't seem any the less terrifying despite the fact that Harris told me it didn't attack people. But I had made up my mind that I was going to do it no matter what. I set my teeth and tried to control the unreasoning terror that welled up in me at the mere sight of that awful thing. I had to keep telling myself, it doesn't eat people. It only looks frightening. It's nothing but a pet—it's just big, that's all.

And then that little voice started its Judas whisper. It's a hallucinact, it said reassuringly. You were only frightened by a vision in your mind. None of this is real. Go on. Nothing will happen. You'll see. There's nothing to it. It's just special effects.

I reached out a tentative hand to touch the giant shark, literally feeling my flesh crawl, then involuntarily jerked it back at the last instant—and a plasma blast slammed into that thick gray hide, pushing the shark away from me as it thrashed, sending great globules of blood bursting out in all directions like dark quicksilver.

For a moment, I didn't know what the hell was going on. I was struck by bubbles of shark blood that burst against me and then I suddenly realized that somebody was shooting at me. I heard Stone yell something and I fired my thruster, sending myself toward one of the struts. I hit it and rebounded, spinning away just as another plasma blast slammed into the strut, shearing it and sending globs of pressurized water and nutrient solution spewing out in all directions.

Someone dressed in the uniform of an SS commando was accelerating through the air toward me, firing a plasma pistol. But with every shot, the burst of plasma coming from the gun sent my attacker flying back in the opposite direction and he had to quickly use his thruster to compensate and correct his glidepath. I saw Harris give Stone a hard shove which sent him flying in the opposite direction, and then use his thruster to accelerate toward my attacker. A couple of the other commandos were also closing in, but they were unarmed and the assassin ignored them, concentrating on me. He was having a difficult time in the zero-G environment and that was the only reason I was still alive.

Harris got to him and "landed" on his back. They went spinning end over end together, but the assassin managed to dislodge Harris and, with a kick, sent him spinning back into the other approaching commandos, which resulted in an abrupt change in his own direction. I had nothing I could use as a weapon, but then neither had the soldiers. There was no reason for the commandos to go armed in their own fish park, yet they were risking their necks going after the assassin unarmed while I was running away again, trying to hide behind an artificial reef. Common sense and a well developed instinct for self-preservation told me to stay exactly where I was and hope the commandos got the assassin but I just couldn't do it. I was furious. I couldn't run away again. And somehow that plasma pistol didn't scare me half as much as those giant shark jaws had.

I pushed off from the reef and went sailing toward the assassin. He was having a bit of a hard time shooting in zero G, but he was learning fast. He fired at one of the commandos and the opposing reaction sent him flying backwards, but the plasma charge took the commando squarely in the chest and he exploded into bits of charred flesh and globules of blood and body fluids. The assassin fired his plasma pistol again to change direction and now he was coming at me fast, aiming . . . I hit my thruster and rocketed sideways just in time. The plasma blast barely missed me and sent him flying backwards into Harris. They struck each other and rebounded in opposite directions, spinning away . . . and then one of the sharks thrashed around and took the assassin's right leg off with one snap of its powerful jaws.

The man screamed horribly as blood bubbles burst out of his severed arteries. The sharks were all going crazy. They were thrashing around, spinning crazily and tumbling end over end through the air, their jaws snapping at anything within reach. Another shark bounced into the assassin, snapped its jaws, and his right arm went floating off into the air, spraying globules of blood behind it.

Harris grabbed me from behind and I was suddenly being pulled through the air away from the grisly scene as he screamed, *"Get out! Get out! Shut down the sector!"*

We went rocketing through the nautilus chamber and several other soldiers came through right behind us, the last one pausing to close off the chamber and shut down that sector of the aquarium. I frantically looked around for Stone, saw that she was safe, and then the reality of that man being torn to pieces by the sharks came home to me and I did something nobody should ever do in a weightless environment. I puked my guts out.

Colonel Renn was not sorry to see us leave Draconis Base. I couldn't really blame him. Two of the men under his command had died. I hadn't killed them, but if I hadn't been there, they'd still be alive. The assassin had killed one and the second man was killed along with the assassin when the sharks went wild with blood frenzy. In spite of what Harris had said, you can only manipulate so much genetically. The smell of blood has been the feeding signal for sharks for thousands of years. The sharks in the aquarium were bred outside their natural habitat and raised in a controlled environment on nutrient solutions and bloodless protein. They were very different from the sharks on Earth, but they still shared a common evolution. The smell of blood had awakened a deeply ingrained instinct.

I tried to convince myself that none of it had been my fault. I tried real hard, but I couldn't quite buy the argument. People were dying around me. The number had gone up to three now, starting with that young bandit shot down by Saqqara's gunmen. If I was going to count the people dying back on the Ginza in a gang war which, in a way, I had initiated, that number would be a lot higher. It seemed as if the only good thing I had accomplished since coming to Earth was a new start in life for Miko and her family. Maybe it wasn't much considered in the balance, but at least it was something.

And then there was Stone. If she had been next to me when that assassin made his move, she might have been killed as well. That was the second time her life was placed in jeopardy simply because she was with me. Breck was right. The only thing to do was take care of Saqqara. The trouble was, so far I hadn't shown much aptitude for taking care of things. My leprechauns had pulled me through somehow, but my Russian archbishops were predicting that my run lof luck couldn't last much longer.

"You're being very quiet," Stone said as we rode the skyhook shuttle to Casino, the largest of the Fire Island habitats.

"I think I lost more than my lunch back there," I said.

"Don't be so hard on yourself, O'Toole," said Breck.

"You've managed to survive a jungle campaign and two assassination attempts. That must stand for something, surely."

"It stands for pure dumb luck," I said, fighting back my anger at his mocking tone. "I've been extremely lucky to have survived this long. If it wasn't for you that night in the hotel, both Stone and I would probably be dead now. As for that jungle scenario, I was so scared, I didn't know what the hell I was doing. And the same thing happened back there in the aquarium. I panicked."

"You don't think I was scared?" said Stone. "I was so terrified I couldn't even move! I didn't do anything to help *you*, did I? Or isn't that my responsibility?"

"Come on, Stone," I said, "this isn't a sex role thing. Well, maybe it is to some extent, I'll admit that, but it would have made no difference if you were a man. The fact is that my fear overcame everything else."

"Fear is a perfectly normal human response to danger," said Breck.

"One which you don't seem to have," I said.

Breck shrugged. "I am not a perfectly normal human. I was designed not to feel fear. Fear is a function of self-preservation. It is nothing to be ashamed of."

"That's easy for you to say. You've never felt it."

"I don't need to experience fear to know something about it," Breck said. "I've seen it many times. SS hybreeds are fascinated by fear, because it is an emotion we can't feel. I have experienced the fear of others through the interface and while it isn't the same as feeling it myself, I think I have an understanding of it. I often wish I had the ability to feel it, because it's clearly a profound experience. Evidently, you can only feel so much fear at any one time. There seems to be a sort of limit, beyond which the mind either dissociates or turns on you completely and shuts down your systems, making you die of fright. When the dissociation occurs, the mind retreats somewhere within itself and becomes essentially dysfunctional. But sometimes you reach the limit of your capacity for fear and you self-protectively and quite unconsciously shift gears into some other emotion. It could take the form of sexual excitement, for example, or it could manifest as anger, an anger so intense that a terrified man pinned down by enemy fire can suddenly charge the enemy batteries in an unreasoning fury. Heroes were often very frightened people. Do you recall what you felt like in the jungle when you made the jump into enemy fire? You were clearly afraid, but you acted with courage, with heroism. You were driven by your fear and you did what was necessary to survive. Now consider what occurred back there in the aquarium. You fled from that shark in terror, yet you went back to face it again."

"Sure, after I thought it was safe," I said.

"But did you go back *only* because you thought it was safe?" Breck said. "You were still afraid, but you went back because you were angry at the fear you felt. A phobia is not a rational thing. People who are claustrophobic are capable of understanding intellectually that they are perfectly safe within a closet, that there is nothing in there that will harm them. Yet try convincing someone with claustrophobia to lock himself inside a closet. You can open it for him, show him there is nothing harmful in there, go in there yourself, and lock the door to demonstrate that it's safe, but you still won't get him to go in and lock the door. His fear controls him. He practices avoidance. That isn't what you did, is it? You used your anger to overcome your fear. You have been experiencing fear incrementally ever since you first arrived on Earth. And you're growing more adept at coping with it. There is an old saying: What does not kill you, makes you stronger."

"Somehow I don't feel stronger," I said. "In fact, I'm more aware of my weakness."

"The more aware you are of your own fears," said Breck, "the more you understand them and the less power they have over you. You're being called upon to use resources you have never needed to develop before. Did you expect it to come easily?"

"I guess I hadn't thought about it that way," I said. "Thanks, Rudy.,"

"For what?" he said. "I am not trying to do you any favors. We are a team and you will not be of much use to us if you're distracted by agonizing over your masculinity. I would rather you concentrated on the job at hand."

Stone shook her head. "You just can't do it, can you?" she said. "The moment you start to show any sensitivity, you have to ruin it somehow."

"I am only trying to keep things in perspective," Breck said, a touch too nonchalantly, it seemed. I had a feeling an old issue between them had been skirted. "But at least we know one thing. This is no illusion."

He turned to me. "It's entirely possible Mondago could have programmed an illusory attempt on your life into this scenario if it were a hallucinact, especially after what occurred at the hotel, but he could not have fooled me with an illusory Bill Renn. We spoke about things only he and I knew, things no playermaster could have pulled out of my mind without my knowing it. So you can postpone your paranoia about induced hallucinations. This is no hallucinact. Whatever it is we'll find down on Draconis, it is going to be real."

Casino was a sphere about one mile in diameter, roughly the same size as Draconis Base. At its poles were the massive external radiators which removed heat from the interior of the habitat and surrounding it like a planetary ring was an array of mirrors directing sunlight through windows near the rotation axis. It was a small habitat by modern space colony standards. The design was originally meant to house between ten and fifteen thousand people, but, according to Colonel Renn, Casino held at least three times that number. It was crowded.

Casino, like Draconis Base and the other three habitats which made up the Fire Islands, had started out as a tachyon drive spaceship. During the late twentieth century and the early part of the twenty-first, there had been much debate about which was the more viable option for the human settlement of space—terraforming or the construction of island colonies. Each side had its champions and the planetary engineering types were often fond of dismissing the island colony proponants as bubble-headed counterculture dreamers while the island colonists regarded the terraformers as "planetary chauvinists," reactionaries bound by inefficient and outmoded ideas. But, as so often happens, the optimum solution was one of compromise.

Humanity evolved upon a planetary body and while some people eagerly responded to the challenge of creating a Bernal Sphere and living in an island colony, most people would always prefer life upon a planet, with its own unique challenges. Some pioneers didn't mind looking up and seeing a town hanging upside down above them, but many found the effect psychologically disturbing. They preferred the vista of a sky and the challenge of taming open spaces.

Terraforming was a long and complex process, involving finding planetary bodies—or creating planetary bodies—with enough mass to hold an atmosphere and asteroids for use as the building blocks of the new world to provide materials for an atmosphere, to reshape the surface by impact, or to "spin up" a planetary body to the desired rotation, following which organisms would be introduced to begin the process of establishing a biosphere. Sometimes it was necessary to dismantle smaller planetary bodies, moons, or even planets themselves to provide the raw materials. These things took time. The people who began the work would not live to see its completion, nor would their children. And they needed a place to live while the work went on.

The advent of tachyon drive made it possible to build an island habitat and use it as a starship to take the pioneers out to the world they planned to tame. Ironically, the planetary engineers would wind up living out their lifetimes in an island colony. Their children would be born and raised there and they would continue with the task. And when the world was ready for human habitation, those who chose to go down to the planet surface would do so while those who chose to remain in the island colony would supply the technology and industrialization to get the new world off to a good start and keep it going without the damage to the biosphere that Earth-based industry had wrought over the centuries.

Such had been the plan with Draconis 9, but when EuroCon pulled out after the disaster, the island colonies remained. They could have been refitted for space travel and transported to a new terraforming project, but what made it more cost-effective for EuroCon to sell them was the discovery of fire crystals on the surface of Draconis 9.

Fire crystals possessed many of the same properties as diamonds, only they were harder and more precious due to their rarity. The first discovery of fire crystals occurred when an asteroid containing them was found in the system of 61 Cygni. Not only did they turn out to be superior to diamonds for industrial purposes, but their haunting beauty and rarity placed them in high demand as precious gems. Supposedly, they had some sort of mystical, talismanic quality. I had never seeen one or known anyone who had one, so I had my doubts on that score. But one thing was certain. The value of fire crystals was enough to make some people abandon everything and emigrate to the Fire Islands, in spite of all the dangers.

The habitats originally meant to house the EuroCon planetary engineers were now home to a wild agglomeration of adventurers. Wherever the prospect of wealth existed, there came those who sought it and those who came to exploit the seekers. Casino was a densely packed orbital city of crystal hunters, saloonkeepers, whores, gamblers, thieves, murderers, and slavers. It made the Ginza Strip seem tame. The entire habitat was a space-borne Combat Zone. There was no more law in Casino then there was in the frontier boom towns of Earth's Gold Rush.

Ideally, island colonies were designed to be self-supporting, with their own industry and agriculture, but Casino had neither. Every available inch of space was taken up by buildings and by people. In the beginning, the island colony plan was followed according to design, but the steady influx of people seeking to get rich soon upset the balance and the companies controlling emigration to the Fire Islands were less concerned with the living conditions in the habitats than they were with the potential profits.

Only one of the island habitats now had agriculture and there was some support industry, but it became increasingly necessary for everything to be imported. Draconis Base was self-sufficient, but life in the Fire Islands was an expensive proposition. That suited the operating concerns just fine. They could maximize their profits by running the island habitats as frontier company towns.

There was a high turnover. Many of those who went down to the planet surface never returned. Some achieved their dreams of wealth and left, but far more became trapped by the harsh realities of life in the Fire Islands. Many died in the habitats themselves. It was a rough neighborhood, full of predators. Those who couldn't pay their way found that there was no shortage of "patrons" willing to extend them credit, but this credit was not given for altruistic reasons. In the Fire Islands, people were a commodity, like everything else. You borrowed against your freedom and if the marker was called in and you couldn't pay it off, you had a very simple choice. Die or become someone's property. You couldn't go to a third party and borrow to pay off your marker, because the human sharks were very careful about things like that. The moment you "established credit" with a shark, he became your "banker" and the information was logged in the computer banks. Other "bankers" consulted their computers before "granting credit" and they didn't poach on one another's interests. Something like that could be fatal. You either paid off your "banker" or he "foreclosed" on you.

Colonel Renn was caught between a rock and a hard place. If it was up to the military, the Fire Islands would be closed to immigration, but it wasn't up to the military. The military had no economic clout. The corporations operating the habitats did. So long as the "quarantine" was preserved, which was the unenviable job of the Special Service, no one cared much what went on in the Fire Islands. Consequently, it was hardly surprising that Colonel Renn did not care much either. However, he had cared enough to allow Psychodrome to show people just what life was like here in the hope that it would discourage would-be immigrants. He felt confident it would. We got a briefing and then we were on our own. Our experience was supposed to frighten people off. I did not find that very encouraging.

Our skyhook shuttle docked with Casino and we entered the habitat through the zero-G access corridor at the rotational axis. We floated through the corridor to the point where it branched out into the axial passageways leading into the habitat. There were directional signs over each of the corridors and we took the one labeled "3rd Avenue South, Administrative, Downtown Residential, New Arrivals." South meant toward the zero-G access corridor and the docking areas, North was uptown, "up" the inner surface of the sphere toward the opposite pole. The main corridor continued on to a point at the approximate center of the sphere, where a club called The Arena was located.

In the early designs for island colonies, this area was set aside for low-gravity swimming pools. Imagine a spire extending out through the center of the sphere, inside of which was the zero-G access corridor. If you think of the habitat as a hollow candy apple on a stick, then the docking areas would be at the end of the stick and this spire would be that part of the stick which went inside the hollow apple. From where we entered the habitat, the "top" of this spire was straight ahead of us. From the point of view of the residences on the inner surface of the sphere, it was straight up at the sphere's center. Surrounding the top or end of this spire was a ring, the inner surface of which had held the pools in the early designs. The rotation that gave the habitat its gravity also kept the water in the pools from going anywhere, but the intriguing design meant that, just as the residents on the inner surface of the sphere could look up and see other residences overhead, so could swimmers in the pool look up and see other pools overhead. Because of the decreased gravity near the rotational axis, it was not only possible to jump off a diving board straight up into an overhead pool, it was also possible to execute porpoiselike leaps out of the water.

Casino, however, had no pools. Instead, there was The Arena, where the ancient concept of the Roman circus had been given a new twist. "Bankrupts"—as the unfortunates who borrowed themselves into slavery were known—sought their freedom as low-gravity gladiators in The Arena. The habitat was aptly named. Once again, I had the feeling I had bought into a game I could not afford.

I hoped there'd be a large audience for this one. I wouldn't want Colonel Renn to be disappointed. If it had been up to me, I would much rather have gone straight down to the planet surface from Draconis Base. Not that I was anxious to get there, but I was anxious to get this over with. Only the idea was to give the home audience an authentic experience. New arrivals did not come to Draconis Base. That was closed to ordinary civilians. New arrivals came in to Casino, made residence arrangements, and then tried to learn the ropes. No one was allowed to emigrate to the Fire Islands unless they had at least enough funds to get started. What happened to them after that was their own concern. The only thing the operating corporations cared about on Casino was collecting bills. And they did not tolerate late payments.

I had been on island habitats before. There were several above Mars. Those, however, had been much larger than the Island One design of Casino. Still, even taking that into account, Casino was not quite what I had expected. It made me think of a modular Manhattan bent in around itself, with all the skyscrapers cut off. Constructing tall buildings inside a

Bernal Sphere wasn't practical design. With anything much over several stories high, there was a decrease in gravity which increased with the height of the building. Most island colonies terraced their residences or, if population density was a consideration, Arcube or other modular types of architecture were employed. On Casino, this did not seem to be a major consideration. There were no skyscrapers, of course, but there were many multistoried buildings. What the hell, just pack 'em in, who cares about their comfort? Long-term health and psychological effects? Why bother. If they want decent housing, let them pay for it.

We didn't go through any sort of customs inspection; that was all handled on the other end. Everything that arrived at an island colony arrived clean. It wouldn't do to introduce insects or plant blights or whatever into a controlled environment, so preembarkation decontamination procedures were pretty thorough. However, one look at Casino made me wonder why they bothered. There was no pollution, of course, but they didn't go to any trouble to keep the island city clean. I began to see what Colonel Renn intended. Even at first glance, Casino did not look particularly inviting.

We followed the signs to the administration complex, where new arrivals were to check in, obtain their residence assignments—which had been paid for prior to embarkation—confirm their credit, and pick up their orientation kits. It was a typically bureaucratic procedure—hurry up and wait in line—but we were quickly spotted and it became apparent that we were not going to be treated as just any new arrivals. We were descended upon by a tall, well-built, handsome and clean-cut character with dark brown hair and a knee-jerk smile.

"Miss Winters! Mr. Breck!" I thought for a moment that I was being ignored, but the slick hadn't forgotten me. "And you must be Mr. O'Toole. On behalf of the Draconis Combine, I'd like to welcome you to Casino."

It didn't take a genius to figure out who this guy was. It was immediately clear that this was Casino's answer to Bob Stiers. It figured. Travel 65 trillion miles and one of the first things you run into is a PR flak. This must have been what the twentieth century treehuggers—pardon me, environmentalists—meant when they warned of mankind polluting space.

"My name is John Rudman, Corporate Liaison for Casino and the Fire Islands community. We've been expecting you. If you'll follow me, I'll see what I can do to expedite your arrival."

I thought we had already arrived, but who was I to argue? Breck looked amused. Stone looked at me and rolled her eyes. Slick Rudman launched into a snappy patter monologue on the wonderful opportunities to be had in the Fire Islands, a monologue I was able to tune out without a great deal of difficulty. He led us to an office suite in a modular complex, past secretaries who gazed at Breck with undisguised admiration—he was a star, after all, and a dashingly handsome one at that—and I noted that some basic facts of life had been exported to Casino from the corporate womb of Earth.

Where women were excluded from the corporate power structure, the men in key positions always selected from the ranks of the drop-dead-beautiful for their secretaries. Women who didn't fit the template didn't have a chance. It didn't matter that the position was almost completely obsolete, with computers able to do virtually all the work required. There was and probably always would be a certain cachet to having a human subordinate to command and the desirability of that subordinate was supposed to say something about the superior. Nor were corporate women any different. When they reached those same positions of power, they often behaved exactly like the men.

The office door opened onto a plush suite with a small garden beyond it on the other side of a set of sliding glass doors. Those doors were open and Slick conducted us through the office and out onto the garden patio, where an older version of himself was seated at a circular glass table. They didn't look alike, but they were cut from the same cloth. Office people. Soldiers of the corporate army. This one was a senior officer, however, complacent and secure. White hair, blue eyes, crow's feet and worry lines from the ascent to power. Executive fitness cultivated through exercise rather than hard work. He wore a dove-gray jumpsuit and a huge fire crystal pendant at his throat.

It was the first such gem that I had ever seen and it was, indeed, spectacular. It really seemed to have a flame burning inside. I couldn't take my gaze away from it as I watched it flicker from bright red-orange to violet-blue to amber-green.

"Ah, I see our stellar crystal hunters have arrived," he said, getting to his feet and extending his hand to each of us in turn, starting with Stone, whose hand he held a bit longer than I cared for. "Miss Winters . . . Mr. Breck . . . and, of course, Mr. O'Toole. I'm Carson Sonoma, Chief Administrator for the Draconis Combine on Casino. Do sit down."

He gave some sort of signal to Slick Rudman and the flak nodded and departed hastily.

"I do wish I had the opportunity to greet you personally when you first arrived," he said, smiling, "but I'm afraid our Colonel Renn co-opted that privilege. I trust your stay at Draconis Base was pleasant. You know, as a civilian, I've never even been there. It must have been a fascinating experience for you."

"It was interesting," Stone said. "Tell me, Mr. Sonoma, do you make a habit of personally welcoming all new arrivals to Casino?"

"Naturally not, Miss Winters," he said smoothly, "but you must admit that you three are not just any new arrivals. You are celebrities, bringing your experience to countless people, some of whom may one day decide to emigrate to the Fire Islands and seek their fortune here. Consequently, the Draconis Combine felt compelled to issue, through me, a statement, as it were. I understand that you are eager to proceed, so I will take up as little of your time as possible."

"We appreciate that," Breck said. "The sooner we are able to go down to the planet surface, the sooner we can attain our game objective."

"Quite so, Mr. Breck," Sonoma said. "Therefore, I will get right to the point. Your home audience should understand that there are fabulous opportunities to be had here in the Fire Islands, but as with most things in life, you get nothing for nothing. The Draconis Combine runs this operation in the spirit of free enterprise and adventure. People who come out here are held back only by their own limitations. Life in the Fire Islands is not without its risks, but to those individuals who seek more out of life than the drudgery of living by the clock, there is limitless stimulation to be found here. Whether one chooses to become a crystal hunter or to engage in any one of the many extraordinary service occupations Casino has to offer, life here is fast and hard and thrilling. To those who can meet the challenge, there is the potential of great reward."

As if absent-mindedly he played with the fire crystal at his throat, turning it so that its inner flame danced brightly. I imagined the scene back on Earth, where the home audience was plugged into their psy-fi sets, dreaming dreams of burning fire crystals buying their way into a better life. Sonoma was playing the scene for its maximum publicity potential, turning us into an advertising medium. You can have one of these, he was saying. All you have to do is squirrel away enough to buy your way out to the last frontier, where men are men and women like it that way. The message was "Come and live the fantasy." It was corny as all hell, but a lot more potent than anything Renn had to say. There was a little bit of Hakim Saq-qara in our friend Sonoma.

"Colonel Renn didn't seem to think that life out here was especially rewarding," I said.

"Colonel Renn has my greatest respect," Sonoma said, "and I won't attempt to patronize you by pretending that life is easy and that people don't occasionally get in over their heads. Fire crystals are not simply to be found lying on the ground down on the planet surface. And it is expensive to live here. We offer a unique life-style, complete with unique pleasures and luxuries. The cost is high, but you get what you pay for. Sometimes people act irresponsibly and overextend themselves, foolishly abusing their credit privileges. We cannot afford to support those who will not carry their own weight and our system may strike some as a bit harsh, but keep in mind that those who have bankrupted themselves have no one but themselves to blame. Still, if they work hard and apply themselves, they can earn their way out of their bankruptcy. Everyone has a chance here. What you make of it is up to you."

"What about the Draconians?" said Breck. "What chance do they have?"

"With a man such as yourself, very little, I should imagine," Sonoma said, smiling broadly.

He had misunderstood the question, though I didn't think he had misunderstood it on purpose. He wasn't the sort of man who would be very much concerned with the welfare of the natives. And it didn't seem probable that he had ever been down to the planet surface himself. He didn't strike me as the kind of man who took the sort of chances he spoke of. Breck did not pursue it. There would have been no point in antagonizing the man. We simply allowed him to finish his little speech uninterrupted so that we could get out of there as soon as possible.

Rudman was waiting for us outside Sonoma's office, full of cheer and excitement for us and ready to "conduct us personally" to our residence—I wondered briefly if it was possible to conduct someone impersonally and I supposed it was—but Breck quickly put a stop to that idea.

"I appreciate the offer, Mr. Rudman," he said, "but I think we would prefer to find our own way."

"Nonsense," Rudman said. "I wouldn't think of it. Besides, you're new here and it can be quite confusing—"

"We do have our orientation kits," said Breck. "And don't forget, the idea is to give the home audience a taste of what it's like to come here and experience the adventure for themselves. Having company officials giving us V.I.P. treatment really would not do. We wish to give the home audience the authentic thing, the undiluted essence of Casino, as seen from the point of view of ordinary new arrivals."

"Yes, certainly, I can understand that," Rudman said, "but surely escorting you to your residence would not detract from—"

"I am afraid I really must insist, Mr. Rudman," Breck said. "After all, you would not wish to disappoint our audience, would you?"

"No, no, of course not," Rudman said quickly. "If you will allow me to direct you, then—"

"We'll find our own way," Stone said, giving Rudman one of her media smiles. "Thank you ever so much, John. You've been wonderfully helpful."

We left an unhappy Rudman behind and proceeded outside on foot, along 3rd Avenue, heading uptown.

"The Combine seems anxious to put its best foot forward," I said. "Why do I feel like a company recruiter?"

"Because that is the role in which Sonoma sees us," Breck said. "But I fully intend to give the home audience the *authentic* experience of Casino, whether the Draconis Combine likes it or not."

"That isn't why we're here, Rudy," Stone said. "I appreciate that Colonel Renn is an old friend of yours, but let's not lose sight of our objective. We came here to get a fire crystal. The game scenario is the important thing. I should think you'd be the last person who'd need to be reminded of that."

"I need no reminding," he said curtly. "I fully intend to

win this game. But I will not do it at the expense of being used as a salesman for the Draconis Combine."

"Does it really make any difference?" she said. "I know how you feel about Draconis 9, but you're allowing the past to interfere with what we have to do in the present. That's what Mondago wants. We can't afford to waste any time. Remember, we may have gained an early advantage, but there are still other teams competing against us."

"I'm well aware of that," said Breck.

"Are you aware that we're being followed?" I said.

Stone glanced at me quickly. "What?"

We kept on walking. Breck frowned. "Are you certain?"

"Reasonably."

"Who is it?" Breck said, without looking around. "That idiot, Rudman?"

"No. Someone dressed in a black jumpsuit. Shorter man, more heavily built. I suppose he could just be heading in the same direction as we are, but then why would he be so careful about it? I've only caught a couple of glimpses of him while I've been rubbernecking like a tourist. Maybe I'm being paranoid, but he seems to be staying out of sight the rest of the time. And doing it damn well, too."

"If we are being followed, I was not aware of it," said Breck. "And that is not good. That is not good at all."

-SIX-

There is something to be said for paranoia. It grows on you. Especially if it improves your odds for survival. Not long ago, I thought I would be safe by leaving Tokyo, but even 11.2 light-years wasn't far enough away from Hakim Saqqara to guarantee my safety. It was typical leprechaun luck with Russian roulette overtones. Only Arkady O'Toole would try to hide out in front of billions of people on the mass media entertainment channels. All anyone had to do to find me was turn on his psy-fi set. I was imagining assassins lurking around every corner.

Saqqara was sparing no expense to kill me. I had always placed a considerable value on my life, but it didn't seem to me that it should be worth so much to Saqqara. Why send assassins all the way out to the Fire Islands? Why not wait until I returned to Earth and have them go after me between scenarios? The assassin who had died in the aquarium must have come out of the same ship with us. He had to have been a ninja. No ordinary man could have infiltrated a Special Service base so effortlessly. He might have made his move while we were still aboard the ship, unless he was concerned about escape—something ninjas were not supposed to be concerned about—but in all probability, he had been on downtime with the rest of us during the voyage and there simply had not been an opportunity. Besides, if he had killed me while I was asleep aboard the ship, it would not have been very dramatic. Saqqara liked to do things flamboyantly.

I kept turning the whole thing over in my mind, thinking I'd be more equipped to deal with it if I could understand it better. Was Saqqara going to all this trouble simply for his own entertainment? Or did he want a dramatic assassination on the Psychodrome channels for the sake of his Yakuza superiors, before whom he had lost face? It was probably a combination of both. And it did occur to me there could be one other reason why he was so anxious to eliminate me. The interface.

The interface wasn't true telepathy. It was chiefly an empathic function. Shared perceptions, physical sensations, and, to some extent, shared feelings. The intensity of the interface, especially in terms of emotions, varied with the individuals involved. As Breck had put it, some people were better broadcasters than others. Apparently, I was a damn good broadcaster. What did that mean in terms of my situation with Saqqara?

People tuning in to me would not know exactly what I thought, but they would have access to my feelings and I had some pretty strong feelings about Hakim Saqqara. At least some of that had to be coming through the interface. What was I broadcasting to the home audience about Saqqara? Fear? Anger? Hatred? The three of us had talked about Saqqara, but we had done it on our own time. Mondago undoubtedly knew all about it, but the company would never broadcast any segment of our experience in which we spoke about Saqqara. Psychodrome wouldn't want to risk a lawsuit. Still, the company could not be held legally liable for my feelings.

I didn't think it was possible to identify Saqqara from my emotions, especially without a perceptual focus for them present in the scenario, as had been the case with Stone. The feelings might come through, but I didn't think the home audience would know those feelings were directed toward a man named Hakim Saqqara. However, Saqqara would know. And so would anyone who knew the details of my association with him—such as the shoguns of the Yakuza.

That might explain Saqqara's eagerness to do away with me. So long as I was still alive, I was a living testimony to his mistake. Every time I experienced an emotion having to do with him, he experienced it through the interface and knew that emotion was directed at him, just as his superiors did. It was an unexpected development. In a strange sort of way, the shoguns of the Yakuza could tune into my adventure and experience Saqqara continually losing face. It was all there for them. I was a man Saqqara should have squashed like a bug, still living, still defying him, rubbing his nose in it in front of billions of people. Perhaps he thought I could expose him somehow through the interface. For all I knew, that could be possible, although I had no idea how. Either way, it had to be galling to Saqqara to experience what I felt about him.

I had started out being scared of him, then, as Breck had pointed out, I began to use anger to dissipate my fear and I started feeling hatred for Saqqara. Could I take it one step farther? How about contempt? Could I work myself around to being *amused* by him? That would drive the bastard crazy. Maybe I could work on it.

It really was funny, looked at in a certain way. There he was, a well-respected businessman, a wealthy warlord of the Yakuza, a Ginza kingpin, owner and operator of the classiest club on the Strip, and he had allowed a nobody like myself to waltz in and take him for a bundle in a card game. The poor sap's ego was so fragile, he couldn't take losing, so he had to even up the score. He went after me and broke me, but I still managed to trump his ace in the end. Alone, completely destitute and with his thugs hot on my trail, I yanked the Pyramid Club right out from under him and turned it over to a bunch of wild kids. The Ginza kingpin got displaced by a down-and-outer and a gang of thrill-crazy scooter bandits. He put a contract out on me and he couldn't even make *that* stick. Two tries by the best assassins his money could buy and I was still alive. It really didn't say much for the dreaded ninjas of the Yakuza. True, I had some help, but these were ninjas, after all, legendary warriors of the Silent Way. And they had been beaten by a one-armed man and a couple of fish.

"What seems to be so amusing?" Breck said.

"What?"

"You've got the most self-satisfied smirk on your face I have ever seen," he said.

"Oh, it's nothing, really. I was just thinking that my situation is not without its humorous side."

Stone looked at me with surprise. "Let me get this straight," she said. "There've been two attempts on your life; we're in the middle of our most dangerous scenario yet; someone's following us who could be another assassin on your trail, and you think it's *funny*?"

"I guess it all depends on how you look at it."

She frowned. "Are you all right?"

I grinned at her. "Hell, yes. I don't know, maybe I'm cracking up from the stress, but I think I'm actually starting to enjoy all this."

She glanced at Breck uncertainly. "Adrenaline-induced euphoria?"

"Possibly," Breck said. "Our friend seems to be testing the limits of his capabilities and stretching them at the same time. Whatever he's doing, it seems to be working. He noticed our tail before I did. And our black-garbed friend is still back there, by the way. I have spotted him a few times out of the corner of my eye. I am not quite sure what to make of that. If he is a ninja, we should not have spotted him at all."

"If you ask me, those characters are overrated," I said. "If these ninjas were everything their reputation says they are, I would have been dead by now."

"Perhaps," said Breck, looking at me strangely.

"I just think it's sort of funny, all this trouble to take out a little guy like me and they can't seem to get it done."

"He's losing it," said Stone.

A slow smile of comprehension spread across Breck's face. "No, I do not believe so," he said. "I suspect he may be gaining something."

"What?" said Stone.

Breck grinned. "A proper perspective, perhaps."

We reached our assigned modular unit and entered, following directions to our apartment. We had agreed to share one. Safety in numbers. Besides, it seemed that damn few people in Casino were able to afford private accommodations. Rent was not cheap and space was scarce. Nevertheless, it was a surprise to see that our apartment was a suite, spacious and airy, complete with a small garden. It was well furnished and clean and far more luxurious than anything I had expected.

"This is a typical apartment for new arrivals on Casino?" Stone said, dropping her bag on the long couch.

"I smell a rat," said Breck.

"I smell the PR department of the Draconis Combine," I said.

"I think you are absolutely right," said Breck. "This kind of apartment, in this part of town—I would say someone was stretching the truth a little. We will not find any other new arrivals in this sector. We should arrange passage down to the planet surface as soon as possible, but before we do, I would like to find out who has been following us. I would also like to give our audience a more accurate picture of life in the Fire Islands. Mr. Sonoma has purposely put us in the best living quarters, in the best residence village. Our neighbors are probably all credit bankers and businessmen. Before we go down to Draconis 9, we should expose our home audience to some of the less fortunate residents out here."

"I don't really see how that's going to help us," Stone said. "I don't like what Sonoma's doing any more than you do, Rudy, but your friend Colonel Renn is trying to use us, too. Everybody has a vested interest. Ours is getting back in one piece with a fire crystal."

"Your point is well taken," said Breck. "However, there are still the ratings to consider. We owe it to our audience to make our experience as interesting as possible. And I think a visit to the downtown sector would be interesting."

He opened his bag and took out a monster plasma pistol, jacked out the power pack and checked it, then snapped it back into the gun. He removed a holster from the bag and attached it to his belt on the right side so he could cross draw with his left hand.

"What do you say we go out for a night on the town, O'Toole?" he said, reaching into his bag and pulling out a similar pistol, snugged down in a holster. He tossed it to me. I caught it in both hands. It was a heavy piece, with a barrel almost a foot long. It weighed close to five pounds. You don't fire plasma from a plastic zip gun. This was the heaviest density nysteel alloy. Serious artillery.

"All right," said Stone, unpacking her own piece and slipping into her shoulder holster rig, "I'm not about to let you two pick up all the ratings points." She took out two long, slim, nysteel-bladed commando knives and slipped one into each of her boottops, fastening the retaining straps on the sheaths tightly around her calves. She also took out a small plastic zip gun and clipped it to her belt.

"What," I said, "no hand grenades?"

"I'm saving those for the planet surface," she said.

I glanced at Breck. "Is she kidding?"

"Difficult to say," said Breck. He snikked out his knives, then retracted them again, checking the action on his arm. "I understand that downtown is a rough neighborhood."

I strapped on the pistol. "Compared to you two, I feel a little underdressed."

"There is such a thing as outgunning your own capabilities," said Breck. "Considering your situation, my advice is to invest in some personal defense and weapons programming when we return to headquarters. You have already picked up a little knowledge from the mercenary program, but you could do with the full course. It is not inexpensive, but you should be able to afford it after this scenario."

"Great. What do I do meanwhile?"

"Aim carefully and try to avoid burning your own foot off," Breck said.

"Thanks. I'll try to remember that."

"And try not to lose the gun," said Breck. "It is my personal property and I will be irritated if you allow someone to take it from you."

"Why do I have the feeling you don't have a great deal of confidence in me?" I said.

"Don't take it personally," said Stone. "He doesn't have confidence in anybody but himself."

"An attitude I recommend," said Breck. "It builds self-reliance."

"I'll keep that in mind," I said. "Where do we start?"

"Why not start where all the action is?" said Breck. "We can take in a show at The Arena. That should give us an opportunity to check out the more successful locals . . . at the same time as the more unsuccessful ones. And if we are being trailed by a ninja assassin from Earth, I would prefer to encounter him in an area of low gravity, where his reflexes will be off."

We locked up our quarters and set off on foot, headed downtown. We wore our weapons in plain sight, but we had already seen that this was not unusual in Casino. Everyone went armed and those who could afford it hired bodyguards, of which there was no shortage.

Casino was an island colony boom town. The uptown sectors, especially the residence village to which we had been assigned, smelled of heavy money. Downtown had the sleazy glamor of a cheap whore. I was not unaccustomed to that sort of atmosphere. Downtown Casino had a lot in common with the Ginza Strip, only on the Ginza, you couldn't look up and see buildings hanging upside down above you.

The Draconis Combine operated Casino on the most cost-effective basis. Build cheap, pack them in as tight as possible, charge them all the traffic will allow, and then leave them to sink or swim on their own. Fire crystals were more valuable than gold, platinum, or diamonds. They were in high demand both as jewelry and as industrial gems. There was money to be made here and wherever there was money to be made, the predators moved in. Those who came to hunt for fire crystal were in the minority, vastly outnumbered by those in the "service occupations," as they were described in the orientation material. There were the credit bankers, the saloonkeepers and the small businesses operating on license from the Combine, the gamblers, the hustlers, those who sold themselves for sex or violence (or both) and those who came seeking their fortunes and now sought nothing but survival. But the crystal hunters were the glamor boys, the *raison d'être* for the entire operation. They were almost exclusively male and the few women among them were frighteningly hard. They had to be, because the fraternity of crystal hunters was not a very friendly one.

They were, after all, competitors. In the habitats, they treated each other with respect and there was an iron camaraderie among them. On the surface of Draconis 9, all bets were off. Down on Draconis, the guy who bought you a drink and backed you up in a bar fight in Casino was just as likely to be the same guy who slagged you and took your crystal. The veteran hunters found no inconsistency in this. They had romanticized their own existence into a sort of gladiatorial mode —comrades in the barracks, fighters to the death down on Draconis. And the ones who couldn't cut it often wound up in The Arena. It was a different field of battle, but the rules were still the same.

The glamor of all this was lost on me, but then I had an unfair advantage in having lived on the Ginza Strip. Casino, like the Ginza, had a certain sleazy glamor to it and no glamor is quite so compelling as the sleazy kind. Take an attractive woman and dress her in the most exquisitely tasteful outfit, one that speaks in subtle tones of charm and sophistication, and then take her identical twin sister and deck her out in a sleazy, garish outfit that shows off more than it conceals and speaks of nothing more complicated than easy availability and see who draws the bigger crowd at a party. Women understand that one far better than most men do, simply because they've got a longer history of being judged superficially. That's why the sex object male is generally of less interest to them than the sex object female is to most men. Women may respond to the strutting rooster on a purely visceral level, but when it comes to laying down the cards, they'll usually look for something more substantial. The pendulum of sexual politics has swung back and forth throughout the centuries, but one thing—unfortunately—has always remained constant. Men are generally less in control of their procreative drives than women are. Ironically, we seem to think it's the other way around. Consequently, we're more susceptible to confusing love with sexual attraction and, perhaps because of that, we're more susceptible to sexual manipulation. I've heard arguments that women use that weapon because it's the one that evolution gave them, but I'm not entirely convinced of that. You get back what you give.

Casino was a lot like a beautiful woman who learned that lesson early and chose to emphasize her superficial aspects because it was the easy way and no one really expected any more of her. So if you looked at Casino superficially, you saw a lot of flash and dazzle, a lot of implied promises, and a lot of trashy charm. But if you looked a little closer, you could see that the mascara had been slept in and the eyes it had been meant to emphasize were vacant. Look closer still and you would see the crow's feet that the makeup tried to hide, the bags concealed by shadow once artfully applied and now put on by rote. Casino was a pretty girl who never took the trouble to grow into a woman. She had skipped that crucial step in her development and now she was a graceless, aging adolescent, still giving pouting looks and hipshots to equally graceless, aging adolescent males pursuing boyhood dreams of wealth and power. It depressed me all to hell because it hit so very close to home and because I knew my presence here was part of a sales campaign that kept the whole thing going.

Colonel Renn thought our being here would expose Casino and her sisters for the pathetic sluts they really were, but I knew better. Carson Sonoma had known better, too. Breck thought we could bypass Sonoma's PR ploy by resisting the temptation to remain in our plush residence uptown and going to the sleazy downtown area, but the damage had been done. The audience back home had seen the luxury Casino had to offer and that's what they would remember. People had a tendency to edit reality to suit their own preferences and expectations. They would dwell upon the trashy glamor and the heavy money, the promise of adventure and the easy thrill, and they wouldn't think about the down side—what it would be like if they were not among the few who made it big here.

I always thought about the down side. My Russian archbishops made a practice of pointing it out to me. They helped to balance out my overly optimistic leprechauns. When I was a little kid, a bunch of us had pooled our allowances and bought a holocube of King Arthur and his Knights of the Round Table. It was used and some of the images were faded from some other kids watching it over and over again. I remember it was the most popular cube around that month and all the older kids were talking about it and acting out its plot. Everyone was talking about how wonderful it must have been to live in those days and dress up in those shiny suits of armor and joust and go on quests and rescue maidens. I mused aloud that it couldn't have been very glamorous to live in a time when there wasn't any plumbing and no one cleaned themselves off after going to the bathroom. I wondered about never taking showers and smelling like something died inside you and suffering from tooth decay and vermin and all sorts of diseases. I wondered about the disadvantages of making love to rescued maidens who had never heard of birth control and I brought up the awkward subject of the much shorter lifespan they would have had in those days. I pointed out that nysteel was a fairly recent invention and that those handsome suits of armor must have weighed a ton and what did you do when you had to scratch yourself in the middle of a joust? I ruined it for everybody. For about a day, everyone went around feeling disappointed, but the next day, they were right back at it again, ignoring everything I had told them. I re-member feeling very puzzled by this. I had researched the sub-ject thoroughly and I knew I had my facts right. The one fact I had overlooked was that people aren't very interested in truths that conflict with their preconceptions. However, I was too young to understand that, so I simply joined everybody else in their games. And as I recall, my knowledge of the facts didn't stop me from playing "let's pretend" and having a good time.

We had reached the downtown "business sector" and people started to accost us, anxious for our business. Some of these people were male, some were female, and some seemed unsure of themselves. In the space of one short block, we were offered every physical diversion I had ever heard of and some that would have raised eyebrows even on the Ginza Strip. We were offered drugs and weapons, "business opportunities" and bodyguard services. A group of these bodyguards became particularly insistent and it looked as if things were about to get ugly. I was about to reach for my sidearm and Breck had stepped forward toward them when they suddenly backed off, looking not at us but at something *behind* us. Not wanting to take my eyes off them, I turned sideways and risked a quick glance, but Breck and Stone were more experienced and she quickly moved to stand back to back with him so she could check our rear and he wouldn't have to take his eyes off the toughs in front of us. It could have been a fake-out ploy by the toughs, but it wasn't.

There was a man standing in the center of the street about fifteen or twenty yards behind us. He was large-framed and muscular, completely bald, and dressed all in black. His effect on the bodyguards so anxious to sell us their services was im-mediate and dramatic. He never even said a word. All he did was stand there, legs spread slightly apart, arms hanging loose at his sides, and they simply made themselves scarce.

Breck turned around, frowning. "I would like a word with you . . ." he began, but the man abruptly turned and walked away.

I drew my weapon, but felt Breck's hand on my arm. "No," he said, shaking his head.

"I wasn't going to shoot him in the back," I said.

"I did not think you were," Breck said. "However, waving that thing around and shouting, 'Stop or I'll shoot' or something equally inane could prove counterproductive. Guns

are for killing people. Unless you are prepared to do that, do
yourself a favor and keep yours in its holster."

I bridled at his tone, which sounded condescending to me,
and then I realized that he was absolutely right. I had acted
like the rookie that I was. There wasn't any point in threatening someone with a weapon if you weren't prepared to make
good on the threat and, if you were, it wasn't very smart to
warn them. I replaced my gun in its holster. Breck looked at
me as if he expected a response, but when I didn't give him
one, he merely nodded.

"What was that all about?" said Stone.

"I am not quite sure," said Breck, "but I suspect our shad-
ower is not what we thought he was. Those men clearly knew
him and they just as clearly thought it prudent to avoid him."

"You think Sonoma's been kind enough to provide us with
a bodyguard?" said Stone.

"It would stand to reason," Breck said. "Sonoma obviously seemed anxious to give us V.I.P. treatment. I would still
like a word with that man, though, somewhere where he will
not be able to walk away so quickly."

We went on to the central axis of the colony and made our
way through the zero-G corridor to The Arena. We floated
"up"—relative to the inner surface of the habitat—toward the
end of the central axis spire, located at the approximate center
of the hollow sphere. It felt strange to be walking normally
one moment and then, a few moments later, to enter the
zero-G corridor and "fly" through it. The corridor was wide
enough to fly a small aircraft through and it was shaped like a
long tube. For the new arrivals who were unaccustomed to
zero G, there were short safety lines that attached to cleats
which moved on tiny rails in both directions, similar in principle to sky hooks or, perhaps more appropriately, to old Earth
ski lifts. You just clipped one end of the line to your belt and
the other to a cleat and you were towed along on the conveyor
to your destination. Otherwise, there were plenty of hand-
holds along the inner surface of the corridor and the experienced habitat residents simply used them to launch
themselves on traverse patterns down the corridor.

The end of the zero G corridor opened out onto the bottom
of a deep, basin-shaped amphitheater. Imagine an impossibly
large, incredibly deep champagne glass with an overturned-
fishbowl covering it, so that the glass extended up inside the

fishbowl. The fishbowl was Casino and the champagne glass its central axis. The inhabitants lived on the inner surface of this fishbowl and the hollow stem of the champagne glass was the zero-G corridor. The corridor opened out onto the glass itself and the curved inner surface of the glass was The Arena. Along the rim of the glass, there was a promenade offering strollers a spectacular, 360-degree panoramic view of Casino. It was like walking around a giant rollercoaster loop-de-loop and the principle was similar. All around you, in all directions, you could see the island colony. You could lean out over the balcony railings, look down, and see residence villages curving around below you. Or you could look straight out and the view would be similar. Then you could look up and see a similar sight, with people walking on the promenade above you. To someone who had never been in an island habitat before, the experience could be profoundly disorienting and disturbing. You could always spot the new arrivals. They were the ones with their hands frozen to the balcony railings, eyes wide with panic, bodies rigid, convinced they were falling even though they were on a solid pedestrian walkway. The nicer people did their best to pry them from the railings and take their arms, walking them around until they grew accustomed to the sensation. The people who were not so nice just chuckled and left them to stand there, immobile and terror-stricken.

The Arena was both a low-gravity amphitheater and nightclub. The tables were arranged like theatrical boxes, tiered on the inner surface of the basin. The domed stage was constructed above the entrance archways from the zero-G corridor.

Most of the fighters were bankrupts who had failed to find their fortunes in the Fire Islands, desperate individuals seeking to free themselves from Casino's credit bankers and stake themselves to one more run or to a ticket home. They provided a constant influx into the gladiatorial ranks. It was possible for a bankrupt to win enough in the arena to buy his way out of debt, but it was rarely possible as the result of only one match. And the combat could be fatal. The odds of that were increased if an inexperienced fighter drew a match with one of the hardcore professionals. Some of these men had begun their gladiatorial careers as bankrupts, had fought successfully enough to pay their debts off, and had chosen to continue in the arena as "independent" fighters. Others were crystal hunters or bodyguards who enjoyed an occasional fight in the arena as a means of supplementing other income. Anyone could enter the arena by registering with the Board of Games. This could be done as easily as ordering a drink from your table. The waitress would bring you a small computer terminal and you would punch in your registration and receive your match in moments, then you could simply relax and enjoy the show until your turn came. Fighters were rated by experience and there was a handicapping system which could apply either to the mode of combat or to an adjustment of the prize money or to both. And if you were really up for gambling, you could go for the big money by selecting the option of combat to the death.

There was nothing illegal about it, largely because Casino wasn't very legal to begin with. It was administered by a multinational combine and its operations were all based upon contractual agreements. Failing to honor a contract was likely to result in another contract meant to enforce the first one. And given the character of the residents, the only quicker way of getting yourself killed would be by trying to pass a law. The corporate advertising of the Draconis Combine made much of the libertarian life-style to be found in the Fire Islands habitats and, strictly speaking, they did not exaggerate, but freedom is a tricky word.

The bankrupts of Casino were free when they arrived, but they did not find quite the utopia they had expected. Freedom did not mean freedom from responsibility. Freedom meant they were exempt from any regulations outside the contractual provisions they agreed to, but it also meant that others were equally exempt and there were no regulations to turn to for protection. One had to accept one's own responsibility for that. There were no social welfare programs to support those who could not support themselves and charity was not widely practiced in the habitats. It was too expensive. There was no police force. The Special Service had unquestioned authority, but only insofar as maintaining the quarantine was concerned. The SS had neither the time nor the inclination to involve itself in the internal matters of the colonies. A libertarian society seemed like an intoxicating idea to many new arrivals, but few of them had given much consideration to how dependent they had been on statist programs. Casino was a harsh and heady dose of freedom, an anarchistic society sponsored by a multinational. A peculiar place; a dangerous life-style. Many new arrivals found they didn't like freedom quite so much when the other guy was just as free. Their unconscious dependence on society's rules often got them into trouble and many of them wound up in The Arena. Nobody forced them. They had a choice. A free choice. But sometimes a choice can be no choice at all.

A dazzling-looking hostess dressed in an outfit that could have been washed in a martini glass led us to a table. In the low gravity, she moved with a practiced sensuality that would have been difficult, if not impossible, to duplicate in Earth-normal gravity. The gravity at the lower end of the basin—that is, nearer to the stage and to the entrance—was less than the gravity at the farther or upper parts of the amphitheater. Obviously, the closer one was to the central axis, the less the gravity and, at the center, there was zero G. The stage was constructed over the zero-G central axis corridor, but it was much wider than the corridor, so that at the outer edges of the stage, there was low gravity while, nearer to the center, there was zero G. There were several matches in progress simultaneously as we entered, the clear domed stage being at least as large as the arenas of the ancient Roman circuses.

The low- to zero-G environment made for interesting combat. It was interesting in the same way that a Spanish bullfight could be interesting. One did not necessarily have to approve of the event to be fascinated by it. A good number of the fighters moved with the grace of ballet dancers in slow motion, though this was an illusion. There was nothing slow about the combat. The new arrivals were painfully easy to spot. It was all they could do to function at all in low gravity, much less zero G, and they lost quickly. I noticed something happening that was straight out of the traditions of the ancient Roman circuses. When one fighter brought another down or disarmed him, he would look to the audience to decide his opponent's fate and they would signal either thumbs up or thumbs down. The vast majority gave thumbs up, but not necessarily because they were disposed to be merciful. Our waitress enlightened me when she brought our drinks.

"Oh, that only happens in the death matches," she said, smiling her friendly service smile, "but the audience usually gives thumbs up because we wouldn't want to run out of gladiators. Besides, the new arrivals deserve a chance to learn, don't they?''

"And the credit bankers who own their contracts deserve a chance to collect their contingency fees," Breck said wryly.

"Well, certainly, sir," the waitress said, smiling at him with unabated perkiness. "After all, they've purchased their clients' debts and it's only fair that they have an opportunity to receive a return on their investment."

"A fascinating way to put it," Stone said.

"Hey, wait a minute," said the waitress. "Aren't you Rudy Breck, the psycho star?"

"I am Rudiger Breck, yes."

"And you're Stone Winters!" said the waitress. "I can't believe it! Can I have your autographs?"

I was totally ignored, not being in the same league, but I didn't mind at all. I minded even less when I saw what happened as a result of this recognition. They signed their autographs for her and she begged a kiss from Breck, which he gave obligingly. He started to give it rather chastely, but she turned it into a meal. The scene attracted some attention and soon other people were aware of who we were—or at least of who Rudy and Stone were—and, moments later, the game announcer was telling everyone about it over the PA and having them stand up and take a bow. Shortly after they resumed their seats, the same waitress returned with our drinks. She also returned with a small portable terminal, which she set on the table in front of Breck.

"What's this?" he said.

"You've been challenged," she said. "Isn't it exciting?"

"Challenged?" Breck said. "What sort of nonsense is this? I'm not fighting anyone, don't be ridiculous."

"Oh, you can't refuse!" she said, looking chagrined. "The challenge is on all the terminals! What will people think?"

"I could not care less what people will think," said Breck, pushing the terminal away. "I have no intention of beating up some fool merely for the entertainment of this crowd."

"Isn't that what you do for a living, more or less?" a soft voice said from directly behind me.

I turned to see the black-clad, bald stranger who had been following us standing at my elbow. He was of average height, but heavy and extremely muscular. He was built like a dray horse, massive and solid. His nose had been broken and poorly set, as if he had done it himself. His features had a chisled look, revealing Mongol or Tatar ancestry. He reached for the terminal and turned it toward him. Deeply set, dark, exotic eyes stared down at the screen.

"The challenge is from Michel Czer," he said, speaking in a soft voice that seemed louder because of its timbre and precise enunciation. "He has little reason to love the SS, and even less to love you, Mr. Breck, who have succeeded so well since your forced retirement."

Breck stared up at him, taking the stranger's measure. "Who are you?" he said.

"My name is Nikolai Razin," said the stranger, pronouncing it *Rah-zeen*. "A soldier of fortune by trade, a crystal hunter by avocation. In this instance, I am something of a corporate liaison."

"You mean Carson Sonoma is paying you to keep an eye on us," I said.

"Yes, and paying me quite well, I might add," said Razin.

"What's this fellow Czer have against me?" Breck said. "I've never even heard of him."

"He has obviously heard of you," said Razin. "As to what he may have against you, I can only venture a guess, but it is an educated one. Czer was once SS himself. He was badly injured in a rocket blast. Enough so that he was of no further use to the Special Service. Like yours, Mr. Breck, his was a forced retirement. Czer is a cyborg. Strictly speaking, he's barely even human. He was not quite as fortunate in civilian life as you, hence his apparent resentment. He came here to hunt crystal, but was not very successful. He became a bankrupt and entered The Arena, where he became very successful indeed. He has fought his way to solvency, but he is not particularly popular. His fighting style is crude and his personality abrasive. And he fights to win. The challenge, you will notice,"—he turned the terminal screen toward Breck—"is to the death."

-SEVEN-

Our table became the focus of a great deal of attention. Many of the tables had portable remote terminals, so the customers could keep track of the upcoming matches. This facilitated betting. For the benefit of those who weren't following the up-coming action via terminal, the game announcer informed everyone of the challenge to "the celebrated Psychodrome star, Rudy Breck" via PA.

We all heard Mondago's sepulchral voice simultaneously through the interface. "*This is an unscheduled interactive gaming option, Mr. Breck. The home audience vote is over-whelmingly in favor of your accepting the challenge. Ap-parently, since your challenger is also formerly of the Special Service and also biologically augmented, they do not consider that you have an unfair advantage.*"

"Screw that," said Breck. "What they're considering is the sight of blood, the ghouls." He sighed. "Very well, I shall oblige them."

Razin frowned. "I beg your pardon? Were you speaking to me?"

"To our playermaster," Stone told him. "We've just been informed through our interface that the psychodroids want to see Rudy pick up the gauntlet."

"And you have no choice in the matter?" Razin said, frowning.

"It all depends on how you look at it," said Breck. "Have a seat, Mr. Razin, and show me how to respond to this challenge."

Razin sat down beside Breck and turned the terminal toward him. "What is your residence registration number?" he said. Breck gave it to him and Razin punched it in. "You're quite certain you want to go through with this?" he said. "I was, after all, hired to watch over you and I feel I should inform you that Czer has never lost a match. I know him well. He is an unprincipled bastard."

"So am I, Mr. Razin," said Breck. "Go ahead, please."

"Very well. Would you please spell your name for me?"

Breck did and Razin punched it in, then punched in the acceptence of the challenge, which was confirmed in seconds over the PA by the game announcer. We watched the odds develop on the screen as bets were placed.

"You said he is cyborg," Breck said.

Razin nodded. "Both his arms are bionic, as are his legs and hips. If I were you, I wouldn't waste my time in targeting his groin. There is nothing there except some rather sophisticated artificial plumbing. It's conceivable that you might damage something, but you wouldn't slow him down much. He would not feel any pain. His trunk is only partially organic. He's had extensive nysteel reinforcement of his skeletal structure, especially in the spinal area. His spinal cord was damaged and it has been repaired and sheathed in nysteel. You won't break his back, in other words. His ribcage is also nysteel and he has an artificial voicebox implanted in a flexible nysteel trachea. Don't bother trying to hit him in the throat; you will only break your hand."

"Where the hell *can* he hit him?" I said. "The man's a bloody robot!"

"I would advise you try for his nose," said Razin. "A hard palm heel strike directed upwards should break it and drive the splinters into his brain. He's obviously aware of his vulnerability there, so he will protect himself. You might consider trying to blind him.''

"You're very well informed," said Breck. "I don't suppose you'd know who did the work on him by any chance?''

"So far as I know, it was all performed in a military hospital," said Razin. "Is that any help?''

Breck smiled faintly. "Some," he said. "It tells me what sort of modifications he *doesn't* have.''

"I don't quite understand," said Razin.

"The service doesn't pay for extras," Breck explained. He smiled and lifted his own artificial arm. "This was not military issue."

"The odds are in," said Stone, looking at the screen. She grimaced and looked up at Breck. They were six to one in the challenger's favor.

"I thought you said he wasn't very well liked," I said.

"He's not," said Razin. "But why should people lose money because of personal prejudice?" He reached for the terminal and punched in a bet. He bet on Breck.

"I appreciate the gesture," Breck said dryly.

Razin shrugged. "At six to one, the payoff is well worth the risk. Besides, I can afford to lose."

"What are the rules?" said Stone.

"What rules?" said Razin.

The game announcer let everybody know that as a result of this "once in a lifetime" match-up, there would be no other competitors in the arena. Breck and Czer would have it to themselves.

"Are you well accustomed to zero G?" said Razin.

"Well enough," said Breck.

"I've seen Czer fight before," said Razin. "He will try to work you all over the arena, from low G to zero G and back, to throw off your reflexes and timing. Don't let him grab hold of you. He could crush you easily. And watch out for his legs. Nysteel bionics pack a powerful kick."

The announcer called for the contestants and Breck went down to take his place in the arena. He went through the entrance at the base and, a few moments later, we saw him enter the dome, stripped to the waist, his nysteel arm gleaming. He was in exceptional physical condition, every muscle standing out in sharp relief. Then we saw his opponent for the first time.

Czer was a giant. He towered over Breck. His legs were covered with skinsuit tights and he wore soft, lightweight boots. His nysteel arms gleamed in the light of the arena. The nysteel reinforcement of his chest made it seem huge and the tremendous muscles he had developed to support it gave him the appearance of a bull. His face had the too-tight smoothness of plastic reconstruction and that somehow made him seem even more of a robot. There was no character in it. The features were handsome, but the expression was blank. His head, like Razin's, was also shaved and he looked like a huge, menacing mannequin. I would have expected him to move ponderously, but the low gravity and his bionics gave him a graceful fluidity that seemed incongruous, given his size.

Each man had been armed with a nysteel gladius, fashioned after the ancient short sword of the Romans, and a small circular shield that seemed to have little practical use. There was no protective armor of any sort, or protective helmets. Each wore identifying crossbelts, white for Czer and black for Breck. They stood across the arena from each other and the game announcer waited until there was silence. He announced last call for bets, waited a moment or two, then said simply, "Gentlemen, the match is to the death. You may begin when ready."

He had hardly finished saying the last word when Czer leaped straight up and out, angling toward the top and center of the dome. He turned in midair, rebounded gracefully off the rounded ceiling, and came down at Breck like a dive-bombing eagle. Breck did a standing back somersault a second before Czer reached him, struck against the wall with both feet, somersaulted again in midair, and snap-kicked Czer as he passed beneath him, sending him smashing into the floor of the arena. Czer struck hard on his chest and bounced. He recovered quickly, tucking up into a ball and spinning with surprising speed, his sword held out away from him. The effect was that of a buzz saw.

Breck kangarooed away from him toward the center of the arena and the zero-G zone. Czer opened out of his tucked position into something resembling a back dive, jackknifed, and reversed motion. He floated down to the floor of the arena lightly and landed on the balls of his feet. The crowd was roaring their excitement. This wasn't some ungainly match involving clumsy new arrivals. This was a battle be-

tween two SS veterans who knew how to handle low gravity
and the peculiar conditions it created for combat. I was
mesmerized. I had never seen anything like it. Even Razin was
watching with rapt attention.

"He's good," said Razin, meaning Breck. "Good moves,
quick reflexes. I might even win my bet."

"What happens if you lose it?" Stone said harshly. "Isn't
your employer going to be upset with you for falling down on
the job?"

"I cannot be held responsible for choices you people make
of your own free will," said Razin. "If you should happen to
be gunned down in the street, Sonoma would be very angry
with me and rightly so. I would have failed to do my job. But I
warned Breck against this match and more than that I could
not do. This is his own responsibility. I do hope he wins,
though. I stand to make a tidy profit on my wager."

Stone didn't seem to appreciate his point. However, I
wasn't interested in their debate. I was fascinated by what was
happening in the arena. Both men had crossed swords only
half a dozen times. Like skilled knife fighters, they used utter
economy of motion, not making a single movement that
didn't have a purpose. In low to zero G, every movement produced an immediate reaction. There wasn't the slash and flail
one might expect of swordplay. There was the wary, careful,
intense watching; the precise anticipation; the exacting movement; the sailing through the air like seagulls on an updraft;
the tumbling like acrobats on a trapeze. It was like watching a
weirdly choreographed underwater ballet, only this dance was
lethal.

They would float toward one another, strike with their
swords, and rebound in opposite directions, sailing across the
zero-G zone slowly, almost imperceptibly losing momentum
as they reached the outer edges of the arena. They touched
down, rebounded, and came back at one another, attempting
to gauge the other's reaction. They would touch down on the
surface like balls bouncing in slow motion and circle each
other, watching for an opening, each trying to manuever his
opponent toward the central axis zero-G zone in a manner that
would place him at a disadvantage.

I began to appreciate the intricacy of the deadly game. It
was better to move quickly across the zero-G zone as part of a
sustained, controlled maneuver rather than be maneuvered

into it unawares. The changes had to be subtle ones, as the entire amphitheater was in a low-G zone close around the central axis and most of the arena itself was zero G. Waitresses kangarooed from table to table, delivering drinks. People floated up out of the entrance to the club beneath the stage, settled gently to the floor, and kangarooed to their seats as two men whirled in midair in the domed arena above them, locked in mortal combat. It was macabre and surreal.

The crowd was loving it. They were shouting, cheering, excited by the uncertainty of the outcome. Neither man had yet drawn blood and the crowd knew it would be sudden when it came—there would be time for only one mistake, an irretrievable one, and it would be all over. And then it happened. Breck misjudged a move that Czer had made and tried to recover, backpedaling and moving, apparently unintentionally, too far into the zero-G zone. He started to float and Czer made his move, committing totally in a fast leap—but Breck flung his shield behind him violently, causing a sudden reversal in direction so that his new course would take him and Czer past one another. He swung his sword with his left hand and as Czer parried him, he snicked out his blades and flicked them across Czer's face.

Czer screamed and the crowd roared, drowning him out. Blood seeped quickly from the five diagonal slashes across Czer's face and floated away in globules as the man writhed in the zero-G zone, covering his face with one hand and swinging his sword around him violently with the other, blindly attempting to keep Breck at bay. But Breck had anticipated the momentum of Czer's leap and he rebounded from the wall, ping-ponged off the ceiling of the dome, and came down directly on top of Czer as he touched down in the low-gravity zone at the outer edge of the arena. He trapped Czer's sword between his blades and pinned him, legs locked around him, his sword poised over Czer's face.

The crowd rose to their feet, screaming wildly, virtually everyone indicating thumbs down. Breck looked at them for a moment, then dropped his sword and gave Czer a quick, sharp uppercut to the jaw. He pushed the limp body away to float off across the arena. He then faced the game announcer's booth and held up his nysteel hand, blades protruding.

"Mr. Breck's option for the nonlethal win," the game announcer said hurriedly over the PA. "Match to Mr. Breck."

"Why didn't you kill him?" Razin said when Breck returned to the table.

"I did not feel like giving them the satisfaction," Breck said. "Sorry if I disappointed you."

Razin shrugged. "Not me. I won my bet. The drinks are on me tonight."

"You will be getting off easy," Breck said. "We will not be staying. I had hoped to let the home audience experience the pathetic spectacle of bankrupt new arrivals cutting each other to pieces in your arena. Instead, they experienced the considerably more pathetic spectacle of two crippled veterans performing like monkeys before a crowd of fools. It was hardly the statement I had hoped to make."

"You were only trying to help your friend, Colonel Renn," I said. "Unfortunately, our presence here can only serve to romanticize the Fire Islands habitats. About the only way we can discourage people from coming out here is to have something highly unpleasant happen to us and that's something I'd prefer to avoid."

"I keep underestimating you, O'Toole," said Breck, smiling. "Remind me to—"

"*You! Breck!*"

Czer approached our table, his face an ugly mask scored with diagonal gashes and streaked with blood. He held a plasma pistol. One eye was caked with blood, but the other stared at us wildly. It became very quiet all around us.

"You humiliated me!"

Breck sat very still. So did we all.

"I merely tricked you," Breck said. "You fought well. You deserve better than to waste your time in the arena, performing for these people."

"Why didn't you kill me?" Czer said, his electronic voice cracking. His hand holding the pistol was shaking. I suddenly felt clammy all over.

"Why should I?" Breck said, keeping his voice even. "I have nothing personal against you."

"I challenged you!"

"And I accepted. And we fought. I won, you lost. It's over. Why not leave it at that? Sit down and join us for a drink."

"You humiliated me!" Czer said again. "The match was to the death! I wasn't worth killing, was that it? I'm just a cripple who's not good enough for you to kill! *You should have killed me!*"

"Allow me to remedy the oversight," said Razin.

A plasma blast burned through from underneath the table and slammed into Czer's chest. Not even nysteel can withstand a point-blank plasma blast. Czer fell to the floor, the stench of charred flesh and slagged nysteel washing over us.

"Damn you!" said Breck. "That was uncalled-for! I could have handled it!"

"I only gave the poor fool what he wanted," Razin said. "Or would you rather I had let him shoot you?"

"I don't need you watching out for me!"

"It's what I'm being paid for," Razin said.

"I'll double whatever Sonoma's paying you," said Breck. "Just get away from me!"

"I'm afraid I can't do that," said Razin. "A man in my line of work loses credibility if he switches sides anytime someone offers him more money. When I hire on to do a job, I finish it."

"You're defeating the entire purpose of why Sonoma hired you," said Stone. "Our experience is transmitted back to Psychodrome through the interface. The home audience knows full well why Carson Sonoma hired you. What does that say about the wonderful life-style in the Fire Islands?"

"Anyone who comes to the Fire Islands can hire a bodyguard," said Razin. "You can hire as many bodyguards as you like, as many as you can afford. No one is attempting to deceive your home audience, Miss Winters. Tell me, who is safer, someone who spends his money paying taxes, a portion of which goes toward paying policemen who will probably be elsewhere when you really need them, or someone who can take the same money he would pay as taxes back on Earth and spend it on exclusive, twenty-four-hour protection? In your case, the only difference is that you are receiving it free of charge, since you are visiting celebrities."

"Does this protection we are being granted free of charge extend to the planet surface as well?" said Breck.

"My job is over when you leave the Fire Islands," Razin said. "My orders are to accompany you down to Draconis 9. You would benefit from my experience as a crystal hunter."

"I think we could do without the benefit of your experience," said Breck.

"It would be unwise to discard any advantage you might have over an opposing team," said Razin. "I understand there are several teams such as yours competing in this game scenario. The Combine has assigned corporate liaisons to each of them. Since I see one of my colleagues over there with those three people, I assume they are your competition."

Breck looked quickly in the direction Razin indicated. Four men were seated at a table several tiers above us. They were watching us. One of them smiled and raised his glass.

"Smythe-Davies," Stone said flatly. "Damn."

Breck nodded back at them. "It seems we have lost our advantage," he said. "You recognize those men, O'Toole?"

I shook my head. "I was never a big fan of the game, remember?"

"Barry Smythe-Davies is the friendly-looking, dark-haired man who toasted us," said Breck. "Don't let his amiable looks deceive you. He is not very amiable at all. The other dark-haired man is Vittorio Panatti. He is rather amiable, but he does not let that get in the way of winning. And the large redhead is John Devlin, one of the game's new players. I don't know very much about him, but Panatti and Smythe-Davies I know well. They should make a formidable team."

"Nice of Mondago to let us know they had arrived," I said.

"Mondago only passes on essential information," Breck said. "Of course, what he thinks is essential may not coincide with our view."

Smythe-Davies was coming toward our table, moving down the aisle with practiced, low-G kangaroo leaps. He was tall and slim, good-looking in a pretty-boy way, with an easy manner and a charming smile.

"Rudy! How nice to see you!" he said, sounding genuinely pleased. He spoke with a British accent. "That was quite an exhibition you put on. Truly impressive. And Stone, my old darling. How long has it been?"

He bent down to kiss her, but she turned her face away.

He raised his eyebrows. "What, have I done something to offend? Or have I been supplanted in your affections?" He looked at me as he said that and winked. I hated him at once. "You must be O'Toole," he said, offering his hand.

I stood and shook hands with him, though I didn't really

want to. He was one of those people whose insincerity was so obvious as to be insulting.

"Doing very well your first time out, I hear," he said.

"I'm trying my best," I said.

"That's the ticket. I was afraid we might have missed you three. You jumped way out in the lead straight off. Had to work damned hard to catch up with you. Been down to the planet surface yet?"

"Not yet," said Breck.

"We were planning to take a shuttle down tomorrow morning. Just got in, you know. Help to get a good night's rest. Understand you've dealt with these Draconian creatures before, Rudy. Any advice, in the spirit of friendly competition?"

"Yes," Breck answered. "Stay here. Don't even bother going down. You might never make it back."

"You seem to have survived no less for wear," Smythe-Davies said with a grin. "Of course, we're not Special Service hybreeds, but I think we'll chance it. May the best team win, eh?"

He left with a jaunty wave.

"Lays it on a bit thick, doesn't he?" I said.

"He's been playing that act so long, I don't think he knows how to stop," said Stone.

"What was that bit about being supplanted in your affections?" I said, in spite of having promised myself I wouldn't ask.

"Nothing you need to be concerned about," said Stone.

"So there *was* something between you?"

She gave me a direct look. "Just sex," she said flatly. "Smythe-Davies used to perform on the lust channels with me. Is there anything else you'd like to know?"

Razin cleared his throat slightly and pretended to be interested in the combat taking place in the arena. A group of bankrupts was involved in a melee. After what they had just seen, the audience was not terribly interested.

"No," I said uncomfortably. "I think that answers my question."

"We should leave," said Breck. "It is a safe bet that those three will be going down tonight. I see no reason to give them a head start."

"I can arrange passage down to the planet surface almost immediately," Razin said. "I have already taken care of the preliminaries and all the supplies."

"Thank you," Breck said. "That was very efficient of you."

"Look, Breck," said Razin, "we don't have to like each other, but perhaps we ought to clear the air. I think I can understand the sympathy you may have had toward Czer, but the fact is he has been trying to get himself killed ever since he came here. Only some men don't die easily, even if they want to. He was in a lot of pain, but he killed many people trying to ease that pain. If I had not fired when I did, he would have killed you and probably your friends as well. You were both disabled and cashiered from the service, only you were able to accept it and adjust. He never could. He challenged you because he resented you and because there was a good chance you would kill him and end his misery. I don't expect your gratitude nor do I desire it, but if you don't wish to be a hypocrite, dislike me for myself, not for having done my duty as I saw it. Or is your own record in such things above reproach?"

Breck gave him a long look. "No," he said after a moment, "it is not. Your point is well taken. You have my apology."

"It's unnecessary," Razin said. "As long as we understand each other. And I think we do. Now, if you don't wish to give your competition a head start, we'd best be on our way. I see they're leaving."

We weren't quite quick enough. The man the Combine had assigned to Smythe-Davies's team was apparently as efficient as Razin. They had shuttled down just ahead of us which technically put them in the lead. I wondered if they too had been briefed by Colonel Renn and if the time we'd spent aboard Draconis Base had cost us, but it was pointless to dwell on that. Razin assured us that the fact that they had gone down before us didn't mean they'd find a crystal first. Besides, getting down to the planet surface was the easy part. Getting back up in one piece was quite another story.

Razin gave us his own briefing as we made the trip, but I was having a hard time paying attention. I kept thinking about Stone. For a while, back on Earth, we had achieved a real intimacy that now seemed to have dissipated. Perhaps it was my fault. It had been none of my business what she had done with Smythe-Davies before she met me and I knew I shouldn't have asked, but somehow I couldn't help myself. The answer I received had only served me right.

The thought of the two of them together was repellent to me, even though she had never made any secret of her past or any excuses for it. She didn't owe me any explanations, but she had talked about it with me back in that hotel room. She had been honest with me and she hadn't asked me for an accounting. I was the one who had been out of line. So why couldn't I let go?

I was reminded of a guy I knew back when I was in the service. We were both in the supply corps. He had fallen in love with a prostitute and had asked her to marry him. He said it didn't matter to him what she was; all that mattered was that he loved her and she loved him. And, to the best of my knowledge, she did love him. She had agreed to marry him, but he couldn't seem to reconcile her being a prostitute with her being his wife. What he said was one thing, but what went on inside was something else. It ate away at him. I believe he really loved her, but the responsibility for destroying that relationship was solely his. She tried. She put up with it as long as she could, but how do you live with someone who can't accept you for what you are? And that includes accepting you for what you were.

It wasn't enough that she stopped seeing other men as soon as they made a commitment to each other. He wanted to know how many men there had been. What kind of men were they? Who were they? What had she done with them and how often and for how much? Never mind that he had been one of those men. I tried once, feeling very youthfully self-righteous, to point out to him that a man who buys the services of a prostitute is on pretty shaky grounds to condemn her for selling herself, but it only drove him into a rage. It wasn't the same thing, he insisted. He *loved* her. Well, didn't she love him? Didn't she leave what was essentially a very lucrative profession to accept a much lower standard of living on a serviceman's pay? Wasn't she faithful to him? He didn't know. How *could* he know? What could fidelity mean to a whore? He punished himself for falling in love with her, perhaps for having gone to a prostitute in the first place. And, in so doing, he punished her and drove her away.

I remember feeling sorry for him and thinking, again with very youthful self-righteousness, that he did not live a very well-examined life. Love, I thought with the simplistic logic of the inexperienced, was an absolute. You either loved someone or you didn't. If you loved someone, you laid down the cards and accepted everything that went along with it. Well, I still believed that, but with the years had come the understanding that love is not a very simple thing at all. It can be frighteningly complex. It can trick you into all sorts of illogical rationalizations because there's nothing very logical about being in love. It can make you forget your own flaws and be less forgiving of the flaws in others. It can cloud your perceptions and make you think reality is the way you think it ought to be and not the way it is. And, perhaps the most deadly side effect of that peculiar disease, it can make you think that because you love someone or they love you, they ought to share your world view.

The Stone Winters I knew was not the same Stone Winters who had been the sex object of the lust channels. She had told me as much and I should have known it without her needing to tell me. She woke up one day and took a look in the mirror and decided she didn't like what it showed her. She looked her reflection squarely in the eye, accepted it, and proceeded to make changes. And what I had just done back in The Arena was tell her that those changes didn't count. It was an indefensible position for me to take. As Razin had said to Breck, was my own record in such things beyond reproach? If you are fool enough to think it is, O'Toole, go ask Hakim Saqqara.

Thinking of Saqqara made me remember suddenly that I was not entirely alone and I wondered, with a guilty embarrassment, exactly how much of my self-recrimination would be broadcast through the interface. And I wondered if Stone would tune in to the rerun—always assuming we made it back alive. I was having a hard time getting used to being a vehicle for the vicarious entertainment of the masses. I kept forgetting they were "there," if not truly inside my mind, then at least accessing some of my feelings. And every time I remembered, I felt as if I had dropped my pants in public.

Get your mind back on the game, O'Toole. It can kill you if you don't pay attention. I had been aware, in a sort of offhand way, of what Razin had been telling us as the shuttle dropped down to Draconis 9. Much of it was a repetition of what had been in our game programming, but Razin either didn't know that or he wasn't taking anything for granted. Probably the latter, I thought, since his survival could easily depend on ours.

There were two ground bases on Draconis 9, neither of which could properly be called spaceports. The Combine had paid for the construction, but they were maximum-security military installations whose Special Service crews were rotated every thirty days. If it had been up to the SS, there would have been no ground bases at all, but since it wasn't their decision and the shuttles had to have a place to land, the SS was forced to supply the ground-base personnel. The frequent crew rotation was necessary because of the constant strain of maintaining the quarantine.

I could understand Colonel Renn's desire to do something to discourage people from coming to the Fire Islands. He was an SS hybreed, designed to cope with the most adverse conditions, but the stress was getting to him. You could see it in his eyes, the beginning of that haunted look that comes to gamblers on a losing streak. I knew the look well—and the feeling. Your stake keeps getting smaller and the best hand you've had all night is a pair of threes. You know you should fold 'em and get up from the table, but you can't. You tell yourself the odds *have* to improve, it's mathematically impossible to keep being dealt such lousy hands, but the cards don't seem to know that. And that's what Renn was going through. There were humans down there, from the original development team. And there were humans down there who had come later, but who had made mistakes and now could not return. And the Draconians were learning from them. Learning how to be more human. Sooner or later, the odds had to improve. A Draconian would break the quarantine. Maybe even more than one. And then what?

The shuttle touched down on the runway. And suddenly my mouth was dry. I was afraid. I wondered if that would make Hakim Saqqara happy.

-EIGHT-

We were taken to the headquarters building of Ground Base Alpha, a thermoplast blockhouse situated in the center of the compound. The shuttle had taken off immediately. It was too late for any second thoughts. Well, not entirely too late. I could still elect to remain at the ground base, but that wasn't really an option, any more than coming to the Fire Islands had been an option. I couldn't quit now. I had to play the hand out.

We were each subjected to a minor surgical procedure involving the subcutaneous implanting of miniature transceivers, each with a specific unique coded frequency. Once we had gone beyond the confines of the ground base, the only thing that would enable us to return would be the transceiver implants. If any one—or all three of us—came back and tried to get into the compound, we would be scanned at a safe distance. If there was no transceiver signal, there would be no entry to the compound and no shuttle back up to Casino.

"And that's only the first step," Razin said as we made our way across the compound toward the skimmer hangar.

141

"There is a three-day quarantine during which you are kept under maximum security and examined more minutely than you have ever been examined in your lives. The military takes no chances."

"Do the soldiers ever venture beyond the compound?" Stone said.

Razin shook his head. "Colonel Renn is not very forgiving of personnel who break regulations. He would treat something like that as desertion under fire and exact the maximum penalty. However, to my knowledge, there has never been a military execution in the Fire Islands, at least not since Colonel Renn took command. There have been other infractions, but nothing very serious and never at a ground base. What happens out there," he said, gesturing toward the countryside beyond the compound, "may be technically under the jurisdiction of the military, but in practice the authority of the SS ends beyond the base perimeter. Here, we play by their rules. Out there, it's anybody's game."

"Do you have any idea where Smythe-Davies and the others might have gone?" said Stone.

"Crystal hunters are not in the habit of confiding in each other when it comes to the locations of their favorite digs," said Razin wryly. "Cameron, the man assigned to your friends, is one of the more secretive ones. Several enterprising hunters joined forces and tried to follow him one time to find out where he found his crystals. They never made it back."

"He'll be sharing the location of his dig with a lot more than several crystal hunters this time," Stone said.

"Not very likely," Razin said. "Cameron will fly them there in such a manner that it's highly doubtful they or anyone in your home audience would be able to follow the course. He knows these mountains well enough to find his way around without benefit of course computer, which has only limited uses in this terrain, anyway."

"Wouldn't that make it difficult for them to find their way back to the ground base if anything happened to Cameron?" I asked.

Razin grinned. "It might give them a good incentive to make certain nothing happened to him."

We reached the skimmer hangar and Razin signed for our transport vehicle. Moments later, we were lifting off in the tiny delta-winged craft.

"The Combine supplies the skimmers," he said. "They lose

them from time to time. They either crash or the hunters experience some other no less fatal difficulty. Others forget instructions and foolishly attempt to land within the ground base compound without following the prescribed approach pattern." He shrugged. "Of course, if the SS has no chance to scan the craft and control its entry, they have no choice but to shoot it down. It pays to follow instructions."

"What happens if there aren't enough skimmers to go around?" I said.

"That doesn't happen," Razin said. "You're not allowed to go down to the surface and make a foray unless there's a skimmer available for your use. So there is a waiting list for surface excursions. Naturally, you being such important guests, you received priority. The skimmers are fairly cheap to build and the Combine has set up a small plant to manufacture them in one of the other habitats. However, use of them is not free. There is something called an excursion fee charged to your account. The longer you keep the skimmer out, the greater the excursion fee. Keeping the skimmer out too long and not finding any fire crystal is a good way to go bankrupt quickly. In that event, one of the credit bankers buys your marker and the company receives its money and stops worrying about you. You, on the other hand, have a whole new set of problems."

"What happens if there's a glut on the market?" I said.

"Too many bankrupts, you mean?" Razin said.

"Yes. What happens if a credit banker doesn't buy up your debts?"

"You might be better off," said Razin. "If the Combine is in need of workers, then you are assigned to a job at the most minimal rate of pay until you work off your debt. That's called 'taking a company mortgage.' That could be preferable to fighting in The Arena under a credit banker's contract. However, if the Combine doesn't require any warm bodies at the time, there is some fine print in the emigration agreement that allows them to sell your contract, usually to a corporate mercenary unit or even to the regular service. That may not sound like such a bad deal, but in such cases, the enlistment contract you 'agree' to undertake is for twenty years and a percentage of your pay during that time is automatically deducted and charged off to your account. It usually takes about twenty years to pay off a debt that way, even if it's not a very large one. Interest, you know."

Stone seemed surprised. "Is that legal?"

"It is if you agree to it," said Razin. "And you do when you sign up for the Fire Islands."

Breck smiled. "You're doing a wonderful public relations job for the Draconis Combine," he told Razin.

"Your sarcasm is hardly to the point, Breck," Razin said. "How much of this discussion do you think will reach your home audience?"

Breck frowned. "What are you talking about?"

"I'm talking about reality, my friend. The reality of business transactions. Did you really think the Combine would give Psychodrome carte blanche out here? Or does it seem more reasonable that they would stipulate—what would you call it?—control over the final cut? What happens, really, when your experiences are transmitted live? Isn't there, in fact, a short delay to allow for what your people refer to as enhancing?"

Breck was silent for a long moment. Stone glanced from him to Razin.

"Can they do that?" I wondered.

"It occurs to me they can," said Breck. "There is nothing in our contracts that says they can't."

"I don't understand," I said. "You mean they edit out what we say if they don't like it? How can they? During live tachyon transmission, the delay isn't long enough to—"

"It is if all they have to do is substitute dialogue of their own for what you're saying," Razin said. "They have enough samples of your voice patterns to duplicate them electronically. Working from any number of sample dialogue scripts prepared in advance, it would be a fairly simple matter to generate enhanced dialogue for you, in your own voices. You see, I make a point of asking about such things. I like to know all the details of the jobs I'm getting into. I wanted to make certain that I would not inadvertently say the wrong thing. I was assured there was no need for concern. For all I know, your computers might be synchronizing my lip movements to a rousing chorus of 'Ninety-nine Bottles of Beer' this very minute. Give or take a moment or two."

"You mean they can literally have us saying whatever they want us to say?" I said. "Have they ever really done anything like that?"

"Not to my knowledge," Breck said slowly.

Stone shook her head. "I never heard of it being done." She paused. "Of course, I've only watched reruns of my own experiences on occasion. Just because they've never done it with me—"

"How do you know?" I said, an unpleasant thought occurring to me.

"What do you mean, how do I know? I'd know it if they changed what I said, wouldn't I? I was there!"

"What happens when you plug into a rerun?" I said. "How do you know you're experiencing it on normal broadcast channels? You either get the company to play it back for you or you plug into a scheduled rerun on a psy-fi set that happens to be in a room the company reserved for you. What if they're transmitting the original, unenhanced recording to you and another one to the home audience?"

"That young man is a Class A paranoid," said Razin, banking the skimmer. "He'll probably go far."

Breck nodded. "You know, that possibility has never even occurred to me in all the time I have played the game, not that I have ever really cared one way or another until now. Yet it makes sense. What made you think of that, O'Toole?"

"Maybe Razin's right and I am a Class A paranoid," I said. "On the other hand, I've had some experience with people making it seem as if I'd done things I hadn't really done."

"Ah, yes," said Breck. "Your friend back on the Ginza Strip. It strikes me that you've served quite an apprenticeship for playing this game. You are not exactly an ordinary rookie, are you?"

"I don't know why that should make me mad," said Stone, "but it does. It's not as if Psychodrome hasn't already used my mind and body, but somehow the idea of having my words changed really bothers me."

"But are they truly *your* words, Miss Winters?" Razin said. "What I mean is, in a sense, aren't you actually playing a part, much as any other actress? The experience you broadcast may be genuine, at least for the most part, but can you honestly say that you are communicating with your audience? There is no real interchange, is there? Rather, you are performing for them, are you not? Playing a part that happens to be Stone Winters, but is nevertheless a role. So what if they change the script? It does not change you, except in the eyes of your home audience, who don't really know you anyway, do they?"

Stone stared at him, then looked at me. "Did you understand what he just said?"

"I'm afraid so," I replied. "That's what worries me."

Razin chuckled. "Don't let it concern you, Miss Winters.
After all, it's only show business, right?"

"I'm not sure I care for your tone, Razin," she said.

"My apologies," he said. "I did not mean to sound condescending. I suspect the only reason O'Toole and I understand
each other is that we are both members of the same club. We
are both cynics. And we are both paranoid, traits which I
would say auger well for our survival. Especially here on
Draconis 9, where you never know for sure if something is
what it seems to be. Rather like your Psychodrome hallucinact, I should think. Who knows, perhaps this *is* a Psychodrome hallucinact. Perhaps I'm not even really here. For all
you know, I might be a computer simulation."

"Razin, give it a rest, okay?" I suggested. "My hold on
reality is tenuous enough, thank you."

Razin smiled. "Really? Well, in that case, as some ancient
personage once said, 'You ain't seen nothin' yet.' "

The skimmer suddenly plunged down into a mountain
chasm and banked sharply, barely missing the rock walls. For
an instant I had a crazy flash of *déjà vu*, as if the scene back
on the Ginza Strip was being replayed in a mountain gorge instead of an urban maze, with Razin flying the skimmer instead
of Kami piloting her tiger-striped scooter.

"Razin!" Stone shouted. "Are you crazy? What the hell are
you doing?"

"Attempting to lose your friends," said Razin. "In case it
has escaped your notice, we are being followed. I assume
that's Cameron behind us, flying the other skimmer."

I twisted around in my seat and saw another skimmer
several hundred yards behind us and closing fast. Razin
banked sharply again and rolled the tiny craft. I felt my body
strain against the seat harness. We were hurtling past rock
walls at an incredible speed, coming so close to them that it
seemed as if at any moment we'd scrape against an outcropping and one of the wings would shear off, but Razin was an
accomplished pilot. Cameron, apparently, was no less skillful.
The other skimmer stayed right on our tail.

We played tag with Cameron among the rocks, zooming
through the mountainous terrain like tiny fish darting among
coral. I had lost all sense of direction. We rolled and banked

so quickly and so many times, I wasn't even certain about up and down anymore. Everything became a fast, disjointed series of blurred images—shrubs and trees and rocks and sky and flashes of a river undulating far below us. Perhaps it was thrilling as all hell for the home audience, but I was feeling incredibly nauseated. They would "enhance" that out, no doubt.

"We appear to be evenly matched," said Razin. "I can't seem to shake him. I was hoping I could make him crash."

"I was hoping we wouldn't," said Stone. "Let them follow us. What difference does it make?"

"It makes quite a difference," Razin said. "Why should Cameron take them to his crystal dig when he can latch onto our tail and follow me to mine? I would prefer not to share its location with him. Unlike Smythe-Davies's team and yourselves, he *would* be able to find it again on his own. I'd rather he didn't do that."

"Lead him away from it, then," said Breck. "Set down somewhere and we'll settle it."

"I was leading him away from it," said Razin. "However, I would prefer not to set down first if I can avoid it. We would present a bit too tempting a target on the ground."

"We could just as easily return the fire," Breck said, patting his pistol in its holster.

"True, but why take unnecessary risks?" said Razin.

Stone glanced at him in astonishment. "You're kidding. After the way you've been flying this thing, you can say that?"

Razin shrugged. "I haven't taken any real risks yet. However, Cameron is beginning to annoy me. Let's see if this won't dissuade him."

He pulled the nose of the skimmer up sharply and it climbed vertically, then looped around and went back in the opposite direction. Cameron had followed, executing the same maneuver, and now we were still in the same relation to each other, only heading back in the opposite direction—whichever direction that was; I was more thoroughly lost than a schizophrenic mouse in a maze. Razin put the skimmer in a forty-five-degree-angle dive, then abruptly cut the engines. I went cold all over.

"Oh, God," I said, my voice sounding somehow very far away. "We're going to die."

"I sincerely hope not," Razin said, "but I confess there is a chance of it, especially if you continue to distract me."

"O'Toole," said Breck quietly. "Shut up, please."

The skimmer dropped down in a very fast, controlled glide. All I could hear was the sound of wind rushing past the wings. I had no idea what Razin was planning and I wasn't sure I wanted to know. I was even more sure I didn't want to know when I saw what he intended, but by then it was too late. I knew. I felt Stone's fingers digging into my shoulders and I tried to concentrate on that feeling, as if it would block out the unreasoning terror that welled up inside me when I saw the opening of the cavern in the side of the mountain directly ahead of us. The cavern mouth was coming up fast. Very, very fast.

"Razin . . ." I said, my voice a horse whisper, "you're *not* going to—"

Stone's hand reached around from behind me and covered my mouth.

We plunged into the mouth of the cave.

Razin hit the engines.

I would have closed my eyes, but it was already so dark inside that cavern that I couldn't see a thing. I kept waiting for the inevitable impact, but it didn't come. The engines braked us and we slowed gradually. I became aware that we were headed downward, going deeper inside the mountain. I still couldn't see a thing. I glanced quickly toward Razin, expecting to see at least the soft glow of the instrument panel, but there was nothing. Pitch blackness. The crazy son of a bitch was flying *blind* inside a mountain. If Stone's hand hadn't been covering my mouth, I would have whimpered.

We turned—turned!—and I felt the almost imperceptible, gentle scraping of the skimmer's undercarriage on something beneath us.

"Damn," said Razin softly, and then he hit the lights.

Even Breck caught his breath.

We were inside a mammoth cavern, so huge it looked as if the entire mountain had to be hollow. It made me think of sailing through some gigantic undersea grotto in a tiny submarine. Gargantuan stalactites hung down from overhead like saurian teeth and we flew between stalagmites the size of skyscrapers. Birds or bats or some kind of creatures with wings darted through the cavern in clusters, avoiding the bright lights of the skimmer. A number of them came extremely close, but didn't strike us, veering off at the last instant. I saw that they were insects of some sort, with darkly glinting carapaces and antennae and multitudinous legs. They flew with a sort of clicking sound not unlike the sharp, professional shuffling of cards.

I could not get over the sheer size of the place. I had been overwhelmed by the grandeur of the mountain ranges of Draconis 9 and made to feel insignificant by their immensity, but nothing had struck me with such force as the experience of being in that cavern system. It was like having been swallowed up into the giant belly of a leviathan. The lights of the skimmer revealed shockingly vivid colors—greens brighter than a parrot's plumage, blood reds, pastel pinks and browns in many shades, dove grays, and bright yellows—all sparkling with dustings and thick veins of pyrites and crystalline formations.

"My God," said Stone softly and it was not until she spoke that I realized she still had her hand clamped over my mouth. I made a sound against it and she withdrew it, mumbling, "Oh, sorry."

I turned to Razin. "You are an absolute maniac," I said.

"You're probably right," he said casually. "It was risky coming through without the lights, but I wanted to give Cameron a bit of a turn. He evidently didn't have the nerve to follow us in."

"It was an impressive maneuver," Breck said. "How many times did it take you to learn the route through the cavern mouth so well?"

"I've done it dozens of times," said Razin, "but that was the first time I've ever tried it without lights. It was a bit of a close scrape there at the end."

"You want to tell me again what you said about unnecessary risks?" I asked.

Razin shrugged. "I felt reasonably confident that I could do this. Besides, you wanted a dramatic experience for your home viewers, didn't you?"

"They certainly got that," said Stone. "Is this the place where you get your fire crystals?"

"Not exactly," Razin said. "When I first found this place, I was convinced I would find fire crystal here, but after exploring this cavern system fully, I found almost every sort of mineral and crystalline substance native to Draconis except fire crystal. Still, I like to come here."

"I can see why," said Breck. "It is magnificent. How did you happen upon it?"

"Entirely by accident," said Razin. "I crashed in this vicinity on one of my first trips out. Stupid, really. I had no business attempting to navigate the gorge without a great deal more experience. I was fortunate and survived the crash, but that left me on foot at the bottom of the gorge, with no way out. I figured I was done for. I was attempting to decide whether I should simply kill myself or die trying to stay alive as long as possible. Purely an intellectual exercise, really. I had always wondered what I would do in such a situation and now that I was confronted with it, I wanted to give it the fullest consideration. Then it started to rain. I decided that I might as well remain dry and reasonably comfortable while I debated the question, so I started to look for shelter. And then I spotted the entrance to the cavern."

The skimmer had slowed so that it was largely hovering, moving forward very slowly. Razin seemed to be following a specific course through the giant cavern.

"It wasn't easy to climb up to it, but I had become curious," he continued. "You can't see the cavern entrance from the air until you're almost right on top of it. You can see it clearly from the ground, but it's quite hard to get to and there isn't any good landing site below it or any reason why anyone should want to land there. The only practical way to get inside it is the way we came—though not necessarily in exactly the same manner, of course. The cavern mouth is deceptive. It looks barely wide enough to admit a skimmer—and it is—but it widens out almost immediately, allowing plenty of room to maneuver a small craft such as this. If you don't know your way, the sudden downward slope that occurs just inside the cavern mouth can be quite dangerous. If Cameron had followed us, chances are he would have crashed, even as good a pilot as he is."

"How did you get back?" said Stone. "You said there was no way out of the gorge except by air . . ."

"There is one other way," said Razin, "and we are about to take it."

Gently, he set the skimmer down, hovering it first, then turning it slowly about its axis as it descended with a diminishing whine of its engines. There was a slight bump on the undercarriage as it touched down and then he retracted the canopy. I felt a damp, cool breeze. It was eerily silent in the cavern, a silence broken only by the chittering flight of the insectlike creatures that nested up in the stalactites.

I pointed at several of them flying past us overhead. "Are those things dangerous?"

"Damned if I know," Razin said.

"I thought you were supposed to be our consulting expert on this junket," I said.

Razin shrugged. "I don't bother them and they don't bother me. It pays not to get too close to the indigenous life forms on this planet. One never knows for sure what they might be." He smiled.

We climbed out of the skimmer and stood on the ledge where Razin had set it down. He took a lantern out of the cockpit and shined it out over the ledge, giving us a breathtaking view of the cavern as he played the wide beam across it.

"Beautiful, isn't it?" he said.

"Have you ever encountered the Draconians?" asked Stone.

"Oh, yes," said Razin. He did not amplify.

"And?" she persisted.

"I am, as I have already told you, a paranoid," he said. "I try to keep my distance. If they fail to respect that, I generally shoot them."

"Even if they have shapechanged into human form?" she said.

"Especially if they have shapechanged into human form, Miss Winters."

"How do you know it's not actually a human?"

"I'm not terribly concerned with that," said Razin. "I have survived as long as I have out here because I watch out for myself. If I warn someone to keep their distance and they seem disinclined to listen to me, then I figure that's their problem. I don't lose any sleep over it."

"You must have an interesting social life," I said.

"Down here, it's each man for himself," said Razin. He smiled at Stone. "Or each woman for herself. And this would be the appropriate time to caution you about keeping very careful track of one another. Do not get out of one another's sight. Especially do not get out of *my* sight. A Draconian could assume your shape in a matter of moments. If I'm not absolutely certain you are who you appear to be, I may develop some acute anxiety."

"So we use the buddy system, is that it?" I said. "Want I should hold your hand?"

"Getting nervous, O'Toole?" Razin asked.

"Why, does it show?"

He grinned. "We may not even encounter any shape-changers. Personally, I would not mind that a bit, but I'd hate for you to feel cheated."

"Oh, I think I could handle it," I said.

Razin reached into his pack and passed out several small, self-contained breathing masks designed to fit over the nose and mouth. "These are extractor masks," he said. "They concentrate the available oxygen in the air. You'll need them. If you haven't already experienced some trouble breathing, you soon will. We will be going to an elevation of approximately sixteen thousand feet. In Earth's atmosphere, this would be comparable to somewhere between eighteen and twenty thousand, so conserve your energy."

We followed him up a steep incline. The passage was narrow, barely wide enough to allow us to pass in single file. Several times, it narrowed so sharply it was necessary to turn sideways and squeeze through. It seemed to be getting colder. I wasn't sure how far we had walked or how long it took. All I knew was that my out-of-shape leg muscles didn't like it very much. It didn't take long before I felt the twitching caused by lactic acid buildup in the muscles. I became more aware of my feet, calves, knees, and hips than I had ever been before. The deficiencies of urban living. I wondered what it was that made people want to to out and hike in mountains for the fun of it. Doubtless, they didn't experience such discomfort. They practiced doing it until it no longer bothered them, which struck me as being similar to bashing your head against the wall on the theory that sooner or later you wouldn't notice the pain anymore.

After a while, I felt the breeze grow stronger. Soon there was light up ahead. We came out finally into what I first thought was a box canyon, but then I realized it was the crater of an ancient volcano, the ridge reaching high into the clouds. We were in the caldera. The mouth of the extinct volcano was shrouded in mist and most of the crater was filled by a large lake. The light was diffused by the clouds and it was like standing in a thick fog.

"This is where I find my crystal," Razin said.

"Aren't you worried about giving the location away?" said Stone. "Couldn't someone find this place knowing they were looking for an extinct volcano at about—what was it you said—sixteen thousand feet?"

"I'm not terribly concerned about it," Razin said. "First of all, as I said before, it's highly unlikely anyone would have been able to follow the course I flew to get there, except an experienced crystal hunter such as Cameron. From the way we went down without our engines, Cameron probably thought we crashed. We disappeared from his view among the lower rock outcroppinngs and if he tried to follow us down, he may have spotted the cavern entrance, but it would be unlikely unless he knew exactly what he was looking for. It's only clearly visible from the ground and from an altitude roughly parallel to it. Even if he spotted it, he'd have to know exactly how to navigate the cavern mouth and if he was able to do that, it would probably take him weeks of exploring the cavern system before he found the tunnel leading up to the caldera. If anyone tried to find it from the air, they'd be hard pressed, because there is always cloud cover. It would be like diving into water without knowing what the depth was or if there were rocks just beneath the surface. Besides, there are quite literally hundreds of volcanos on Draconis 9, some extinct, some dormant, and some active. The records are by no means complete. I found this place purely by chance. Someone else trying to find it from the record of your experience would have a difficult time of it."

Breck was looking all around at the sides of the caldera. "How did you get out of here the first time, after you crashed your skimmer?"

"I climbed," said Razin.

"Up *these* walls?"

"It took me over a week to climb up out of here," he said. "Most of that time was spent scrambling, looking for hand- and footholds. I would get partway up and then there would be nowhere else to go, no purchase whatsoever. I would be forced to climb back down the same way and start again, looking for another way out. It was not the most pleasant experience I've ever had, but several pocketfuls of fire crystal kept me going. I've been coming back here to get more ever since."

"Where do you find them?" I said.

"Sometimes you will find a vein of the crystal," Razin said. "That is comparatively rare. More often, you might find pieces of a shattered crystalline formation, either lying around loose as rubble or on the bottom of stream beds. But the rarest find of all is what is known as an intact formation."

He moved over to a large outcropping of dark volcanic rock and, unexpectedly, plunged his fingers into it, as if he were tearing a hunk of bread from a giant loaf. The thick dried mud caking the rock crumbled easily, revealing the shimmering clusters of faceted crystal formations underneath.

Stone stared at it with disbelief. *"That whole thing is . . ."*

"An intact formation of fire crystal, Miss Winters," Razin said, "standing over twelve feet tall and six feet in diameter, extending an undetermined distance beneath the surface. It was brought up from below during the last eruption, but it was never carried out over the rim. I imagine it was deposited here as the lava subsided and then, when it cooled and the caldera formed, the lava hardened into a basaltic outer skin over the formation. It took me months to carefully chip it away from this one formation. This entire caldera is full of them. They are all around you. I've found thirty-seven so far."

Stone gasped. Breck stared at Razin with utter disbelief. My mouth had gone completely dry.

"You fool," said Breck, in a low voice. "Do you have any idea what you've done?"

"I have created a legend," said Razin, smiling. "A legend of a place where, if you could only find it, you would discover enough fire crystal to make you rich beyond your wildest dreams. And it is a reality, not just some tale told by drunken crystal hunters. Through you, millions of people have seen it, experienced it for themselves."

"And since you're the only one who knows how to find this place," said Breck, "you're going to be a marked man for the rest of your life."

"Perhaps that would concern me a great deal," Razin said, "if I were a man." Before any of us could react, his weapon was in his hand and pointed at us. "Please make no sudden moves. I honestly have no wish to kill you, but I will not hesitate to do so if you force me."

-NINE-

"Is this some sort of joke?" said Breck. "If it is, it is not amusing."

"Nikolai Razin is dead," the ambimorph said. "But in a sense, he's also here. I have assumed his personality—his memories, his thought patterns, his bioplasm—and what you see before you is indistinguishable from the original, except it is not strictly human."

"I don't believe it," Stone said. "You were on Casino with us. You haven't been out of our sight since we left. The transceivers—"

"Are a stopgap measure at best," the Draconian said. "The transceiver implants prevented me from simply assuming any human form and attempting to enter your ground bases by passing myself off as a human. They do not, however, prevent me from taking the place of a specific human if I am able to kill him."

"How?" I said.

"We survive by assuming the forms of other creatures," the Draconian said. "We duplicate them down to the last detail.

155

In this manner, we are able to live as they live. Possessing their interior organs, their biochemistry, we are able to adapt to their life functions. We can breathe as they breathe, feed as they feed. Our adaptability has always been the key to our survival. But in what you would call our natural state, we feed in the same manner as the unicellular protozoans native to your planet."

"You mean you absorb your food like an amoeba?" I said. Suddenly I understood and I felt sick. "My God. You ingested him."

"You seem horrified, O'Toole," said the Draconian. "And yet you humans saw nothing wrong with hunting us for food. In the form we had adopted, we were even considered something of a delicacy by many of those who first came here, which is more than I can say for the taste of human flesh. I became quite ill after consuming Razin. It is an experience I have no wish to repeat, so you can rest easy on that count." The shapechanger grimaced wryly. "I promise not to eat you. I killed Razin only because it was necessary. He tried to kill me. Consuming him was the only way I could absorb his transceiver implant into my own system."

"Then you've broken the quarantine," said Breck. "But by telling us, you have also alerted our authorities."

"Which was precisely my intention," the Draonian said. "I have no wish to harm you. You are my vehicles for communicating with the human race, through your psych-fidelity network. I am aware that your playermaster, Tolliver Mondago, is monitoring your experience along with officials of the Draconis Combine. Mr. Mondago, I have information which will be of vital interest to the human race, but I shall divulge none of it unless I have your assurance that this transmission will not be interfered with by the Combine. I await your reply."

I held my breath, waiting for Mondago's contact. It did not come right away. The tension increased as the silence lengthened. Finally, Mondago's voice came to us across the vast distance of space.

"*Forgive the delay*," he said, his well-bottom voice sounding, in my mind, perfectly calm and controlled. "*It was necessary to have the Combine observer removed from the game control center. He became quite agitated and wanted to censor the transmission, insisting it would cause widespread panic. He may be right, but under the circumstances, I feel that I must override him on the grounds of the public's right to know."*

I didn't think Mondago was especially concerned about the public's right to know, but the ratings would definitely be on his mind. He was speaking to the telepathic shapechanger directly, through us.

"You have my assurance that there will be absolutely no interference with the transmission of the players' experience. Your message will be broadcast live over the psy-fi network, for which I accept full responsibility. In return, I trust you will remember your promise not to harm my players. Now, what is it you want?"

I was surprised by Mondago's apparent concern for our welfare until I realized that he was probably not speaking for our benefit alone, as he usually did, but for broadcast purposes as well.

"We want only to survive," said the shapechanger. "We Draconians, as you call us, do not wish to be perceived as dangerous, xenophobic monsters, yet we are all too aware that we will probably be portrayed in that light. When you humans first arrived here, we did not engage in any hostilities against you. We were peaceful, until humans began to kill us indiscriminately, to hunt us for food. We were forced to act in a manner that would ensure our survival, which has always been dependent upon our ability to assume what you would call protective coloration to adapt to our environment. When confronted by a predator, it is our first instinct to take that predator's form. We began to take human form instinctively at first, merely to protect ourselves, but also to learn everything we could about this new predator which had appeared. The result was a form of mutation for which, in a curious way, we should probably thank you.

"You are the most advanced species we have ever encountered and through our defensive transmogrification into human form, we evolved into something much more than what we were. We understood that, to you, we were initially nothing more than animals and that it was not unnatural for your predatory instincts to cause you to act as you did. We also understood that among many of you, there was considerable regret for your mistake. Yet, while there may have been regret, there was also fear. Fear which would have led to the genocide of our species, only our nature renders us difficult to detect. Mr. Breck, as one of the soldiers sent here for that purpose some time ago, can testify to that.

"A quarantine was the only logical alternative," the shapechanger continued, "but there was something here you humans wanted and a quarantine—a real quarantine—would have denied you access to it. Fire crystal means nothing to us. We have no use for it. We would gladly have given you all you wanted, but you chose instead to come and take it for yourselves, as if it were your right to do so. We would not have objected to that, either, only your greed caused you to come here and kill one another for it and your fear caused you to kill us as well. If you had your way, you would have wiped us out, not just because you were afraid of us, but because this planet could be terraformed and we were in the way. You have done this even with those of your own kind.

"Well, we have learned much from you and one of the things we have learned is how to deal with you in terms you would understand. We want no more humans on our world. You may keep your ground bases and use them to negotiate with us for fire crystal. You may think of them as embassies. But we do not want you to set foot beyond the confines of those ground bases and we will not give you fire crystal for nothing. We have learned that humans value only that which costs them dearly. And to strengthen our negotiating position, we will appeal to your fear.

"We have broken your quarantine. We succeeded in breaking it some time ago. The method is not a very pleasant one for us, but it has proven effective. Even as I speak, some of us are in Casino and the other habitats which comprise the Fire Islands. Some of us have gone on to your colonies and even to your home world, Earth, where we can easily pass as human and where, just as easily, we can reproduce.

"We can live among you peacefully as humans," the shapechanger said, "even as there are now humans living peacefully with us, trapped here by your own quarantine. Or we can embark upon a program of terrorism the like of which your world has never seen before. It is not something we wish to do, but you have shown us how and we are uniquely suited to it. The choice is yours. We have had enough of being slaughtered. That is all I have to say. I have now accomplished what I had set out to do."

The Draconian looked at each of us in turn, gauging our reactions, as if he were trying to guess from our thoughts how the rest of the human race would respond upon hearing this ultimatum.

Breck stood looking at him. He walked over to the crystal formation, removing his glove as he went, snikked out his blades, and struck the formation a sharp blow at the bottom of a cluster. An obelisk-shaped crystal broke off and dropped into his other hand. He held it up briefly and looked at the fires dancing within the perfectly formed, natural facets.

"We have also accomplished what we set out to do," he said. "Now we had best be on our way."

The shapechanger hesitated a moment, then nodded and holstered his pistol. "I will take you back."

"I would not advise that," Breck said. "You have delivered an ultimatum that will not be received easily or well. If the Combine's representative had time to get off a tachyon transmission to Casino, you will never leave the ground base alive. They will want to interrogate you thoroughly and they will not be particular about how they get their answers."

"It is a risk I was prepared to take," the Draconian said. "Someone needs to represent our case to your people."

"What if our people decide to kill you?" Stone said.

The Draconian gave a very human shrug.

Part of me was wondering why we were concerned about his safety. This alien had just threatened the human race with terrorism. Yet another part of me—the part I tried to focus on—was reminding me that we were the aliens here and that we had been the ones who taught him. I tried to imagine how I would have felt if the Draconians had come to Earth to claim it for their own. How would I have felt if they had considered us nothing more than animals? What would my reaction have been if they had started hunting us for food? Would I have been content to have them quarantine my world?

One of the first and most important steps in any conflict in our history was always the dehumanization of the enemy. An Indian became a wog; a Native American became a redskin; an Asian became a nip, a gook, a chink, a kraut, kike, wop, spic, nigger . . . it was all the same, one category, one subrace, one something-less-than-human which made it easier to oppress or even kill. In this case, it was really easy because there was no question of humanity involved. This time, we were really faced with *other* and the emotions brought into play keyed off "us" and "them."

Part of me was emotionally outraged at the Draconian's belligerence and part of me kept pulling in the reins, reminding me that *we* had taught them this. "We have learned how to deal with you in terms you would understand," the Draconian had said. It was infuriating to be told what terms we would understand, it sounded arrogant and condescending, yet how was it possible to dispute knowledge gained through telepathic contact? How could it be dismissed as arrogance? What was arrogant was that we had imposed our sensibilities and our perceptions upon another race of beings, we had even had the arrogance to name them after the human who had "discovered" their world.

And then there was the question of responsibility. By coming to their planet, we had changed them. Our interaction with them had forced a mutation. They had learned, been forced to learn, to become like us, to look like us and act like us and think like us. I looked at "Razin" and saw the Razin that had been, the human template for the new model I confronted. The mimicry was perfect, both inside and out. Inside that chest there was now a heart that beat just like a human heart, lungs that breathed like human lungs. Cut him and he might bleed. Would a chemical analysis reveal a composition unlike that of human blood or was this so plastic a life form that even the molecular structure of human blood could be duplicated? Could they even be what they were if their molecular structure were not plastic, radically different from anything we had ever encountered before? How much was really known about them? Did they merely take the form of humans or did they, in fact, *become* human? If so, then maybe they were better at it than we were. The real Nikolai Razin would probably have killed his enemy. This one had chosen not to.

None of us spoke as we made our way back through the tunnel to the cavern where we had left the skimmer. There was a lot to think about. Our experience had become much more than simply an entertainment for the masses. I wondered how the news would be received back home. I thought I had a pretty good idea of the answer and that made me afraid.

Breck and the Draconian were in the lead. Stone walked directly ahead of me. I suddenly felt an overpowering need to reestablish the closeness there had been between us. I reached out and took her by the arm. She stopped and turned to face me for a moment. In the darkness of the tunnel, we could barely see each other.

"Stone," I said, speaking in a voice not much louder than a whisper, "I just wanted to say . . . about what I said back in Casino . . ."

I felt her fingers briefly touch my lips and then, a moment later, I felt her lips brush mine. Then she turned and continued down the tunnel.

That soft contact, so brief and yet so full of meaning, was more important to me than anything we could have said to one another. Sometimes there are things you have to say that can't be said with words. I wondered if paranoia was a trait unique to humans. It was hard enough, among yourselves, to develop trust. It was hard enough to just believe in someone. Does this person really think well of me? Are these people really my friends? Do they really like me? Does she really love me; does he really understand me or is there some secret truth being kept from me? What is he *really* thinking? What does she *really* want? Wasn't what psychologists called being "well-adjusted" actually nothing more than a functioning methodology for dealing with our insecurities? How "well-adjusted" would we be now, knowing we had been invaded? To all those other questions directed at seeking reassurance would now be added a terrifying further doubt—is this person really *human*? And how would anybody really know?

We reached the end of the tunnel and stepped out into the giant cavern. The skimmer sat on the ledge just below us. I wanted to believe that none of it had really happened. We had come here to obtain a chunk of fire crystal and we had done that. Now we would leave. Would the game go on as before? I didn't like the rule changes. I didn't want to play. I wanted to yell out that universal, wonderful, childlike demand, "Do over!" It was an unacceptable reality. I didn't want to deal with this.

We were almost to the skimmer when the shots were fired.

The first plasma blast slammed into a rock formation just in front of us, between us and the skimmer. Superheated rock chips and chunks of molten crystal flew like shrapnel. The second one, coming fast on the heels of the first, blasted the cavern wall above and to the left. The entire wall came down in an avalanche of rock and dust. Something struck me and I went down. I heard someone shouting, but it was drowned out in the echoes of the plasma blasts and falling rocks. I covered my head with my arms, expecting at any moment to be crushed beneath tons of rock.

I was dazed. There was a ringing in my ears. I wasn't sure how much time had passed, if I had lost consciousness or not. I felt the wetness in my eyes before I felt the pain. Blood was trickling down from a gash in my forehead above my left eyebrow. My right shoulder felt numb. Rock and crystal dust was everywhere. I tried to breathe and it triggered off a spasm of coughing.

The first thing I saw as the dust slowly settled was the skimmer, half on and half off the ledge, crushed beneath fallen boulders. I couldn't see any of the others. There was a huge pile of rubble in front of me. I had just missed being buried beneath the stone. Stone!

Breck came scrambling toward me over the mound of rubble. "O'Toole!"

"Here," I said, coughing and struggling to my hands and knees, wiping blood out of my eyes. "Stone—"

"She's alive," he said. He didn't look well. "She didn't quite make it clear, but I was able to pull her free. Both her legs are broken. She has some cuts and bruises, possibly internal injuries, I cannot be certain."

"The Draconian?"

Breck looked over his shoulder at the pile of rock. "Under there."

"What happened?" I said. "Who—"

"Cameron," said Breck. "Who else?"

"Razin?" someone shouted. "Razin, you alive?" The voice echoed weirdly in the cavern. "O'Toole? Breck!"

Breck glanced at me and shook his head. "Make no sound," he said, drawing his weapon.

"Razin, if you're alive, you'd best answer me, boy!" The voice had to be Cameron's. "Your skimmer's destroyed. You people aren't going anywhere. You want me to just leave you here?"

"Can you move?" Breck said softly. "Is anything broken?"

"I don't know. I may have a concussion. I can't move my right arm, but I think I can walk."

"Stone needs help," said Breck. "The only way we can leave here now is with their skimmer. Us or them. They made the choice. You understand?"

I nodded. "What do you want me to do?"

"Get over there with Stone," said Breck. "Try to keep them

occupied while I work around behind them. Can you make it?''

"I'll make it."

"Good man." He clapped me on the shoulder, giving it a hard squeeze.

"Rudy?" I swallowed hard. "What do we do if you don't come back?''

"I will be back," Breck said.

I smiled weakly. "Promise?"

"I promise."

I crawled around the mound of rubble piled before me, under which the Draconian was buried. I wondered what would happen now. I found Stone in the shelter of a large stalagmite, where Breck had left her, her back propped up against. it. She held a plasma pistol in her hand. The expression on my face must have said it all, because she grimaced at me wryly, clearly fighting back pain, and said, "Sorry. Didn't have time to fix myself up."

Her face was caked with blood and rock dust and her matted hair hung down in her eyes. She made no move to brush it away as she reclined against the rock, breathing heavily. She shut her eyes tightly, grimacing with pain. Her legs were splayed out at odd angles. There had been no time for Breck to splint them and nothing to splint them with. I took her hand and she squeezed hard.

"I guess we blew it," she said, gritting her teeth.

"Not yet, we didn't. It isn't over 'til it's over."

She managed a small grin. "It isn't over 'til it's over. I like that. Did you just make it up?''

"It's something my father always used to say. I never knew if it made any sense or not until I started playing cards for money.''

"Well," she said, gasping with pain, "I can't say I care much for this hand. You're the gambler. What do you suggest?''

"We can't afford to fold. We'll have to bluff. Only in this case, we make them think we're holding even worse cards than we are. And with any luck, our partner will slip us an ace or two under the table.''

"What happens if they catch him at it?''

I shrugged. "That's why they call it gambling."

"I see. Remind me not to play poker with you."

"Cameron!" I shouted, trying to make my voice sound as if I had been badly hurt. I didn't have to try too hard.

"O'Toole?"

"Yeah. Don't shoot. Please."

"Where's Razin?"

"Dead. So's Breck. They were both buried when the wall came down. Stone's hurt real bad. She's unconscious. She may be dying. I can't move. My legs are broken. I'll do anything you want, just don't kill me. Please. I'll tell you where the fire crystals are. That's what you want, isn't it?"

I heard him laugh. It was a very unpleasant sound.

"What's so goddamned funny?"

"You don't have anything to bargain with, O'Toole. Look above you."

I glanced up to where the wall of rock had come down, burying the Draconian. The avalanche caused by the plasma blast had exposed a face of shimmering crystal, a thick vein of faceted clusters glowing with a lambent, inner fire of dazzling colors.

"I just struck it rich, O'Toole," Cameron's voice came back, echoing off the walls. "I *knew* Razin would lead me to it! This whole cavern must be full of fire crystal! There's enough here for a man to buy his own damn planet!"

"What happens to us?" I shouted back. "What about Smythe-Davies and the others?"

"Funny thing about that," Cameron called back. He sounded closer. "Seems there was an accident. Guess their team didn't do so well."

"Damn you, Cameron! That's murder! You'll never get away with it."

"That's the way the game is played, rookie. You shouldn't have bought into this one. The hell of it is, no one will ever know. They use fire crystals to focus tachyon beam transmission, did you know that? There's enough crystal in this cavern to keep your signals bouncing around in here for years. It's just you and me in here."

So that was why the Draconian had led us through the tunnel to the surface. If the cavern was full of fire crystal, there was no need for us to hike up to the caldera, but he wanted to be certain his message would get through. We couldn't broadcast from inside the cavern.

"Cameron!" I shouted, holding my weapon ready. It sounded as if he was trying to work his way up to us. I glanced at Stone, put my finger to my lips, and pointed to where I thought he was coming from. Then I pointed at the mound of rubble, thinking if I could get up above him, I might get a clear shot at him. Stone nodded that she understood. "Cameron, please! I'll do anything! I don't want to die!"

"Sorry, O'Toole. That's the way it goes."

I started to crawl toward the mound of rubble.

"Toss out your weapons, O'Toole! I'll make it quick and painless."

I started to drag myself up the mound of rubble. I grabbed hold of a rock and started to pull myself up, but it came loose and started a small slide, taking me down with it. It broke other rocks loose and they cascaded down over the ledge, starting a small avalanche down into the bottom of the cavern. I almost went over with it. I caught myself just in time.

"It'll never work, O'Toole!" yelled Cameron. "I know exactly where you are! Give it up!"

A large part of the rubble mound had broken loose and fallen over the ledge. I was in the open, an easy target, a fact that was confirmed when a plasma blast plowed by so close to me that I felt the heat wash past me and the rocks I was clinging to suddenly grew very warm to the touch. The rocks started to slide again and I scrambled for purchase. I was obscured by the shower of rock chips and dust.

"You want it the hard way, O'Toole?" Cameron shouted from somewhere below me.

I cursed Breck. Where in hell was he? Stone was on the other side of the mound of rubble and couldn't cover me from there. I was completely exposed, unable to fire. If I let go even for an instant, I was sure to slide down over the ledge and it was a long drop to the bottom.

"Say good-bye, O'Toole," I heard Cameron say from behind me.

I heard a plasma pistol fire and wondered what it would feel like to be incinerated, but the hellfire never came. I glanced quickly over my shoulder and caught a glimpse of something wreathed in blue flame falling down into the abyss below me. It was a moment before I realized it was Cameron.

"Hang on, O'Toole!" shouted Breck from somewhere off to my right.

I shut my eyes and pressed my face against the rock, clinging to it like a bug to a wall and hoping it wouldn't start sliding again. I had nothing left. That look down into the abyss and the sight of Cameron's burning body falling, tumbling end over end, had taken all the fight right out of me. I had been ready to die and had resigned myself to it, but miraculously, my death had been postponed. It left me feeling giddy, wanting to sob with relief.

I heard rocks skittering down as Breck came closer, moving carefully. I began to believe the man was indestructible.

"Easy, O'Toole," he said, directly above me. "Easy now. Stretch out your hand."

I was afraid to let go. I couldn't move.

"Come on, damn you," Breck said, "give me your hand or must I pull you up by your hair?"

The crazy image of Breck hauling me up by the hair, like some sort of caveman with his latest conquest, made me chuckle in spite of myself and it broke the freeze. Cautiously, I extended my hand to him. I felt his gloved, nysteel fingers clamp around my wrist like a vise and suddenly I was being pulled up effortlessly, as if I didn't weigh a thing. Rocks started to slide under me, but Breck held me firmly in his grasp and a moment later, I was pulled to safety.

"I found their skimmer," Breck said. "That bastard actually had the nerve to follow Razin in. There's no sign of the others. I think he must have done for them."

I nodded.

"Are you all right?"

I took a deep breath. "I thought I was a dead man back there."

"You almost were. All things considered, I thought you handled yourself rather well."

"You know," I said, "this is going to sound crazy, but for a moment there, while I was clinging to the rocks, wondering if Cameron was going to get me first or if another slide would dump me over the edge, I had the wildest temptation to just let go."

Breck nodded. "The magnetic attraction of fear. I am told it literally pulls at you. It can be quite seductive."

"That's what it felt like. A sort of . . . pulling."

"But you did not give in to it."

"I don't know why. Too scared, I guess. Scared to let go."

"Clinging to life," said Breck. "I envy you the intensity of that experience. Sometimes I wish I knew what it was to feel afraid. Do you feel euphoric now?"

"Yes, I suppose I do. I don't know whether to laugh or cry.

I'm trembling. How do you feel?''

Breck sighed. "Weary. And savagely bitter." He looked at the pile of rock beneath which the Draconian was buried. "That poor creature never had a chance. You know what will happen now?''

I shook my head.

"We are going to finish what we started here, we humans," Breck said. "And my friend Bill Renn is going to be the man saddled with the job. No one will look at what the Draconians have done as self-defense. It will be considered an invasion and we shall react accordingly. What a waste. What a damnable, criminal waste.''

"Maybe we can do something," I said.

"Perhaps," said Breck. "But I cannot see how. In any case, we first have to figure out how to get out of here. Can you fly a skimmer?''

I stared at him with a sinking feeling in my stomach. "No. Can't you?''

"I have never flown one of these small, civilian models," he said. He shrugged. "What the hell, how different can it be?''

"I think I'm going to be ill," I said.

"In that case, do it and get it over with. I will need your help to carry Stone. I am not about to hike out of here with both of you on my back.''

"Okay. Give me a second.''

I turned around, leaned forward, supporting myself on a stalagmite, and emptied out my guts. It made me feel better, though I still felt a little light-headed. When I was finished, I looked up and my gaze fell upon the shimmering vein of fire crystal exposed by the plasma blast from Cameron's gun. The clusters gave off light in thousands of directions; the fires danced within them, giving the illusion that the crystals were filled with multicolored liquids pulsing through them. I was staring at a fortune. All I had to do was break off a few chunks and fill my pockets and I would have enough to set me up for life, enough to buy off Saqqara or, if he would not be bought off, enough to pay battalions of ninjas for his assassination. But I couldn't reach the vein. It was on the other side of the chasm and the rock slide it had been exposed by, which had rained down on the ledge where we stood and crushed our skimmer and buried the Draconian, had also blocked off the entrance to the tunnel leading up to the caldera.

Cameron had said the cavern was full of crystal. We could

undoubtedly find more. But strangely enough, perhaps irrationally, I didn't care. I had yet to touch a fire crystal and now I didn't want to. I was suddenly afraid that if I held one in my hand, something would happen to me. The dancing fires within the crystal had a hypnotic beauty that was now completely lost on me, but if I actually touched them, they might burn me with their cold flame and ignite something within me that would turn me into someone just like Cameron. That scared the hell out of me.

"Some people are players," Sean O'Toole had told me once, "and some people are played. If you ever find yourself standin' at a wheel, watchin' the ball goin' round and round, unable to take your eyes off the bloody thing as if that were your heart bouncin' around down there, or if you're ever sittin' at a table with your stake reduced to eatin' money, holdin' a hand all full of nothin' and you know you ought to throw 'em down and leave, but somehow you just can't bring yourself to do it, then you'll know you've got the fever and it's not you holdin' the cards, but the other way around. If that ever happens to you, son, then you'll know that you should never, ever play again. Take your lumps and drag yourself away and if ever anyone asks you to sit down to a game again, then shoot the bloody bastard, because he'll be askin' you to hang yourself."

I was a player, a man who was used to taking risks. But a real player knew when to cut his losses and walk away. I looked down over the edge, into the chasm where Cameron had cashed in his chips. And then I started walking.

-TEN-

There is something called a night terror, a nightmare so intense, so realistic, that when you awaken from it, the dream imagery briefly remains engraved upon your consciousness, etched so sharply that the border line between the states of wakefulness and dreaming is momentarily erased. Imagine being trapped deep within the REM state, tossing and turning in your sweat-soaked sheets, pursued across the dreamscape by some slathering demon conjured up from your subconscious. The reality of the experience seems indisputable, there is no awareness of its being a nightmare, no urgent feeling that you must wake up because you do not realize you are asleep. Fear drives you to the breaking point and some involuntary mental circuit breaker finally clicks over to prevent the overload and you are suddenly wrenched out of your dream so quickly that you linger for a moment in a sort of double exposure state—you *know* you are awake, and yet the nightmare won't let go. It has pursued you into reality and there that demon stands at the foot of your bed, grinning at you horribly.

169

It is hard to convey to someone who has never suffered night terrors exactly how awful the experience can be, not so much because it's frightening in itself—although it is extremly so—as because it shakes the very foundations of what you consider to be real. Repeated doses can drive you over the edge. People who regularly suffer night terrors become afraid to go to sleep and their raveling reality frequently results in schizophrenia.

When I woke up, someone had erased the borders. I remembered everything with an incredible clarity and couldn't bring myself to question its reality even while some part of me was vigorously trying to deny it. I knew it had been real, yet I had awakened from a dream. I saw the by-now familiar surroundings of the Psychodrome game center and I thought it had all been a hallucinact and felt relief that it was over. Only the night terror had followed me into my waking state and I knew it had not been a cybernetic dream. My shoulder was still sore from where the rock had struck it when the cavern wall came down and I felt the wound on my forehead, still there, no longer bleeding, but no less real for that. I sought relief, an explanation, a way to make the conclusion fit the facts. I had been tossing and turning on the couch and I had fallen off, striking my head on the edge of the couch, causing the gash, and then hitting the floor in such a way as to cause the shoulder injury. It was a convenient scenario, one I clung to gratefully until Mondago injected a harsh dose of reality and blasted it to pieces.

The first thing I saw upon opening my eyes was the ceiling, then the walls with their banks of instruments, then Breck lying on the couch next to mine. He was already sitting up before I became fully conscious. I didn't want to move. I shut my eyes and opened them again, taking inventory, trying to decide if it had been a real experience or an electronically programmed hallucination. Then Mondago's face moved into frame. He was staring down at me, his face intent, concerned.

There was someone standing close beside him, someone I had never seen before, a middle-aged man wearing an Army officer's uniform with a powder blue fourragére around his shoulder and about ten rows of ribbons over his left breast pocket. I moved my head and saw another man standing beside the Army officer, this one dressed in a dark, expensive suit, severe and elegantly tailored in conservative, executive fashion. Both men looked very serious. I sat up, fully awake, and it was only then I noticed the empty third couch.

"How do you feel, O'Toole?" Mondago said, sounding incongruously like an anxious father.

I nodded. "All right, I guess." I glanced at Breck, sitting on the edge of his couch, staring thoughtfully at the two strangers. "What's going on? Where's Stone?"

"These gentlemen insist on speaking with you now," Mondago said, accenting the word "now" slightly.

The man with the dark suit did not bother to introduce himself. Neglecting to introduce himself had probably become a habit, acquired with years of having one's power unequivocally accepted, one's word unquestioned, one's status as Authority taken as an irrevocable fact of nature. The simple courtesy of giving somebody your name became superfluous when that somebody didn't matter to you in the slightest. You don't introduce yourself to a chesspiece you move upon a board.

He looked from me to Breck and spoke in the manner of one who spends his life issuing directives. "First of all, I want you both to understand that what goes on in this room, every single word that's said, is classified information. Top secret. You are to discuss it with no one. No one, is that clear? Any breach of security will be treated as a treasonable offense and—"

"Wait a minute," I interrupted. "What the hell is this about? And who the hell are you?"

He gave me a look of extreme annoyance. I had questioned the unquestionable. "My name is Coles, Mr. O'Toole, and this is General Tynan, from the Pentagon. And that's already more than you need to know. Who I am should be of less importance to you than the fact that I have the power to confine you for the remainder of your life, the duration of which could also be at my discretion. If I were you, I would remain silent and pay very close attention. Nod your head if you understand me."

I nodded, by reflex more than anything else, and by doing so confirmed his authority over me. The command had been given; I had instantly obeyed. It had been done quickly, smoothly, and efficiently and it had the desired effect of reducing my brief rebellion to a pliable submissiveness. I had always known there were people like this but this was the first time I had ever met one. This was one of "Them," the ubiquitous "They" people always refer to, as in "They'll never

let you get away with it'' or "They're wise to that one'' or
"They don't care, They make the rules.''

"We were unable to monitor the transmission of your experience while you were in the cavern on Draconis 9,'' he said,
"so I want you to tell me, without omitting a single detail, exactly what went on there and the manner in which Stone
Winters died.''

I felt as if I had been gut-punched. "What are you talking
about?''

"Mr. O'Toole, we reviewed the transmission of your experience in the volcanic caldera. That portion of the transmission, of course, was not broadcast over the psych-fidelity
network. Mr. Mondago realized that would have resulted in
mass panic and he wisely contacted us immediately. However, from your behavior and particularly from your reactions
through the interface, it seemed obvious that both you and
Mr. Breck felt a not inconsiderable sympathy for the shapechanger. You certainly made no attempt to kill it when you
found out what it was. You may be faced with a charge of
treason and conspiracy and possibly accessory to murder after
the fact. I would strongly advise you to cooperate voluntarily.
You would not find involuntary cooperation very pleasant, I
assure you.''

"I'd be happy to cooperate,'' I said. "I just don't know
what you're talking about. Why are you threatening us with
charges? And what's this about a murder? Stone isn't dead!
She came back with us! Breck, tell him!''

"It seems it was not Stone who returned with us,'' Breck
said slowly in a level voice, watching the two men very carefully. "And they apparently think we are responsible.''

"That's crazy! She was hurt! We carried her back to the
skimmer! Her legs were broken! She was treated by the doctors in Casino—''

"And 'she' somehow managed to heal rapidly enough to
knock out three technicians and walk right out of this room,''
said General Tynan. "Two of those men are in the hospital;
one is in critical condition. That thing came out of downtime
before the revival signal was transmitted and now there's no
telling where it may be. It may have left the building complex
or it may still be here somewhere, posing as one of the em-
ployees. It could have taken any form at all. For all I know, it
may be that chair over there or a desk in one of the offices.
You people brought a shapechanger back from Draconis 9 and

now it's loose somewhere in the city. For all I know, you could be shapechangers yourselves. If the creature was able to fool the doctors on Draconis 9, right down to the broken bones showing on the medscan, how do I know *you're* human?''

"For that matter, General," Breck said, "how do *we* know *you* are human? If we were to indulge our paranoia, we might just as easily assume that Mr. Coles is the Draconian. After all, Draconians can shapechange with surprising speed. How do we know the *real* Mr. Coles was not intercepted somewhere in the corridor by the Draconian and killed?''

General Tynan frowned, then glanced at Coles uneasily.

Coles smiled mirthlessly. "I see that Mr. Breck, at least, appreciates the gravity of the situation. Though he describes it in somewhat iconoclastic terms, that is nevertheless precisely the position we find ourselves in at the moment, which is why not a word of this can go beyond this room. If we are to accept the creature at its word, then there is no way of telling how many shapechangers may have infiltrated us. No one will have any way of knowing who is human and who—or what—is not.''

"If you had listened to the military in the first place," Breck said, "you might have dealt with this threat years ago when it all started. The SS has been telling you people all along that your half-assed quarantine was a certain invitation to disaster. Well, it has finally happened. Frankly, Mr. Coles, whoever or whatever you are in the governmental heirarchy is of no consequence to me and I am not at all inclined to listen to any allegations that we were somehow responsible for this.''

"Now listen here, Breck—" Coles began.

"No, *you* listen," Breck said. "If you wanted a couple of scapegoats for this, I have no doubt you would hang O'Toole and me out to dry, but you would only require scapegoats if word of this got out. I assume it has not. Now, I could go on making assumptions, but it would be very much easier for everyone concerned if you ceased flexing your bureaucratic muscles and got directly to the point.''

Coles was momentarily taken aback. People like Coles do not have many weaknesses, but there is one thing that always catches them off guard and that is a man who simply doesn't care. People whose power base is money, political clout, or legislative control or any combination of the three grow to depend upon that power because it is damn near omnipotent. A wealthy man can call his lawyer, mention your name, and say, "Make his life miserable, hurt him!" The result would be a

fallout that makes the trials of Job look trivial by comparison.
A man like Coles could probably wield the power of in-
numerable governmental agencies against you, deprive you of
your livelihood and liberty. People like that are not moved by
threats of lawsuits. They have more than enough money to
employ batteries of lawyers to squash you like a bug. You
can't threaten them with laws, because they own the system.
But there is one thing that pulls the rug right out from under
them—someone who doesn't care about all that they can do.
Someone who looks them squarely in the eye and say, "Yeah,
I know you've got the power. I know you can bring the system
down on me. But how is that going to help you when I come
across this desk *right now* and go directly for your throat?"

Breck wasn't threatening the man, but what he did
amounted to the same thing in a way. He was recognizing the
power Coles had, accepting it and merely shrugging his
shoulders. He was saying, in effect, "So what?" Power can
intimidate only when someone is scared of it. And Breck did
not get scared.

I was following all this in a sort of distanced way, as if it
were all happening to someone else. Part of me still refused to
believe it. Stone dead. How was it possible? Unfortunately, I
knew all too well how it was possible, but that meant accepting
an unacceptable reality. When the cavern wall came down, it
had come down on both Stone and the shapechanger. She had
not managed to get clear at all. She had been buried, crushed
beneath tons of rock. She had probably died instantly. At least
I hoped to God she had.

The shapechanger must have reverted to its natural form
and somehow survived the rockfall in its plastic, protoplasmic
state. Then, in that same state, it must have oozed between the
rocks to where Stone's body had been buried and . . .

I recoiled from the thought.

I remembered her leaning back against the rock formation,
grimacing with the pain from her two broken legs, her hair
matted and her face caked with rock dust—it had been Stone.
It couldn't have been the shapechanger.

I remembered helping Breck carry her back to the skimmer,
arranging her carefully so as to minimize the pain, strapping
her in so that she would not be moved around unnecessarily.
She had smiled at me and made little jokes, self-deprecating
comments . . .

I remembered that frightening passage back through the

tunnel, Breck flying the skimmer as slowly as possible, almost hovering, until we were out in the open and rising rapidly out of the gorge, flying for hours through the mountains, running low on fuel, trying to find our way back to the ground base, and finally establishing radio contact and asking to be brought in . . .

I remembered the first aid she was given at the ground base, how we were forced to remain in quarantine there for the prescribed period of time while they observed us carefully, despite the fact that she required further medical attention. I recalled Breck being debriefed and telling them about how Razin had successfully circumvented all their quarantine procedures and how frightened they had looked, but no one had ever suspected Stone, who suffered through her ordeal and kept her spirits up despite the pain. Even in Casino, when we came to see her in the hospital, she had been sitting up in bed, complaining that the doctors were keeping her too long . . .

The shapechanger had fooled everyone. The broken legs were real, a subterfuge, executed perfectly. The medscan showed broken bones and no one even thought to question if those were human bones or not. And even if they had, would there have been any way for them to tell? Logic said there had to be. On some level of their molecular biology, the Draconians had to be visibly different than we were. At some point, their imitative faculties had to break down. But where? How closely would they have to be examined before the simulacrum revealed itself? There was so little known about them, it was difficult even to theorize. And they knew ever so much more about us than we knew about them.

I felt an immeasurable sense of loss, but I couldn't grieve for Stone, for the woman I had loved, for the relationship that might have been. Things were happening too fast and they were giving me no time. Coles and General Tynan debriefed us exhaustively. Finally, apparently satisfied that we had no conscious part in smuggling the Draconian back to Earth, they outlined their plan for trying to apprehend the shapechanger. It centered on the biochip which had been implanted in Stone's brain.

"We are still receiving signals from the biochip," said Coles. I didn't fail to notice how casually Coles and the megacorporate entity that was Psychodrome had become "we." Nor did I fail to notice how Mondago now remained almost completely in the background. Coles had taken over.

"That biochip is the key to capturing the shapechanger. The signals coming in are peculiar and intermittent. Apparently, the people in your engineering section can't seem to decide if this is a function of the different life form it is now interfacing with or if the biochip was damaged in the process of Stone Winters's death and subsequent assimilation."

Assimilation, I thought. Trust someone like Coles to come up with a word like *assimilation* as a euphemism for being eaten. My stomach churned.

"We don't know exactly how the biochip is interfacing with the alien," Coles continued. "We are working under the assumption that since the shapechanger seems to function on the basis of absolute mimicry, that is to say, perfect duplication of another life form down to the last excruciating detail, it somehow flows into that form during assimilation in a manner that assumes the same positional characteristics. In other words, since the biochip was implanted in Stone Winters's brain, it is now in the exact same location within the shapechanger—interfacing with the so-called human brain the alien has shaped or mimicked rather than being located in its stomach, say, or large intenstines. This raises the question of why. If the alien life form is so plastic, why couldn't it have somehow arranged for the biochip to . . . 'flow' within its organic structure so that it *would* wind up somewhere in its digestive system, from where it could be easily expelled? Perhaps it was not aware of the biochip's function."

"Of course it was aware," said Breck. "Draconians are telepathic. It knew we were capable of broadcasting our experiences back to Earth via the biochip. That was the whole point of its interaction with us."

"That wasn't what I meant," said Coles. "Perhaps I phrased it badly. What I meant was that maybe it could not recognize the biochip for what it was, even though it was aware that there was such a thing. We are assuming that the creature possesses no sophisticated knowledge of cybernetics. It would probably have to spend some time in telepathic contact with an engineer in order to acquire such knowledge. However, as a result of its telepathic contact with you and other crystal hunters on Draconis 9 and in Casino, it could be aware that there are many humans who have such devices implanted within them, either to maintain some natural function which would otherwise be impaired or to augment normal abilities. Like a pacemaker, for example. It might not be able to differentiate between them. Perhaps even now it is working on identifying the biochip for certain as being what it is, so that it can expel it from its body. If that is the case, then we don't have much time."

"Or else it already knows and has chosen to retain the biochip," said Breck. "That seems like a much more likely possibility to me."

"Why would it do that if it knew that the biochip would give us the ability to track it?" Coles said, frowning.

"Perhaps because it wants to maintain contact," said Breck.

"For what possible purpose?"

"I have no idea," said Breck. "I can only guess, as you are doing. But it strikes me that what the shapechanger wanted to accomplish through its contact with us was to reach the human race. The biochip will allow it a certain ability to accomplish that, even if you censor the transmission and keep it from being broadcast over the mass media. It would still have contact with *you*. That may be precisely what it wants."

"Interesting idea," Coles said. "However, that would make the creature vulnerable, wouldn't it? Surely it must know that."

"I do not doubt it," Breck said. "Still, a biochip is not exactly a homing transmitter. Having access to the Draconian's perceptual experiences is not quite the same as knowing precisely where it is. Admittedly, the biochip would help you track it down, but Draconians are very good at hiding. There is yet another possibility you seem not to have considered. You said you were receiving peculiar, intermittent signals. The biochip is partially organic and the Draconians have a great deal of organic flexibility. Has it occurred to you that the Draconian may be learning to control it?"

General Tynan glanced at Mondago nervously. "Is that possible?"

"I don't know," said Mondago, frowning thoughtfully. "Ordinarily, I would say no, but we are faced with something very different here. I am not a cybernetics engineer, but I'm not even certain that our staff engineers could answer such a question and we employ some of the top cybernetics specialists in the world. At the moment, they're attempting to diagnose the cause for the peculiar biochip responses we're receiving from the alien and they don't seem to be making any headway."

"Terrific," Tynan said with disgust. "We've been invaded and we can't even *find* the goddamn enemy."

"On the other hand, perhaps we can," said Coles. "Assuming these two gentlemen will help us."

It wasn't exactly a request, but it was nice of him to phrase it that way. Considering what was at stake, I wondered what Coles would have done if we refused. Perhaps it was best not to wonder about such things. The plan he outlined was fairly simple and there was no guarantee that it would work, but it was probably the best that anyone could do, given the situation. We would be taken out of the gaming round and some sort of explanation would be broadcast as to why the third scenario, which would undoubtedly have been the hallucinact, had been deleted. Technical difficulties or something. On the basis of that, we would be awarded the win and our broadcast transmissions would cease so that the audience could then concentrate on the fight for second place. In the meantime, we would be on indefinite loan to the government, as ambulatory scanners.

There was nothing wrong with the signals from our biochips, so while the engineers worked to diagnose the trouble with the biochip inside the Draconian, we would be sent out in an effort to track down the alien's location based upon the intermittent flashes of data that came in from it. In turn, we would be monitored ourselves and since our signals would not be intermittent, Coles or Tynan or whoever was in charge of keeping track of us would have our location at any given time, so that a strike by standby SS troops could be called down at any moment. The whole idea sounded vaguely familiar to me. I think it was based upon an ancient hunting ploy—staking out a Judas goat.

"You think you can handle it?" said Coles.

"Suppose we find the shapechanger," I said. "When this so-called strike is called in, I assume someone will warn us to get out of the way?"

"Every effort will be made to minimize the risk to you," said Coles.

"In other words, no," Breck said dryly.

"So we're expendable, is that it?" I said.

"Strictly speaking, yes," said Coles. "I'm not going to mince words with you. If it comes down to a choice between letting the shapechanger escape or taking out all three of you, it's not going to be much of a choice. However, keep in mind 'that it's of paramount importance for us to take the alien alive. If we're to have any hope of dealing with this invasion, then we have to have at least one of the creatures in custody, in a secure environment where it can be studied and interrogated."

"And how, exactly," Breck asked, "are you planning to capture a creature that can assume a protoplasmic shape and slip out of restraints or seep through cracks?"

"We're working on it," Tynan said. "You leave the worrying about catching the damn thing to us. You just concentrate on finding it."

"When do we start?" I said.

"Right now, Mr. O'Toole," said Coles. He went to the door and opened it for us. "You brought that thing here. Now get out there and help us find it."

It still hadn't really hit me. Soldiers—and not only soldiers, but anyone who has been subjected to a traumatic experience —sometimes suffered something known as Delayed Stress Syndrome. It was a condition that had been pretty much unknown prior to the Southeast Asian conflict of the twentieth century. It had existed, but no one had ever bothered to characterize it until veterans of the Vietnam War started to succumb to its effects in large numbers. Profound depression, suicidal tendencies, psychotic behavior—those were only a few of the results of Delayed Stress Syndrome. An "atypical depression with psychotic features" was the clinical way of describing a terrifying hallucination in which the victim relived the experience which had caused the trauma. I wondered if that was what I had to look forward to.

I felt nothing. Absolutely nothing. No grief, no pain; it simply wasn't there. The woman I had been in love with had been killed in a horrifying way, her body consumed by an alien creature which had then taken her form, and I had taken it all in, it had registered, I had accepted it, and now I was simply going on. I felt a vague sense of guilt at even being able to function. I felt no hate for the Draconian. It hadn't killed her, after all; it had merely taken advantage of her death. It was only trying to protect itself. It was struggling to save its species.

"What do you think they'll do?" I said to Breck as we left the building and went out into the streets of New York City.

"About what?" he said.

"About Draconis 9. They can't keep running the Combine operation as they have before. The quarantine's been broken. They'll have to put it on for real now, won't they? Nobody goes down to Draconis 9. The ground bases get closed and the habitats evacuated—"

"To where?" said Breck. "How would they know who they were evacuating? They wouldn't want to risk bringing back any more ambimorphs."

"I hadn't thought of that. So what do you think they'll do?"

"I suspect they'll probably quarantine the habitats," said Breck. "No one will be going home until they arrive at an infallible test to determine if someone's human or not. If it were my decision, I'd quarantine the ground bases as well. No one else goes down and nobody comes up. However, it is what will happen afterward I am afraid of."

"Afterward?"

"They will never accept a situation in which they had to hear terms dictated by a bunch of intelligent amoebas. I suspect they will probably hold off as long as possible, on the theory that it may forestall these terrorist acts the Draconians have threatened, but you can be sure that it will not be long before they move to exterminate all life on Draconis 9."

"*All* life?"

"They call it a surgical strike," said Breck. "We have had the capability to do it ever since the invention of the neutron bomb. The technique has been refined considerably since then. There will be severe damage to the ecosystem, to be sure, but nothing a well developed terraforming plan cannot repair in time. They will justify it on the grounds of preventing an alien invasion, safeguarding the peace and security of the human race, manifest destiny or some such thing. The result will be a sterilized planet ready to be either terraformed or disassembled. But not until all the fire crystal has been mined."

"You know, there's something else that just occured to me," I said. "The Draconian had said something about how they can easily reproduce here. Amoebas reproduce by binary fission."

Breck stopped and stared at me. "There's a highly unpleasant thought. However, they would have to effect some profound changes to the human physiology they have mimicked in order to do that . . . assuming that is the way they reproduce."

"Unless they revert back to their original form to reproduce," I said.

Breck nodded. "Perhaps, but they would be vulnerable during the process. And if they reverted to their natural form, they would lose their protective coloration and that would make them easy to spot."

"Maybe," I said, "but in a city like New York, or any other large city for that matter, who'd pay any attention to some sludge lying in an alley?"

Breck raised his eyebrows and nodded. "A good point. It seems we are giving our friend Mr. Coles a great deal to think about."

"I hope it gives him one hell of a migraine."

"*I already have one hell of a migraine, thank you, Mr. O'Toole*," Coles's voice came to us through the interface. "*You have indeed given me a lot to think about. In the meantime, we've been picking up some scattered images from the alien's biochip. We've strung them all together and we'll be feeding them to you momentarily. Are you ready to receive?*"

Breck looked at me and nodded. "Anytime," said Breck.

Disjointed images started flashing through my mind like a collage. I "saw" a technician turning around and looking at me with surprise and I "heard" him shout as he was grabbed and thrown across the room. I experienced a brief flash of feeling as if I had been the one who threw him and then there was a mad flurry of images and perceptions all blurred together, impossible to differentiate, followed by a sensation of movement and I saw the corridors of the Psychodrome headquarters building from the alien's point of view as it moved quickly, running past people who turned to stare at it with surprise—I wondered if they were staring at Stone or if the alien had already taken another form—and then the creature was out in the street, looking around, a feeling of puzzlement, disorientation—more fuzzy images, light refractions, a dizzying cornucopia of unidentifiable sensations—was I experiencing the alien's thought patterns through the interface?—more running, seeing people passing by, some responding to the alien's flight, some not, some being shoved out of the way—crossing a spanway against traffic, stopping in the middle as vehicles screamed past, their computer guidance systems making handling decisions faster than human thought could and avoiding a collision by stark millimeters—the experience of standing out upon the spanway with the spires of the city towering above, the levels down below, the sheer mass and complexity of it overwhelming all ability to cope—and then the siren of a police skimmer, the urgent feeling of needing to escape, the PA system on the police skimmer barking out a command and then flight, running quickly down the spanway, being pursued, and then a DIVE over the side!—plunging!—falling!—spinning end over end and hurtling down into the city's depths, another spanway coming up below and then— the sounds of flapping, the sensation of air pressing upon wings, lightness, speed, gliding, soaring, swooping down to . . .

It stopped.

I held my breath.

"Dramatic, wasn't it?" said Coles.

"Jesus."

"Mondago says the engineers have been unable to isolate those blurred sense impressions you experienced," said Coles. *"I've got xenobiologists en route from Clarke Station, but their shuttle hasn't landed yet. As soon as they arrive, I'll plug them in and feed it to them, see what they can make of it. Apparently, the biochip is, to a certain extent, functioning exactly as it's supposed to. It's giving us not only perceptual feedback from the alien, but some of its feelings as well. If the thing even has feelings. The engineers are calling it APT, 'Archetypal Persona Transference,' whatever the hell that means. If we can make some sense out of it, maybe we can get some sort of handle on how the creature thinks. What did you make of it?"*

"It scared the shit out of me," I said.

"I was hoping for a somewhat more analytical reaction," Coles responded.

"I experienced the strongest identification with the early part of the transmission," Breck said, "while it was still in human form, in roughly familiar surroundings. Keep in mind the Draconian had been in Casino, so a human urban environment would not be completely strange to it. However, the environment in an orbital habitat is considerably smaller and more closed in than New York City. The moment the creature reached the outside, I experienced a distinct sensation of agoraphobia . . . and something else, I'm not sure what. Fear, perhaps. Uncertainty."

"If it's telepathic, shouldn't it have expected what it would be like outside?" responded Coles.

"Having telepathic knowledge of something may be one

thing," Breck said, "but actual, direct experience is something else."

"Makes sense to me," I said. "I thought I experienced a strong sensation of feeling disoriented."

"What struck me most," said Breck, "was that there was absolutely no perceptual difference or sensation associated with the shapechange. It leaped over the railing of the span-way, fell—and there was the familiar sensation of falling, or at least it was translated into that familiar sensation in my mind —and then I was aware of the Draconian flying, having wings. It clearly shapechanged into some sort of bird, but I experienced no sense of transition."

"Neither did I," I said. "One moment it felt as if I were falling and the next I was gliding like an eagle. I wasn't really aware of the exact moment the change took place."

"*Scary little beasties, aren't they?*" Coles responded. "*Well, at least we know roughly which way the creature's headed. It's heading downtown, toward the lower levels. We're still receiving intermittent transmissions. As soon as your people have something edited together, I'll send you an update. Meanwhile, at least you've got a direction as a start-ing point.*"

"Downtown lower levels," I said. "Good thing we brought our guns."

"Just try to keep yours hidden beneath your jacket," Breck said. "We would waste valuable time explaining things to a vigilant policeman. We would probably be better off hailing a cab."

"Good luck getting one to go down there," I said.

A skimmer came down and settled in front of us. The canopy slid back and the pilot flashed his ID at us. "Mr. Coles said you might be needing a ride."

I glanced at Breck. "The man doesn't waste any time," I said.

Breck grimaced. "I do not think he can afford to."

We got into the skimmer and it took off, climbing fast and banking sharply. The pilot put it in a hard dive toward the lower levels.

"Take it easy," Breck said. "Are you in that much of a hurry?"

"Mr. Coles said—"

"Forget about what Mr. Coles said," Breck said. "I would like to get down in one piece."

The skimmer built up speed, continuing its dive.

"Look, this thing was not built to be flown like a combat vehicle," said Breck. "Pull up."

"I'm trying," said the pilot.

"What do you mean, you're trying?" I said.

"I mean I can't pull out!" the pilot shouted. "Something's gone wrong! I've lost control!"

"Get over!" Breck said, reaching over the seat and pushing the pilot aside so that he could grab the joystick. The city was coming up at us with alarming speed. We were fast approaching the interlacing spanways of the middle levels. "Damn," Breck said, fighting the panicking pilot and the joystick. He clipped the man on the side of the head with his artificial fist and the pilot slumped down on the seat, unconscious.

We started to spin.

"Christ, Breck, do something!" I said.

"The joystick is frozen," Breck said.

We barely missed one spanway and continued plummeting toward the lower levels, the wind screaming past us as the skimmer screamed down in an almost vertical dive, rolling, corkscrewing as the ground rushed up to us—

"*Breck!*"

"I cannot pull out," he said, straining against the frozen joystick. "We are going too fast."

"*No, goddamn it! I don't want to die!*"

"I do not see what we can do about it," Breck said, still fighting the stick, refusing to give up even though it was clearly, horrifyingly too late.

"*Shit! Shit!*"

A spanway came up fast, too fast, unbelievably fast, we were going to hit, we were going to auger right into the damn thing—

I screamed . . .

The impact never came. Someone was holding me down, pressing on my shoulders. I was still screaming. I fought that hold, trying to get up, and then suddenly I realized I was lying flat on a couch in the game center and one of the technicians was shaking me, trying to snap me out of it. The night terror had followed me into wakefulness and the dream would not let go. I stopped screaming and struggling.

Mondago was bending over me. "How do you feel, O'Toole?"

I blinked and took a deep, ragged breath. "All right, I guess." I glanced over at Breck, sitting up on the edge of his couch. I felt an indescribable sense of relief. "Jesus. Jesus, that was awful. I thought it was all over."

It had all been a hallucinact. A devastating one and I hated Mondago for it, but at least it wasn't real. I had survived. And Stone—

I glanced over at the other couch.

It was empty.

I sat up quickly.

And then I saw General Tynan.

And Coles.

I looked from them to Breck to Mondago.

"I'm sorry, O'Toole," Mondago said. "I had no choice in the matter. These gentlemen insisted."

Coles came forward. "It had to be done, O'Toole," he said. "For security's sake. Nothing's changed, but I had to know for certain that you and Breck were what you seemed. We were blind while you were in that cavern. I couldn't take a chance. You two could have been shapechangers as well. I figured if you were, then faced with imminent death, you'd change—"

I hit him. Hard. With everything I had. I came right off that couch and landed on his chest, swinging, screaming at him. It took both Breck and General Tynan to pull me off him.

"You son of a bitch! You son of a bitchin' bastard . . ."

Coles slowly got up off the floor, wiping the blood away from his mouth. "I'll give you that one," he said. "But that's all you're going get. Now pull yourself together. That alien is still out there somewhere and you two have a job to do."

-ELEVEN-

It was a while before I could speak. I was so tightly wound that one wrong word from anyone, one perfectly innocent gesture might have set me off. The emotions coursing through me were so strong I felt as if I were vibrating like a tuning fork. It felt as if I had been taken up, then down, then brought back up and then slammed down again and I didn't even know what was real anymore. What's more, I wasn't even certain that I cared. All I knew was that I felt angry, more than angry, furious, like a heat-seeking missile looking for a target to destroy.

"Did you know?" I finally asked Breck when I thought I could control myself well enough to handle a normal conversation. He had understood. He had given me the time I needed and now he answered cautiously, gauging my reactions to see just how close to the edge I really was.

"That it was a hallucinact program?" he said. "No, of course not."

"You handled it much better than I did," I said.

"I would not say so."

"I panicked. Lost my nerve."

"So would I have panicked, had not that particular circuit been bypassed in my genetic programming," Breck said. "I merely reacted in the only way I could react. I want to survive as much as you do. The fact that I do not have the ability to feel afraid does not make me more courageous than you are."

"Funny," I said. "You seem fascinated by the emotion of fear, just because you can't experience it. Right about now, I'd give a lot to be wired the way you are. I don't seem to be handling this very well. I wanted to kill that bastard, Coles. Still do. But even if I got my hands around his throat, how do I know he'd really die? It all seemed so goddamned real. How do I know *this* is real, right now? I mean, what if all this is still the same hallucinact? What if we're still lying back there in the game center, only *thinking* we'd come out of it? Maybe we never came out of it at all. Maybe *none* of this has happened. Maybe it's all been a programmed hallucination right from the very start. How the hell does anybody tell?"

"I cautioned you before," Breck said, "when all this started. I warned you not to think about it. Forget about hallucinacts. Treat everything as if it were absolutely real. Chances are it is. If it is not and you have approached it with the sensibility that it was real, then no harm has been done. On the other hand, if you begin to doubt the reality of your experience, you will stop trusting your senses or at least you will develop the tendency to question your perceptions during moments of stress. That could prove fatal and that way also lies insanity."

"You mean you never wonder about it?"

"No," said Breck. "I have learned to force it from my mind. It is not very difficult to do. It is far easier to trust the evidence of your senses than to question what they tell you. Suppose I had succumbed to doubt while that illusory skimmer was spiraling down in a crash dive. Suppose it had *not* been a hallucinact. What then? I might have found something to cling to in the face of such a desperate situation. I might have attempted to convince myself that it was all an illusion because what my senses were telling me was real seemed so hopeless. And since it had seemed hopeless, I might have simply given up and hoped that I would wake from it in one piece. But if it *had* been real, we would have been dead. Instead, I treated it as real; it never occurred to me to question its reality and so I continued fighting to pull out of that dive right to the very end . . . because I might have managed it, you see."

"Yes, I see. No false hopes that way."

"Precisely."

"I'm surprised it doesn't drive the players crazy."

"It often does," Breck said. "A high percentage of the players in high-risk scenarios become insane. For what should be obvious reasons, the company does not release those figures. That would not make for very good publicity."

It seemed utterly ridiculous. Here we were, part of only a handful of people who knew that humanity had been infiltrated by alien life forms and we were talking about what might or might not be favorable publicity for Psychodrome. I was filled with a sense of *déjà vu* again. We were flying high above the city in a skimmer piloted by one of Coles's men, the very same man who had piloted the skimmer in the hallucinact. The intricacies of cybernetic reality programming in the hands of a man like Coles was a frightening thought.

Nothing had been wasted. The hallucinact had been designed to maximize the flow of data so that we could immediately respond to the situation without delay when we woke from it. Coles was not concerned about the recommended rest interval following a programming. The data feed from the alien's biochip had been incorporated into the illusion and it had been real, even if our experience was not. We hadn't lost much time. And if we had proved to be Draconians in human form, well, then Coles would have accomplished a large part of his objective by inducing us to shapechange while still under his control. A complicated thinker, Mr. Coles.

"Well, at least there's one good thing about all this," I said. "So long as they're not broadcasting our experiences, Saqqara's assassins don't know where I am."

Breck glanced at me sharply. "Would you believe I had forgotten all about that?"

"Things have been a little hectic lately," I said.

"I would not advise relaxing yet," said Breck. "In some ways, we are even more vulnerable now than we were before. We still have the ambimorph to deal with and just because our experiences are not being broadcast does not mean we are safe from your Egyptian friend. It has been announced that we have returned from the Fire Islands. Anyone watching for us at game headquarters will know we are back. We must be careful.''

"We?" I said. "It's me they want, Rudy. This isn't your fight.''

"A commendable sentiment, O'Toole, but we are in this thing together. Besides, I have a bone or two of my own to pick with your Mr. Saqqara. Several of my fellow hybreeds were killed back at Draconis Base by his assassins. In a sense, that is like losing family. As soon as this is over, I think you and I should take some time off to go to Tokyo and do something about Mr. Saqqara. Something rather drastic.''

"*Sorry to interrupt your private business, gentlemen,*" Coles said through the interface, "*but there are somewhat more urgent matters to attend to. We've got another data feed we're going to boot up to you. The signals are starting to come in less frequently. We may be losing the implant. Stand by for an update.*"

The first image to come in startled me so badly that for a moment I thought I was having a flashback from the hallucin-act. Suddenly, it seemed as if I were spinning downward in the skimmer once again, plummeting toward the ground. It didn't help that we were sitting in the back of an airborne skimmer as the data feed came in. It took me a moment to realize that what I was experiencing were the perceptions of the shape-changer in its bird form as it swooped down for a landing. It was a wild sensation as I suddenly "felt" myself gliding earthward with great speed, "saw" the ground rushing up to-ward me, and, with no awareness of transition whatsoever, it seemed as if I were walking down a street, my eyes roughly level with those of other pedestrians around me.

There had been no awareness of size at all, no difference to speak of between the way it felt to be in bird form and what obviously had to be human form again, walking down the sidewalk. Either it had been one heck of a large bird or the Draconian was able to alter its size effortlessly, with no more awareness of the process than I had of my hair growing. That did not seem possible. It was a volitional change; there *had* to be some sort of awareness. What was more, how could it alter its size without affecting its mass? In human form, it seemed to have normal mass for a human. When it had disguised itself as Stone, it had not seemed any heavier or lighter than it should have seemed. I hadn't paid any real attention to it then, but Breck and I would surely have noticed if "she" was significantly lighter or heavier than she should have been. That meant that, as a human, the Draconian had approximately the same mass and weight as the human whose shape it had adopted. Yet it had shapechanged to a bird. Unless the bird had been something the size of a California condor, how could the Draconian have become smaller without dramatically increasing the density of its mass? And in that case, how could it have flown? What the Draconian did, apparently as effortlessly as I could blink, seemed to contravene known science. The laws of physics were no different for Draconians than they were for us. Were they? No, that was impossible. But then what the hell did I know? I wasn't a physicist. Just trying to follow secondary school physics had left me hopelessly confused and feeling like a moron. I had a feeling that the Draconian was about to provide me with an exquisite revenge. Wait 'til those physicists get a load of *this*, I thought.

There was a blurring, dizzying effect, then the image changed—dim light, a cacophany of street sounds, a strange, inexplicable throw-focus effect that came in and out, as if someone were literally playing with the focus on a camera. At first the focus was directly to the front, with areas on the periphery blurring into indistinct shapes and colors, then the effect was reversed, then reversed again, then the field widened, then narrowed again.

"Would you believe it?" I heard Breck's disembodied voice say, as if from somewhere quite far off instead of right next to me. "The creature is experimenting, learning to control the biochip."

I suddenly felt cold. Then warm. Then cold again.

It wasn't supposed to be able to do that.

"What the hell is it doing," I asked Breck, hoping to receive some reassurance, "changing its body temperature?"

My voice sounded normal to me, but Breck's reply again seemed somewhat distant. "Your guess is as good as mine," he said.

"I thought you were supposed to be the resident expert on shapechangers," I said.

"I suppose I am," he said. "That does not sound very encouraging, does it?"

"*According to the cybernetics staff here,*" Coles said

through the interface, cutting into the feed, *"the creature is probably—emphasis on the word probably—altering the bio- chip signals rather than its own body temperature. The visual effect, the blurring focus and so forth, seems to support that theory. The engineers aren't very happy about this develop- ment. Apparently, it isn't supposed to be able to do that."*

"That's what I thought," I said.

The data feed resumed.

Whip pan. The effect was not unlike that of a video techni- cian executing what's known as a wipe, in which the camera appears to pan very swiftly, as if mounted on a speeding vehi- cle, so that there was the visual sensation of blurred movement all in one direction, going from one scene to a completely dif- ferent one.

Ground level. Very dim. Shadowy. Foreboding. Concrete jungle of the lower depths, not unlike Tokyo's Junktown— *déjà vu* again—proceeding down a dark alleyway, past slither- ing shapes and prostrate derelicts moaning in piles of refuse —descending down a flight of steps and going through a door- way—VOLUME—driving beat of electronic frenzy—bodies moving—amplified voices in staccato monotone—the lost children of the urban basement ghetto congregating in nihilis- tic tribal ritual, most of them very young, slack-jawed, glitter-eyed, robotic-motioned dancing, colliding with each other and rebounding aimlessly to the rhythmic tempo of a mechanistic heartbeat—a blasted stage elevated high above the floor—musicians standing in the rubble, wired for sound, fingers plucking strings and dancing over keyboards hard- wired into garish costumes, vocals processed through vocoders surgically implanted into throats, interface of man and instru- ment, the child and the city, the ambience of hopelessness and dying dreams.

Moving through the crowd—being jostled by the swirling bodies—scanning—smelling—feeling—standing at the bar and drinking—recoiling from the harsh, unpleasant taste —throwing down the glass—it shatters on the bar—no sound —drowned out by the driving music —bartender sweeps away the shattered glass without a thought, such an act not remarkable in such a place, where violence is part of the at- mosphere to be partaken of—

A hand touching the shoulder softly, lingering, sliding

slowly down the upper arm and stopping at the elbow, moving up again and down in a caress—a voice close to the ear—very close—

"Touch me. Touch me now. Right here."

A hand closing on the wrist and moving it toward a breast barely contained by an open jacket of synthetic skin, almost like human flesh—the feel of it, the flap of the jacket being brushed aside as she moved the hand directly to the breast, now bared—

Shining eyes in a hard little face, feral-pretty, tall crest of golden hair ending in a long tail cascading from behind the neck and down the right side of the chest, body slim and youthfully coltish, moist lips parted, shallow breathing, the feeling of a young heart beating, seeking nothing more complicated than momentary physical fulfillment—

End feed.

The skimmer had landed.

"Let's go, you two," the pilot said. "I want to be airborne and out of here before the screamers in this neighborhood strip this thing for parts."

"*We're losing it,*" said Coles. "*The creature's practically got the biochip under its control. Best estimate places it at somewhere within half a mile of your current location. We're activating every available biochip implantee with the sector. Be prepared to receive update feeds at any time. I'm going to boot data up to you as fast as it comes in.*"

"Wait!" Breck said. "What do you mean by 'available implantees'? And how do you expect us to function if we start receiving perceptual transmissions without warning? Do you have any idea how disorienting—"

"*I haven't got time to explain everything as I go along,*" said Coles. "*I'm going to say this only once, so pay attention. You two are going to have to think fast on your feet. These are combat conditions, Breck. I'm having all the company records of former Psychodrome players pulled and sorted, classified by sectors of the city. We're going to be tapping into every available biochip in the vicinity where the creature was last seen. I want to be able to cover every available—*"

"Wait a minute!" I said, astonished at what Coles was proposing. "Have you lost your mind? You can't do that! You can't just arbitrarily start tapping into people like that! It's against the law!"

"We're faced with an alien invasion, O'Toole," said Coles. *"If it would safeguard national security and the interests of the human race, I'd break every damn law ever written in this or any other country. Okay, over to your right there, that looks like the place where the creature landed. You should be getting close."*

"I don't think he has any idea what he's doing," I said to Breck. "He's talking about the most massive invasion of privacy in human history! The minute he starts tapping into those people, he's going to have every lawyer in the country screaming bloody murder. Can he really *do* that?"

"I think he can," said Breck. "And I fear he knows exactly what he is doing. Think about it. Are you aware of being monitored during the game scenarios? You know it is happening, of course, but are you actually *aware* of it happening?"

"Jesus," I said. "He's just going to start accessing people and they're not even going to know it's happening. It's a paranoid's nightmare."

"It makes you wonder," said Breck. "There are a great many wealthy, influential individuals who have played the game at one time or another. People with access to all sorts of interesting information."

It was a chilling thought. I realized that something like this had occurred to me before, but I had never followed it through. Maybe because I had been afraid to. I remembered thinking when the whole thing started about what Psychodrome might one day do with all the people it's been wiring up. If the government had ever tried to pass a law that every citizen had to be wired with a biochip capable of interfacing with a centralized computer network, there would have been an instant revolution. But make it all a glamorous game with fabulous sums of money at stake, a recreation for the rich and famous, a media event, an entertainment, and they'll line up to buy lottery tickets to take a chance on "winning" the ultimate fascist prize.

My Russian archbishops were nodding knowingly somewhere at the back of my subconscious. This was nothing new to them. The method was different, but the results were still the same. My Russian ancestors had lived under the most autocratic, most repressive regime in all of human history. Absolute power resided in one man or woman—the czar or the czarina. Absolute power backed up by divine right in a country that had no conception whatsoever of what freedom meant. Catherine the Great had thought nothing of gifting a departing lover with a palace and four thousand or so peasants. People had been sold in the marketplace like furniture. Entire families regarded as possessions, capable of being bought more cheaply than a horse or hunting dog. Even the nobility were subject to the whims of the autocracy, told where and how to live, whom to marry or divorce, even when to live or die. The Soviet state which had replaced the monarchy had not been very different. One czar had been replaced by a council of small-time czars—the Politburo—and things went on much as before.

Things like this were not supposed to happen in our country in these modern times. Freedom was a guarantee, taken for granted. Or had we, after all, merely been sold a bill of goods, conned into thinking ourselves superior and more privileged, more liberal and enlightened than our predecessors and all the other nations of the world? A man like Coles was like a pail of cold water thrown into the face of all my notions of democracy and inalienable rights. And a man like Coles did not spring out of nowhere. He had been nurtured and developed by a system, a power structure I had never really been aware of until now.

My great-grandfather, whom my father had been so fond of quoting to me, had been one of the great iconoclasts and cynics of his time, an unregenerate technophobe who had disdained the rules and had a hatred of what he called "the microchip mentality." He despised the buzzword glorification of the technostate and had lived on the fringes all his life. He did not fear computers, but he was afraid of what could be done with them. He protested against drivers' licenses with photographs and social security numbers on them, bank cards with built-in memory, cashless economy and bureaucratic centralization. "They've got your number" was an ominous phrase to him and he had passed on his fringe philosophy to all his sons and daughters. I had always thought of him as a paranoid and harmless old eccentric. Now I saw that he had not been harmless. He had been a dangerous man. The trouble was there hadn't been enough men like him.

We found the alleyway the creature landed in, the place where it had shapechanged back to human form. As we walked down the darkened corridor between two buildings, several forms detached themselves from the shadows and stood in the center of the alley, blocking our way. I glanced over my shoulder and saw more behind us. Young people. Cyberpunks. We were trespassing on their turf and that made us fair game.

With these kids, artifice was art. They went all out to cultivate the image of the technoman. Spiky hair in multicolored rooster crests, the skin of their shaved heads corrugated with the look of subcutaneous cyberwires, ball-bearing eyes shining in the dark, teeth bared to show glittering steel incisors . . . it was all cosmetic. In the morning, the corrugated scalps peeled off, the steel tooth caps were removed, the silvered eye cups painstakingly taken off and the kids went off to work, if they were lucky enough to have jobs, or to while the afternoons away in the labor pool, which basically meant wasting time standing in line to get their dole. Even if they could afford the expensive process of cybermodification, the sort of external appearance they favored would have left them unemployable. So they settled for the cosmetic look and spending money on vocoders, which could be surgically implanted or worn externally (not quite as much cachet), turned on or off as the occasion warranted. In this case, an ominous presence called for the vocoders to be on and we were greeted with a grating, electronic overlay of snake voices hissing from the leader's voicebox.

"Wassss' worth t'ya t'keep ahn li-vin'?"

"I have no time for you," said Breck. "Get out of the way."

"Wasss thisss, hahd mahn, lookin' fuh fasss time, hahd trade? Dump thissss mu-tha's file!"

Breck pulled off his glove and five long, gleaming nysteel blades sprang out. He held the blades inches away from the cyberpunk's face. "If you want hard trade, son, I will be happy to oblige."

I pulled out my plasma pistol and snapped off a charge at the feet of the punks behind us. They leaped back from the explosion of blue flame and scattered. The snake-voiced cyberpunk suddenly found himself alone, staring wide-eyed at Breck's blades.

"Dohn cut me, mahn, pleasssss, pleasssss . . ."

"Turn that ridiculous thing off," said Breck.

"Anything you say, man, just don't cut me, all right? Please?"

"We are looking for a girl," Breck said. "Young, very pretty in a hard sort of way, golden hair worn in a very long crest. She was wearing a scarlet skinjac and high black boots, tattoo of one blue teardrop right here," Breck said, touching the cyberpunk's cheek with his blades.

"That's a hard-time ride, man. She kills people just for juice. You're no vark, man, what you want with her?"

"Never mind what I want with her. Where can I find her?"

"I don't owe that damn slit nuthin', man. She's likely back to her place, picked herself up some new hard meat, radical lookin' mods, heavy hardware—"

"*What the hell is that moron talking about?*" Coles said through the interface.

Breck ignored him and got directions to the girl's place.

"The girl picked up someone new, someone these kids didn't know," I translated for Coles. "The other terms were meant to be complimentary, I suppose, describing cosmetic modifications. Perhaps not so cosmetic in this case. It seems the alien's shapechanged to a cyberpunk, the better to blend in down here."

"*Okay, it checks,*" said Coles. "*We just received an update from an implantee in sector three on Ground Level. A former lottery winner who's a compartment manager in a box warren on Saint Marks. Visual readout matches the description of the girl. She was seen entering a building with a young male cyberpunk, hold it, let me get you a visual . . . got it. Stand by . . .*"

Coles was learning quickly. He was using the system as well as a playermaster and coming up with wrinkles even Mondago didn't know about. At least I didn't think he knew. I was no longer sure. I imagined that what Coles had done was activate every biochip in the ground-level neighborhood he had designated as sector three, then initiate a centralized scanning program to monitor every one of them. He had directed the program to flag a readout containing a visual matching the girl's description and now he isolated it, enhanced the image of the male she was with, and booted it up to us.

It was an image like a still frame, enlarged and enhanced from the original, seen through the eyes of the compartment manager across the street, who probably had nothing better to do than sit at the window of his box warren cubbyhole and stare outside all day, thinking about the one time he had his shot and blew it. He had walked away from it with nothing but the memory of whatever his Psychodrome experience had been and a biochip implanted in his brain, a semi-organic microcomputer that had grown together with his brain matter, always a part of him, always representing his potential. He could buy computer interface time and have himself programmed with knowledge that would gain him a new and better life, but there was, of course, a catch. There always was. First he had to be able to afford it. If he saved a little every year, perhaps in another five or ten years he'd have the necessary funds to buy himself an education. But living where he lived was not very conducive to saving money. A life-style such as that required anesthetic. I saw his in the form of the bottle his hand held before his face. He had been in the process of lifting the bottle to his mouth when the readout had been frozen. In the background, a girl dressed in a scarlet skinjac and high black boots walked arm in arm with a young male cyberpunk.

Enhance.
Zoom in.

I could no longer see the bottle the man was drinking from. The scene across the street was closer, the focus on the couple.

Enhance.
Zoom in.

Their upper bodies and their faces now, close together, apparently talking to each other.

Enhance.
Zoom in.

Now just their faces.

Enhance.
Zoom in.

It was Razin. Only a much younger, cyberpunk version of Razin, with a tall black crest of spiky hair crowning a corrugated scalp, exaggerated cheekbones, silvered eyes, snake fangs protruding over the lower lip.

"It's him," I said, automatically thinking of the Draconian as "he" when, in fact, I had no idea of its gender or if it even had one.

"Curious that it should use that face again," said Breck.

"Almost as if it were expecting . . . damn! Coles! If the ambimorph has learned how to control its biochip and you have directed the computers to activate every known biochip in the sector, then—"

"*Shit!*" Coles said. "*The son of a bitch knows we're scanning for it! I'm calling in the strike force. Get over there fast. Move!*"

We started running hard. The place was only a couple of blocks away. Breck was in better shape than I and he started outdistancing me quickly, even while speaking to Coles.

"Coles," he said, "try to feed the Draconian a hallucinact program. See if you can disorient it. Confuse it long enough for us to get there."

It was all I could do to stay with him for the first ten or twenty yards while he spoke to Coles and then he was off and I couldn't hear him anymore, but I heard Coles replying through the interface.

"*It's no good. We've already tried it. We can't even access the creature's biochip anymore. It's figured out some way to block out incoming signals. We've done all we can do from here.*"

Breck was outpacing me rapidly, running like a streak toward Saint Marks Place in one of the most ancient and run-down neighborhoods of New York City. He was already a full city block ahead. As I turned into Saint Marks Place, a dimly lit, blasted avenue with huge cracks in the long untended pavement and rubble from wrecked buildings lying everywhere, I saw Breck running full speed into the ruined building where the cyberpunk girl and the Draconian had gone. I had to stop for a moment, gasping. I simply couldn't match Breck's hybreed body for speed and strength and stamina. I fought for breath, telling myself that I probably wouldn't be much help to him in any case.

And then I saw the girl leaving the building.

It didn't hit me for a second, then I started running, pulling out my plasma pistol as I ran. I dodged among the wreckage of what had once, centuries ago, been a stately neighborhood —handsome building facades on tree-lined streets beneath a pale blue sky. Now it looked like the aftermath of a fire bombing, everything cracked and peeling, fallen down and wounded, no blue sky visible above, not even a polluted brown sky, just the dark weight of the city overhead, pressing down on this sorry excuse for a neighborhood and its even sorrier inhabitants.

I followed a scarlet skinjac and long sleek legs in high black boots. I was so winded from the run I could barely breathe, yet I forced myself to keep on running, unable to cry out, hoping Coles was scanning me. I was gaining, getting closer . . .

The girl heard my running footsteps coming up behind her and she turned around . . .

And it was Stone.

I froze in the act of pointing the pistol at her.

"Arkady! Don't! It's me, Stone!"

"O'Toole! Don't kill it! I want that thing alive!"

"Let me go, Arkady. Please. They'll hurt me."

Five skimmers swooped down low over my head and landed in the street, canopies sliding back, disgorging soldiers armed with plasma weapons—

And suddenly all hell broke loose. Several plasma blasts slammed into the street close beside me and one passed so low over my head that it set me on fire. Instinctively, I dropped down to the ground and returned the fire, shooting blindly in the direction from which the plasma blasts had come. I slapped at my hair and clothing and I rolled, trying to extinguish the flames. My skin felt scorched from the close passage of the plasma blasts and I realized I had come within millimeters of being incinerated.

I was completely out in the open, no cover anywhere. The best I could do was roll into a huge pothole that only partially concealed my body. As if lying in a trench, I tried to squeeze down into the hole and looked quickly from side to side, trying to find out who was shooting at me and then I saw them, dodging from doorway to doorway on the opposite side of the street, black-suited ninjas converging on me and firing as they ran. There were at least five of them, maybe more.

The soldiers had responded to the fire and they returned it, some dropping to the ground, some deploying in doorways and in crumbling basement stairwells.

"Saqqara!" I screamed in an agony of frustration. "God damn you! Not now! Not now!"

The street became a war zone and I was caught right in the crossfire. I couldn't move. Plasma blasts were passing so low over my head that I could feel their heat. They slammed into the building walls behind me and the ancient tenements began to burn. I heard screaming.

I was back in the jungle, slogging through the swamps as auto pulser fire and plasma rockets landed all around me. I saw insects buzzing in front of my eyes and I seemed to feel them crawling up on me, I felt them right through the combat armor, I felt the heat, the sweat running down my body, I couldn't breathe and I began to scream, a long, drawn-out, throat-rending scream of killer fury.

My scream was suddenly joined in chorus with another and I looked up to see a ninja, black garments wreathed in flames, wailing like a banshee as he dove down at me. I fired. The plasma hit his chest point-blank and he became a fireball.

I ducked beneath the burning human remnants and started running in serpentine, looking for cover. I dove into a doorway and pressed myself flat against the wall, firing across the street. Another ninja went down in flames. Plasma charges were whumping into building walls and panicked people were running out into the street, right into the line of fire. One woman was stark naked. She took five or six steps before a stray blast hit her and a flaming hulk fell to the cratered street.

The soldiers had no idea what was happening. They were merely reacting as they had been trained to do. They had been sent in to capture an alien creature and now suddenly they were facing heavy opposition from an unknown enemy. So they did the only thing they could do, which was to turn their attention on the unknown attacking force. The ninjas couldn't have known what it was all about. Breck had been right. Someone had been watching for us at game headquarters and we had been tailed expertly by warriors of the Silent Way. They had chosen their time to strike and, without warning, their lone target had suddenly been joined by several platoons of SS commandos. And the innocent paupers who lived down here in squalor and quiet misery now had a war in the street outside their homes.

I don't know how long it lasted, but it must have been over fairly quickly. It hadn't seemed quick, though. As I huddled in the doorway, staring wildly out into the street, trying to separate the fleeing bodies of civilians from any black-clad assassins running toward me, the plasma fire died away and left only the screaming of the people in the burning buildings.

It was over. The ninjas were all dead, as well as a good number of the soldiers. There was no sign of the alien.

I forced my mind to block out the image of the burning jungle and mercenaries moving ponderously in heavy combat armor. I now saw only the flames, the blackened stone of ancient buildings, and the ruptured street littered with burning bodies. Breck!

I ran back toward the building where the girl had lived. I racked my brain for the apartment number the cyberpunk had given us. *What was it*? Third floor! 3-G! I took the littered stairs three at a time, slipped in a pile of garbage on the stairwell, caught myself on the railing, and lunged up the final flight of steps, the breath rasping in my throat. The door to 3-G was open.

Breck was lying on the floor inside, his head bleeding. He was stirring, groaning softly. I found the girl inside the filthy bedroom. The room was bathed in blood. She had been slaughtered like an animal, her chest torn open, entrails hanging out upon the floor. Written on the wall, in blood, was the chilling phrase "Now it begins." I doubled over and became violently ill.

I felt someone steadying me and when I straightened up, I saw Breck standing beside me, staring into the bedroom with glazed eyes. Blood was running down the side of his face.

"My God," he said.

I turned away from the horror.

"You're hurt," said Breck. "What happened?"

"I had it," I said. "I had it cornered. The soldiers landed and I thought we had the thing and then a squad of ninjas came out of nowhere and opened up with plasma weapons. The whole damn neighborhood's on fire. Everywhere, people dead . . . Saqqara. That son of a bitch Saqqara!"

"Coles?" said Breck. "Coles!"

There was no response. Coles had lost the alien and he was probably beside himself. He had no time for us.

I started crying. I clung to Breck and wept like a baby. He held me in his arms. I felt his blood dripping down onto my face.

Breck took a deep breath and let it out slowly. "Come on," he said. "Let's get out of here. You and I have a score to settle on the Ginza Strip."

-TWELVE-

The Ginza looked the same as I remembered it. There was no reason for it to have changed, but it felt as if I had been away for years. The light show still illuminated the Strip with a symphony of color, the shills still worked the sidewalks, the scooters still terrorized pedestrians. One thing had changed, though. The Pyramid Club was under new management.

The young lycra-suited bouncers at the door did not look as elegant as Saqqara's people had, but they looked just as tough. One of them remembered me. He buzzed the office and spoke a few words too softy for me to overhear, then Breck and I were politely escorted inside the club.

I remembered hearing they had trashed the place, but it had been rebuilt the same way as before. Business was brisk, even though the patrons were not quite as stylish as the crowd Saqqara had once catered to. We were escorted up a plushly carpeted stairway to an office on the upper floor, the same office where I had once stood before Saqqara, with his bodyguards behind me, desperately trying to fast-talk myself into a few more hours of life. A lot had happened since then. That frightened con artist I remembered seemed like a completely different person. It was hard to believe that had been me.

Coles had been livid. He had lost all track of the Draconian. His only lead to the shapechanger infiltration and now it was gone! There had already been one "incident." One of the offices of the Draconis Combine in Paris had been blown up and the news media had received a message claiming responsibility and threatening more terrorist acts "if humans did not abandon their interests on Draconis 9." The news reports had made no mention of anyone claiming responsibility for the explosion. Apparently, Coles had hushed it up, but no one would be able to keep it under wraps for long if it continued.

"I don't have time to waste on petty criminals in Tokyo," Coles had said, "but I have a personal grudge against one in particular. Do what you have to do and get back quickly. Don't worry about any consequences. I'll arrange to clean up after you. But get the job done. Permanently."

Our escort knocked at the office door and someone opened it from inside. The bandit stood aside to let us enter and I saw the new proprietor of the establishment seated at the desk, dressed in high boots and a sleek black lycra suit that left little to the imagination.

"Hello, Kami," I said.

She got up and came around the desk, leaned back against the front of it, and stared at me for a moment, then she smiled. "*Konnichi wa*, O'Toole."

We stood staring at each other, not saying anything, then she reached out and grabbed a fistful of my shirt and pulled me to her. Our arms went around each other and, after a long time, I finally remembered to introduce my friend, Rudiger Breck, who seemed to find the whole thing quite amusing.

The gang war was all over. Apparently, the shoguns of the Yakuza saw no percentage in wasting time and money and receiving lots of unfavorable publicity all over a few gaming interests on the Ginza. They were not very happy with Hakin Saqqara. Word had come down to stop the nonsense and get back to business. For a man of his position, he had exercised poor judgment in the whole affair and his stock in the organization was not high. According to Kami, he kept a very low profile these days, even lower than before, which meant he had become a virtual recluse. He had a great deal of ground to make up, a reputation to rebuild, and all the money in the world would not buy back the "honor" he had lost because of me. I had become his grand obsession, the *bête noire* of his existence, and word on the street was that a person could secure some valuable connections and make a tidy piece of change if they brought reasonable proof of my demise.

Fortunately, I had the "tiger lady" on my side, as Kami was now referred to on the Strip. The bandits ruled the Ginza now and they had made it known that they would not be very pleased with anyone who undertook a contract against me. Needless to say, this did not intimidate the ninja guild, but it was a strong deterrent to the independent contractors. I was safer on the Ginza than I would have been back in New York. Especially with Kami's bandits to protect me. She had brought all the bandit gangs together when the war had started and she kept them together now, under her leadership and that of a "senior council." She had become a warlord in her own right and she wore the mantle well.

Her new role in life had changed her. She was learning how to be a businesswoman. She was a bit more talkative, though still on the quiet side by most people's standards. She did not waste words. She still did not own a dress and she still took pride in her status and appearance as a bandit shogun. The long scar on her face was still there, though she could now easily afford to have cosmetic surgery remove it. I was glad she hadn't. For me, it had become a vital part of her.

We spent that first night back together making love and catching up. Breck had not been left entirely to his own devices. The bandits have their own ways of making an honored guest feel welcome and Kami had seen to my friend's comfort. The Pyramid Club still boasted a full complement of lovely ladies.

In spite of being sworn to secrecy by Coles, I told her everything. To hell with Coles. I was on my own time and I was never much for following orders. I make my own decisions about whom to trust and I trusted Kami more than I would ever trust a man like Coles. If he was keeping tabs on me through my biochip, I'd soon find out by breaching security. But no voices came to me through the interface and I began to think he meant it when he said he would respect my privacy. Strange man. I couldn't figure him out at all.

Kami listened to it all without comment and when I got to the part about Stone's death, my voice broke and she gently touched my cheek. It was a long unburdening that took most of the night, but when I had finished, I felt much better and we held each other for a while, enjoying that same special closeness we had shared before. It wasn't the same as it had been with Stone, but in a strange way, it felt somehow better. And as I thought about it more, it seemed less strange.

The Ginza had shaped us both and made us what we were. We understood each other. There was no need for questions, explanations, or verbalizing feelings. We were both street people and we would remain street people, no matter where we went or what our fortunes were. Ours was not a great romance. There was no unbridled passion, no emotional outpourings, no driving need to form an artificial bond we'd have to work to reinforce so that it would still hold us together when the novelty wore off. Instead, there was companionship, shared warmth, natural trust, and understanding, that indefinable something that made us both together a better thing than we were on our own. After all this time, we were back together and it was like we never left. There was a lot to be said for a relationship like that. It was not important to define it, but it was important to think hard before walking out on it again.

"We have unfinished business with Saqqara," she said at the end, "but we do not know where he is."

"I know," I said. "There is a man named Coles who's very good at finding things."

She nodded. "Good. Tomorrow, then."

Saqqara had done very well with the seeds I had provided him. He now had a penthouse suite high atop Hamamatsu Tower. It was a security building in one of Tokyo's most expensive districts and Saqqara had augmented the security considerably. The sole way up to the penthouse was via lift tube and the tube only went as far as the floor below Saqqara's penthouse. That floor was controlled by Saqqara. It held his corporate offices and security staff headquarters. There was a separate lift tube connecting that floor to the penthouse suite above. The only other access to the penthouse was by the skimmer pad, which was covered by gun emplacements. The entire complex was heavily guarded and scanned at every conceivable access point by cameras. Not a few bandits had died trying to get inside. Only Saqqara wasn't there. Coles had tracked him down and located him in the least likely of places —Junktown.

It was the last place anyone would have thought of looking for him. The war with the bandits had made Saqqara paranoid and had brought home to him the knowledge of his own vulnerability. He had counted on his power and position, on the fact that only someone truly crazy would risk trying anything against a warlord of the Yakuza. The bandits were truly crazy. They just didn't give a damn.

Saqqara had lost a good many of his people in the conflict and he had almost lost his own life on at least three separate occasions. He had gone underground—literally—in a ground-level block of Junktown he had purchased through a number of false fronts so that his ownership was almost impossible to trace. Under ordinary circumstances, it would have been impossible, but ordinary circumstances did not take into account the resources of a man like Coles.

From the outside, Saqqara's new headquarters looked no different from any other seedy residence in Junktown—a crumbling block of box warrens, tiny cubicle apartments. Little closet-sized coffins for the living, just like the place where all of this had started for me when I woke in the cramped living quarters of Miko's nonreg family. No one ever saw the light of day down here. The poorest of the city's poor dwelt in a perpetual urban night. Few could afford power. Campfires burned in the middle of the streets, surrounded by tattered tents, home to those who could find no other housing. People lived and died here and they died more often than they lived, buried beneath a city which had closed its eyes to their existence. But behind the ruined facades of the block Saqqara had purchased, there was a luxurious complex built inside the gutted buildings. Here Saqqara lived, in palatial splendor, isolated from the squalor all around him. He had withdrawn to lick his wounds and shore up his power base, to prepare for his next move in the tangled world of corporate high finance.

Coles had a staff of highly trained investigators take a can opener to his corporate interests, stripping away the covering layers by raiding data bases and corporate computer records, bypassing sophisticated security programs and tracing down the leads that led to the spider at the center of his web. Saqqara had disappeared in Tokyo, but he was getting ready to resurface. While he ran his financial empire from his secret hideaway, he had been buying real estate and establishing new businesses, few of which could stand very close scrutiny. It seemed he was about to liquefy his Tokyo assets and reappear in Los Angeles, with a new identity and new corporate holdings which he had been carefully establishing. He was going to impress his bosses in the Yakuza with his massive upward mobility and gift them with new territory all at once.

Not if I could help it.

Breck had surveyed the outside of Saqqara's hideout with a practiced eye and he returned to us where we were waiting around a campfire built up in a rusted barrel in the ruins of an old tenement building across the street. We looked like a miserable group of derelicts in shabby, tattered robes. Beneath the robes, we were wearing lycra suits and leathers, belt and shoulder holsters, concha belts holding the deadly buzz discs. We had our helmets wrapped up inside the shapeless bags we carried. No one could tell that spread out in small groups among the city's nonregistered derelicts were over one hundred young scooter bandits, spoiling for a fight.

"Your friend Saqqara seems to know his business," Breck said as he warmed his hands over the fire. "The building entrances are probably all false fronts. Security personnel disguised as very unfriendly nonreg tenants, box warren cubicles masking the interior construction strategically placed to cover the street from all angles, like fortified pillboxes. My guess is that none of the entrances we see from the outside are actual entrances to the complex. They've probably been sealed. The real entrances are camouflaged."

"How can you be sure?" I said.

"I saw several men leaving the building," Breck said, "going in different directions. I followed one of them and he doubled back to join up with the others a block away. They went down into one of the old underground subway terminals. It looked like a change of shift with the security, disguised to look like ordinary comings and goings in the building."

"There has to be a tunnel connecting to the subway," I said. "There's no other reason why they'd be going down there. *Nobody* goes down into the old subways."

"Unless, perhaps, they are armed with plasma weapons," Breck said. He looked at Kami. "It took a great deal of trouble and expense to set this up. You must have really frightened the poor man."

She smiled.

"We have watched his home in Hamamatsu Tower for months," one of the other bandits said. "We never thought to seek him here."

"Small wonder this man was so upset with you, O'Toole," said Breck. "You cost him prestige with his organization and when they refused to support him in his personal vendetta, he was forced to leave his penthouse and make a nest for himself here in the slums. A comfortable nest, to be sure, but it must have been quite an affront to his dignity and pride. One of the wealthiest and most powerful men in Tokyo, forced to hide out from a band of street urchins."

"Is that how we seem to you, Breck-san?" Kami said.

"Sorry, I meant no offense," said Breck. "It takes nerve to go up against professional talent."

"We have our own talents," Kami said.

"Do you?" Breck said. "All right, then, how do you plan to gain access to Saqqara's stronghold without alerting him? You can be sure he has at least several escape routes. If you try a frontal assault, he will be long gone before you can break in."

"Then we will not do it that way," said Kami. She turned and spoke to several of the bandits in rapid Japanese. They nodded and departed quickly.

Breck looked at me and raised his eyebrows.

"There's going to be a changing of the guard," I said. "This should prove interesting."

We followed Kami to a spot opposite the crumbling entrance to the subway and waited in the shadows. "Make yourself comfortable," I told Breck. "This may take a while."

We waited until it was time for the next security shift change. The shift coming on came up out of the subway and split up, going in different directions. After a short while, the shift coming off duty appeared. Two men dressed in shabby hooded coats approached the subway entrance. From across the street, another two men came. Two more appeared from a side street and another two from an alleyway. They all converged a short distance away; then all eight started to come directly toward us. Breck reached for his sidearm, but Kami caught his hand and shook her head, smiling. The men reached us and started to remove their cloaks. They were all bandits.

Breck chuckled. "Nicely done," he said.

The bandits had taken advantage of the weak point in the arrangements. In order to make the change in shifts appear like normal arrivals and departures from the box warren, the security men did not leave all at once and they always went in different directions before they reformed about a block away by the subway entrance. They had grown careless, dependent upon their weapons, contemptuous of the beaten-down people of Junktown, even the most desperate of whom were no match for a trained pro with a plasma weapon. The bandits had followed them as they left the building complex and taken them out one at a time. They stripped them, took their weapons, and rendezvoused as planned outside the subway entrance. We took their hooded cloaks and put them on, then joined the other bandits and went down into the subway.

We walked in total darkness for a while, moving slowly and cautiously. Once, many years ago, these underground tunnels had been a vital part of Tokyo's mass transit system. Crowds of people moved through these subterranean passageways, hurrying to catch electric trains which wound ceaselessly through the tunnels underneath the city, delivering citizens to various terminal points beneath the streets. The spanways and the conveyer tubes had changed all that as the city had grown upward, the only direction left for it grow, and as the towers of Tokyo reached higher and higher, the nether sections of the city had fallen into disrepair until now, like the floor of Tokyo Bay beneath the pilings that supported the floating cities, there was only mire and darkness here and the inhabitants moved through the murk like scuttlefish. The subway tunnels, many of which had long since collapsed, leaving gaping fissures in the ancient streets, wound through the ground beneath the city like catacombs.

There were creatures down here, creatures who had long since ceased to be people. Like trap-door spiders, they preyed on the unwary, on the weak, on those too tired or too desperate to flee. They kept to the darkness of the tunnel entrances and if anyone was careless enough to venture too close, they would swarm out in small groups and drag the hapless victim underground and, for a while, they would have food.

We saw no such creatures, however. No doubt they had

learned to avoid this section of the subway. We encountered no one as we walked through the passageway, hearing only the echo of our footsteps. Breck, who saw better in the dark, spoke softly to us when we were about halfway down the passageway.

"Careful," he said. "Keep your hoods over your faces. There are infrared scanners mounted on the wall ahead."

As we passed that point, Breck gave a casual wave. Soon we saw a light at a bend in the passageway. It opened out into a well-lit plaza. There was a glass-enclosed booth with a guard stationed inside, watching a small bank of screens.

Kami grabbed our arms. "Support me," she said.

She sagged down as if hurt or ill. We supported her on either side, practically dragging her forward. The guard in the booth saw us approaching and frowned. He stuck his head out.

"What's wrong?" he said, speaking in gutter Japanese.

Kami moved swiftly. She reached inside her cloak and straightened up fast, letting fly with a buzz disc. It whirred toward the guard and embedded itself in his forehead, the tiny spinning blades slicing deeply into the bone.

Breck ran to the glass booth. Two guards came running into the plaza from a side tunnel and a couple of the bandits hurled their buzz discs, dropping the men in their tracks. Kami and I joined Breck in the booth. He was studying the control panel.

"We appear to be in luck," he said. "These screens are monitors for the tunnels in the immediate vicinity. This is the centralized station for all the scanners to the tunnel entrances. There are three more besides this one, all connecting to this terminal. Here's the alarm switch. This was not very well thought out. They should have had the monitor station located within the complex itself rather than the subway terminal." He grinned. "This is what comes of cutting costs."

Kami spoke to a couple of the bandits and they went running back down the passageway toward the subway entrance. Within a short while, armed bandits were streaming down the passageway and filling up the plaza. We went out across the platform and jumped down onto the tracks, moving silently into the subway tunnel, leaving bandits stationed along the way. We were moving back in the direction of the complex. There was a flood of light up ahead, coming from the side of the tunnel wall. We approached it cautiously. It was an open passageway, branching off from the subway tunnel and heading straight back beneath Saqqara's complex. There was a heavy door at the far end.

"Scanner just above the door," said Breck. "No way to avoid it. This could pose a problem."

Kami beckoned a couple of the bandits forward and spoke to them quickly. Then, to Breck's astonishment, she started to strip. She took off her cloak and removed her weapons, handing them to one of the other bandits, who hid them underneath his cloak. In moments, she was completely naked save for her boots. She issued a curt command to one of the bandits, who said, "*Hai*," and then struck her hard across the mouth. Her head snapped back and her mouth started to bleed.

"What the hell . . ." said Breck.

Another carefully executed blow bloodied her nose. She didn't cry out once. Two of the bandits held her between then, one holding each arm; two more took up position behind them. As she pretended to struggle, they started walking with her down the tunnel, half dragging her, laughing loudly and talking among themselves.

Breck shook his head as he watched them heading down the passageway toward the scanner above the door. "That is an amazing woman," he said. "I have no idea what she sees in you, O'Toole, but allow me to give you some advice. Never make her angry."

They reached the door. It opened. We waited a moment, then heard the high-pitched whine of zip guns. I shouted and we went running down the tunnel at top speed. It was all over by the time we got there. The guards had been disposed of and Kami, ignoring the blood running down her face, was quietly and quickly getting dressed and buckling on her weapons. There had been no time for them to sound an alarm. We had breached the complex. Several of the bandits came forward, holding a wounded guard between them. Kami wiped the blood away from her face and approached him.

"Where is Saqqara?" she said in Japanese.

The guard spat at her.

She calmly reached out with her right hand and, with a quick flick of her index finger, popped his left eye out of its socket. The man screamed horribly. I felt my gorge rising and I fought it down. She repeated her question. This time, she got an answer. The interrogation was very brief. One of the bandits grabbed the guard by the hair and jerked hard, snapping the man's head back. Kami hit him hard across the throat and finished him.

Saqqara's people never knew what hit them. The bandits fanned out through the complex, pouring out of the lift tubes and the stairways, slaughtering everyone in sight, trashing the place. We found Saqqara in his bedroom on the top floor of the complex, wearing a long black brocade dressing gown. Two terrified young girls were huddled together on the bed, clutching the covers to themselves. In spite of being surrounded by armed bandits, Saqqara seemed calm and self-possessed as we walked in. He turned to face us, utterly in control, self-assured, as elegant as ever.

"O'Toole," he said softly, his eyes widening slightly. "And the Tiger Lady herself." He smiled wryly. "This is all quite impressive, my dear," he said to Kami. "I had truly underestimated you. My congratulations. And O'Toole, it seems I had underestimated you, all along. I never thought you would be so difficult to kill, much less that you would wind up killing me. That is, of course, the object of this exercise, I assume?"

"You didn't leave us any choice, Hakim," I said.

He nodded. "I suppose not. I really should have called your bluff when you drew to that inside straight. You were good. I was convinced you had it. It *was* a bluff, wasn't it?"

"You didn't pay to see the cards," I said.

He smiled. "Once a hustler, always a hustler," he said. "But you were small-time, O'Toole. I made you. Always remember that." He glanced at Breck. "Mr. Breck, is it not? I haven't had the pleasure. I have been quite a fan of yours."

He came forward toward Breck and held out his hand, as if we were guests in his home. Breck wordlessly held out his hand, then suddenly released his blades. Saqqara hesitated, staring at their razor-sharp edges, his hand still held out, motionless.

"Ah, yes, that interesting hand of yours," he said. "I had thought that you, at least, being a former military officer, would have the grace to observe some of the courtesies."

"Your hired assassins were not very courteous toward my fellow hybreeds at Draconis Base," said Breck. "I do not forget such things. And you have interfered in a great deal more than you realize."

"Indeed? Well, that is a pity. I had not meant to offend you. It was only O'Toole I wanted. I regret the loss of your comrades. It may not be much, but allow a dead man to offer his most sincere and abject apology. Please."

He carefully reached around the blades and took Breck's nysteel wrist in both his hands. "I *am* sorry," he said, looking into Breck's eyes. "It seems I have not played my cards well. But at least I can deny O'Toole the trump."

He suddenly jerked forward and impaled himself on Breck's hand. He gasped and his eyes opened wide. Breck, startled, started to pull away, but Saqqara held onto him with all his strength. Breck jerked his hand back, breaking Saqqara's hold, and the man slowly sank down to his knees. He looked up at me and smiled.

"Perhaps not the formal way to observe the old tradition of *seppuku*," Saqqara said, gasping with pain, "—but one does what one can."

I watched him as his life ebbed away and it occurred to me that he had died as he had lived. With style. And I didn't understand it. I didn't understand it at all. I gained no satisfaction from it. I just stood there and watched him die.

-EPILOGUE-

The game was over and I had somehow managed to survive. Purely by chance. Everything in my life seemed to have happened by chance. Chance led me to marry Miko while I was in a drunken state; chance saved me from a life of quiet desperation down in Junkdown; chance led me to The Pyramid Club and made my path cross Hakim Saqqara's. I took a chance, bet everything on a turn of the cards and won, but I had lost my winnings in the large game Saqqara played with me. And when everything seemed blackest, I won the one chance in a trillion at the lottery and escaped Saqqara's men, thanks to a chance encounter with Kami's bandit squadron. But I had escaped only to play another, even larger game of chance, one that had come close to killing me. The game was over, as far as the home audience was concerned, but for me, it was only just beginning. One game ends, another starts, the stakes keep getting bigger. It seemed I had no control at all. Does anybody?

It all came down to chance. I could not escape the strange

tricks of my leprechauns nor the gloomy fatalism of my Russian ancestors. The leprechauns were gamblers; the archbishops were survivors. Somewhere between the two there was a balance point on which I was precariously perched, compelled to spend my life forever taking chances, living on the ragged edge of dreams.

The shuttle to New York was leaving in ten minutes and I was going to be on it. Breck and I sat in the bar, drinking coffee. We hadn't said a word in half an hour.

"It's still ten minutes," Breck said, breaking the silence finally.

"What?"

"That was the fourth time you've checked your watch in the past thirty seconds."

"Oh."

"Would it help to talk?"

"I don't know."

"You want to stay?"

I shook my head. "I can't. It's not my my world anymore, Rudy. Maybe it was once, but not anymore. Even if Coles would let me stay, which I somehow doubt, there's a little thing inside my head that's changed the game on me. I can't just pretend it isn't there. I can't go back."

"I know the feeling," Breck said.

"I guess you do. You know, it's funny, but the first time I met you, I didn't like you very much. I didn't trust you. I thought you were only out for yourself. You had this big reputation as the game's number-one villain, but you've proved to be a good friend, Rudy."

He smiled. "And the first time I met you, I was convinced you would quit after the first scenario. That is, if you managed to survive it. You talked a good game, but I did not believe you had the nerve for it. I am glad I was wrong. I suppose it only proves that people are not always what they seem."

"Unfortunate choice of words, under the circumstances," I said, thinking of the ambimorph. I stared into my coffee. "I wonder what our friend Coles, the thought cop, intends to do with us. You think we're going to be drafted into his spook army?"

"We know much more than we should," said Breck. "That

puts us on the inside, as Coles would probably say. It appears you have bought into yet another high-stakes game, O'Toole."

"Yeah, and I probably can't afford this one, either. But what the hell, that's never stopped me before."

Breck grinned, then became silent for a moment. "You wanted to know about me and Stone—"

I shook my head. "Forget it."

"It seemed important to you at the time. I know it bothered you. Perhaps it makes no difference now, but if it would help settle anything between us—"

"Friends don't need to ask for explanations," I said, "and you don't owe me any. Stone didn't, either."

Breck nodded.

"What's bothering me right now is something a great deal more important," I said. "You think Coles or whoever was behind him was in on this thing all along?"

"I'm not sure what you mean. You're referring to the game?"

I nodded. "I just keep thinking about how quickly they moved in. Coles seemed to adapt to the process as if he'd been a playermaster for years."

"I've thought about that, too. The game seems to have the potential to be far more than a mere game. It makes me wonder how far that potential has been explored by Coles or by people like him. It's an unsettling thought."

"It's all a game in the end," I said. "The game of power. People like Coles seem to control all the pieces. They write all the rules. But the ambimorphs are going to add a few new wrinkles. It's a whole new game now and I've been thinking about how the rules are going to be rewritten. What you said about them sterilizing Draconis . . ." I shook my head. " . . . I don't think they're going to do it."

Breck raised his eyebrows. "What makes you think so? It would be the logical thing to do. They would be crazy not to."

"Yes, well, I haven't noticed that the universe is particularly logical, but I *have* noticed that it's crazy. If they sterilized Draconis 9, it would be essentially unusable for years, wouldn't it?"

"I should think it would take at least several generations to repair the damage," Breck said, "assuming an all-out commitment."

"You think anybody really wants to pay for that?" I said.

"I doubt the Combine will have much choice."

"It isn't only the Combine that would be affected," I said. "It's Coles and the people he represents, as well. They need the fire crystals for their tachyon drives and weapons systems and whatever. They might well find another source, but it would be expensive, as would be the clean-up of Draconis after a surgical strike. Plus there's one other consideration. There's no way of knowing how many ambimorphs have managed to break the quarantine. A surgical strike against their home world is the one thing Coles has to hold over them. It's the one basis for some kind of negotiation. Burn out Draconis and there won't be anything left to hold back the ambimorphs who've made it to Earth and to the colony worlds."

Breck stared at me for a long moment. "You are beginning to sound like Coles."

"I'm trying to figure out how the man thinks," I said. "All of a sudden, I'm sitting down at the table with him and he's got all the chips *and* all the cards. I could have burned that ambimorph, but Coles wanted it alive. You're a soldier, Rudy, you're trained to think in terms of defeating the opposition. Try thinking like a politician, in terms of cost-effectiveness, deals and trade-offs. It's a lot like being in a poker game, when you come to think of it. We've got 'x' number of ambimorphs who've broken the quarantine and are posing a threat —that's the hand the other player's got, the cards you can't see. You know the other guy's got a good hand, but you don't know how good. You have no way of knowing if what you've got can beat it."

Breck nodded.

"So what do you do?" I said. "If you call and he's got you beat, he takes the pot and you're effectively out of the game, because if you lose the pot, you've only got enough to maybe make it through another hand or two and it'll cost you everything you've got left. Odds of coming out ahead are nonexistent; odds of coming out even are poor, at best. What you've put into the pot is Earth and the colony worlds. What he's put in is Draconis 9. You haven't put in everything, you've each got some left in reserve, but not a lot. Not enough that either of you can afford to throw in your hand."

"So what does the prudent gambler do?" said Breck.

I grimaced. "There's no such thing as a prudent gambler.

There are only amateurs and pros. The amateur plays hunches. The pro goes with the odds. And we're all pros at this table. Suppose we act like amateurs and throw in everything we've got on one big raise and call his bluff. We snuff Draconis. Call. And he lays down a royal flush. A staggering number of ambimorphs infiltrated into human society, penetrated into key positions, nothing holding them back from all-out war. Read 'em and weep. But being pros, are we going to take that chance? No. That isn't smart. Instead, what we're going to do is call on everything we've got, all our professional experience, and test each other's nerve. We're going to raise each other a little at a time, watching the other guy's face carefully, looking for anything, the slightest tick, the smallest bead of sweat, the tiniest flicker in the eyes that gives us a better idea of what the odds are, of just how good a hand he's got and just how confident he is. And we're going to hope like hell our own poker face won't crack and that his will before we've used up all of our reserve. We're looking for a break in his concentration—one ambimorph or more, to lock away somewhere in a lab and study, figure out how to detect the bastards so we can get the infiltrators and wipe them out on Draconis without having to resort to a surgical strike that would damage the planet for years to come.''

"And where do we come in? You and I? How do we fit into this game?" said Breck.

"We're the bluff cards that are filling out the hand," I said. "Or maybe we're the ones Coles is thinking of discarding. Depends on how things go, I guess. Maybe he'll throw out some other cards and draw something that will reinforce us. Who the hell knows? But he's the one holding the hand, the way I see it. And Psychodrome just happens to be the table we're all sitting at. We know there are a lot of people out there with biochips hardwired into their brains. And at least one ambimorph, who has apparently learned how to control it. And other ambimorphs could probably get biochips the same way ours got his. That links us all in the same game. Them, us, and the public out there who tune into the game.''

"Only the moment word gets out about this," Breck said, "the public will panic. At the very least, they'll stop tuning in.''

"I've thought about that," I said. "I tried thinking about it the same way Coles would. And you know what I decided I'd do in his place? I'll tell you something, I don't know what scares me more, the fact that I could think this way or the fact that this is probably just what Coles will do. Instead of trying to stop any of this from getting out, I would go public with it. Only I would go public with it as a lie. It isn't really happening. It's all part of the game, a brand new wrinkle, a new and continuing scenario for Psychodrome—the alien invasion."

"Now you're getting carried away," said Breck. "It would never work. The moment the ambimorphs committed their first significant terrorist act, it would all be out in the open."

"Not if it's part of the game," I said. "That's the beauty of it. And the horror of it, too. Anything you can hush up to large extent, you pass off as a hallucinact. Otherwise, you establish that the game is incorporating reality into its scenarios, something it's already doing anyway, only now various 'isolated incidents' of violence are going to be incorporated into one so-called conspiracy, a fictional alien invasion—some building blows up somewhere, killing 'x' amount of people, and it was actually some sort of accident, you see, but it becomes incorporated into the alien invasion scenario. Any statement claiming that the Draconians were responsible becomes accepted by the media and the public as a press release from Psychodrome, taking advantage of a real-life event to publicize a game scenario."

"They'd never get away with it," said Breck. "At the very least, relatives of those killed in terrorist acts would institute legal proceedings against the game."

"On what grounds?" I said. "There's no law against basing a fictional entertainment on real-life news events which are public domain. Besides, Coles and his people own the system. If anyone got in their way and threatened to expose it all, they'd simply be squashed like a bug. Remember what Coles said? He'd break every law ever written to safeguard the security of the human race. He sees himself as the man with the Holy Grail. And for all I know, maybe he is, God help us. He's already co-opted us. Do you recall him asking? You want to test his resolve? Miss the shuttle. Go to the press. See what happens."

They announced the boarding call for the shuttle to New York. For a moment, Breck acted as if he hadn't heard it. For a moment, I thought he was actually considering my suggestion, but then he looked up at me with a strange expression on his face and got up to leave.

"It appears she didn't come," he said, looking around.

I thought back to the last time I had left Japan. It seemed like a century ago. I wondered if there would ever be a next time.

"Kami's not much for good-byes," I said.

As we stepped onto the slideway, Breck gave me a nudge. I turned in the direction he was looking and I saw her, dressed in black and silver lycras, standing at the bottom of the ramp, flanked by a couple of young bandits. She wasn't the type to wave, but she gave me a slight nod, then turned on her heel and walked away without a backward glance.

"Unusual young woman," Breck said.

"Yes. She certainly is that."

I was still smiling as the shuttle lifted off. Maybe it was crazy. I was just a little ball in a runaway roulette wheel, popping into one slot after another as it went around, one with a homicidal youth gang leader who was both the most frightening and the most compelling woman I had ever known; one with an ex-commando of the Special Service who was far better equipped to deal with the hammerblows of life than I was, so I wasn't sure how I'd ever manage to keep up; one with a man named Coles, who saw me as nothing more than just another chip in the very large pile of chips he played with and one with Hakim Saqqara—who had started out holding all the cards and had wound up busted. You win a few, you lose a few. I had won that one. I had won it big. But the game continued at a breakneck pace. Perhaps I should have been afraid, but I was smiling. Look at me now, Sean O'Toole, you old bastard! Talk about rollin' high! You ever see a game like this?

All right, so deep down inside, I was scared out of my mind, but I was just too high to feel it. Breck would never understand, but Sean would. I had the fever.

I couldn't wait to ante up.

Made in the USA
Columbia, SC
07 June 2024

36796404R00122